PRAISE FOR
Love's New Beginnings

This is the perfect start to the series and a perfect book for
the Christmas season.

Jenny, Reader

Love's New Beginnings is a tender, gentle, faith-filled romance
that will sweep the reader into the world of two uncertain
characters and the captivating Wyoming Sunrise series.

Madisyn Carlin, Author

A lighthearted read set in the mountains of Wyoming Territory,
you'll be left smiling and sighing throughout its entirety. Perfect
for readers of Janette Oke.

Abbigail Raine B., Author

In today's world, the chance of finding good clean fiction that is
sweet and a joy to read is rare indeed...I highly recommend this
book and series.

Chat With Vera, Blogger

PRAISE FOR
Forgotten Memories

With themes of forgiveness, grace, and second chances, this story is sure to touch your heart.

Cover Lover Book Review, Blogger

This was the first time I have read a book by the author, Penny Zeller and I was captivated from page one.

Michelle, Reviewer

This book is a wonderful read! It's well written and holds your attention from the first page until the last.

Ann, Reviewer

Fantastic book! The story line is unique and the setting comes alive with Penny's descriptions. The characters are so realistic and relatable.

Jeanette, Reviewer

PRAISE FOR
Dreams of the Heart

This story was a delight to read and if you like tender historical and inspirational romance then you're in for a treat.

Ivonne, Reader

I read this book in about two days. I did NOT want to stop reading. I can't wait to read book 3!

Terri, Reader

I had a hard time putting this book down. It was a wonderful combination of adventure, heartache, and joy.

Cynthia, Reader

This is an outstanding story and one that will keep you turning the pages.

Phyllis, Reader

PRAISE FOR
When Love Comes

Penny Zeller's latest creation is a radiant addition to
Christian historical romance, leaving readers enraptured by
the echoes of love and grace that resonate long after the final
page.

Luann, Reader

One of the best things about this book, is that it really can be
read as a stand-alone, even though it's part of a series. (But
honestly, the books are too good to miss any.)

Becky, Reader

The story draws the reader in with more than romance,
unsavory characters and some tense moments keep you on the
edge of your seat.

Shonda Czeschin Fischer, Author

The author's ability to bring life to every word, hope to every
challenge, all the while consistently pointing the reader to the
God of love, life and liberty is nothing short of divine guidance.

Evelyn, Reader

When Love Comes

When Love Comes

PENNY ZELLER

When Love Comes

Book Cover Design by Mountain Peak Edits and Design

Rough Draft Critique/Developmental Edits by SnowRidge Press

Copy Editing by Mountain Peak Edits and Design

Proofreading by Kristina Hall

All scripture quotations are taken from the King James Version of the Bible. All song lyrics for the hymns as found in the public domain.

Print ISBN: 978-1-957847-18-4

ALSO BY PENNY ZELLER

Maplebrook Publishing

Standalone Books
Love in Disguise
Love in the Headlines
Freedom's Flight
Levi's Vow

Wyoming Sunrise
Love's New Beginnings
Forgotten Memories
Dreams of the Heart
When Love Comes
Love's Promise

Love Letters from Ellis Creek
Love from Afar
Love Unforeseen
Love Most Certain

Chokecherry Heights
Henry and Evaline (Prequel)
Love Under Construction

Horizon Series
Over the Horizon
Dreams on the Horizon
Beyond the Horizon

Whitaker House Publishing

Montana Skies
McKenzie
Kaydie
Hailee

Barbour Publishing

Love from Afar
*(The Secret Admirer
Romance Collection)*

Freedom's Flight
*(The Underground Railroad
Brides Collection)*

Beacon Hill Press
(Nonfiction)

77 Ways Your Family Can
Make a Difference

Dedicated to my daughters—the decades-younger
inspirations behind the characters of
Aunt Myrtle and Aunt Fern.

I will lift up mine eyes unto the hills, from whence cometh my help.
My help cometh from the Lord, which made heaven and earth.
~ Psalm 121:1-2

CHAPTER ONE

PRUNE CREEK, WYOMING, 1895

MA WAS RIGHT. SOME time away from Willow Falls would be just the antidote to her broken heart. "After all," Ma surmised, "how can anyone remain melancholy when spending time with the aunts? Just be sure not to eat Aunt Myrtle's baking, and you'll be fine."

Charlotte didn't plan on eating much of Aunt Myrtle's baking as she knew full well her great-aunt's reputation when it came to such matters, but she did wonder if Ma was accurate about the melancholy part.

The couple across the aisle, a handsome duo around Charlotte's age of twenty-two, gazed tenderly into each other's eyes. Charlotte overheard the woman telling another passenger that she and the gentleman were on their honeymoon. Tears welled in Charlotte's eyes and she blinked them back.

Unannounced envy crept in at the most inopportune times. Lest they discover her staring yet again, Charlotte tore her eyes away from the smitten couple and averted her gaze to the book in her lap, rereading the same paragraph for the sixth time. She'd never struggled with covetousness until a despicable man named Cyrus Keller entered her life and exited it, leaving pain and sorrow in his wake.

Her brother, John Mark, would tell her she was dramatic for entertaining such thoughts, but the ache still lingered from what she'd eagerly anticipated would be a godly and loving marriage.

Not only had she been foolish to believe Cyrus's affections for her, but she'd also been daft in ignoring the warnings of those closest to her.

Hadn't she always desired to be a wife and mother? To follow in her ma's steps as a kind and giving soul who loved her family only second to the Lord? A marriage to Cyrus would have filled that longing in her heart. Her former beau, just like a hero in a book, was dapper and charming. However, he lacked the most important characteristics—godliness and integrity.

Now slightly older and hopefully wiser, Charlotte Eliason would never allow herself to fall in love again. If she was to be a spinster, so be it. Not everyone could have a happily ever after reminiscent of the characters in one of her favorite dime novels.

Ma mentioned that, once upon a time, Aunt Fern's heart had been broken by a scoundrel named Mr. Wilkins. If Aunt Fern could survive a broken heart, then so could Charlotte. And if it was God's plan for her to be a spinster, then she'd accept her fate, albeit begrudgingly. Being a spinster wasn't the worst thing in the world, was it? She swallowed the lump in her throat and instead attempted to focus on the adventure that lay ahead.

Charlotte adjusted her posture, prayed for the Lord to set her focus on anything but her fragmented dreams, and determined that very moment that she would set her sights on caring for and assisting Aunt Myrtle and Aunt Fern.

At least the train ride portion was a much smoother and more efficient ride than the first part of her journey by stagecoach had been. Several areas of Wyoming still lacked travel by railway, and Willow Falls was one of the towns still without a train depot. Pa had worried that he should perhaps take Charlotte over the mountain to Prune Creek, but Charlotte requested she do this on her own. Ma mentioned something to Pa about Charlotte being much like the aunts in that regard, and perhaps, just like the stories she'd heard about them arriving from Minnesota so many years ago for a fresh start, Charlotte would experience a fresh start as well.

Excitement bounded through her as the train entered the Prune Creek depot. Trees on either side of the tracks gave way to a clearing that marked the town that had obviously grown since Charlotte's last visit years ago.

Brakes screeching, the train slowly came to a stop. Charlotte's heart pounded in her chest, and she could barely wait a moment longer upon the hard bench seat. She fingered the purple heart-shaped pendant necklace around her neck, a gift from her family. What did the future of this time away from home hold? She peered out the window, searching for her aunts among the swath of people.

When folks, waiting to disembark, crowded the aisles, she reached for her heavy, overly-filled carpetbag and Ma's worn brown trunk and perused the crowd awaiting the passengers. Were Aunt Myrtle and Aunt Fern among them?

"Charlotte! Oh, Charlotte!" Two jubilant voices garnered her attention as she deboarded. Aunt Myrtle and Aunt Fern waved at her from the north end of the boardwalk, and Charlotte bustled her way through the crowds and toward the aunts.

My, but if they hadn't begun to share a strong resemblance in their older years! Both had completely gray hair, and while Aunt Fern wore spectacles, her round face and pert nose matched her sister's.

"Best never say they resemble each other even if they do," Ma had told her before she embarked on this trip. *"For you might find yourself sleeping in the chicken coop for such a comment."* Ma and Charlotte had laughed over that, even as Ma insisted it would be detrimental to suggest their likeness.

"Look at you! You've grown into such a lovely young lady." Aunt Myrtle wrapped her arm around Charlotte. "We're so glad you're here."

Aunt Fern gave her a hug next. "Yes, we are. It's been too long since an Eliason was here in Prune Creek. The buggy is thisaway. It's a slight bit too far for us to walk to the Peabody house these days."

"Too far for you, maybe." Aunt Myrtle fingered her decorative hat. "What do you think about my hat, Charlotte? Mrs. Peabody was about to discard it, and I salvaged it."

Since she was taller than Aunt Myrtle, Charlotte could see the top of the hat and the fake bird immersed in a portable flower garden. "It's charming."

"Well, it is not," declared Aunt Fern. "Who wears a hat with a bird on it?"

Aunt Myrtle lifted her chin, nearly causing the hat to topple off her head. "Women of high society who take a fancy to the latest and most elegant fashions."

"But you're neither."

"Pshaw. Hush, Fern."

They strolled down the boardwalk on the way to the buggy. As they passed the barbershop, a balding man with the thickest spectacles Charlotte had ever seen stepped into the entryway. "Well, hello, Fern. Would you like a haircut?"

"You know full and well, Mr. Gorman, that I do not need a haircut." Aunt Fern fluffed her gray curls and tossed him a disgusted look. "That vexing man asks me if I would like a haircut every time I walk by the barbershop. Far be it from me to allow someone with magnifying glasses for spectacles to see well enough to fashion my coiffure."

They loaded into the buggy, Charlotte sandwiched between the aunts, and rode along without incident until Aunt Myrtle's hat blew off in a gusty breeze. Aunt Myrtle steered the buggy to the side of the road, and Charlotte retrieved it.

"Do assist me with this," Aunt Myrtle requested of her sister.

Aunt Fern set it nicely on Aunt Myrtle's head—backwards. She cast a warning glance Charlotte's way and shook her head, finger to mouth to say nothing. Charlotte did her best not to smirk. The hat looked even more hideous backwards.

"Dear me, there's Mr. Clifford Quimby." Aunt Myrtle slowed the buggy next to a tall, thin, older man carrying a stack of papers. "Hello, Mr. Quimby." Was it Charlotte's imagination or did Aunt Myrtle blush when she spoke?

"Well, hello, Miss Beauchamp."

Aunt Myrtle held a hand to her heart. "Oh, hello," she tittered again.

The corners of Quimby's mouth turned upward. "Miss Beauchamp, what brings you out and about on this lovely summer day?"

"Our niece is visiting from Willow Falls. May I present to you Miss Charlotte Eliason."

Mr. Quimby removed his hat. "Pleasure to meet you." He stared for a few moments up at Aunt Myrtle. "I do declare, Miss Beauchamp, that is the most interesting hat I've ever seen."

"Do you like it?"

"Well..." Mr. Quimby tilted his head to one side. "Do lean this way, Miss Beauchamp."

Aunt Myrtle leaned carefully to the left so as not to tumble from the buggy. Mr. Quimby reached up, removed the hat and set it on her head the correct way. "There, now it looks exquisite on you."

"Oh!" Aunt Myrtle's cheeks flamed with a red hue the color of raspberries.

"I best be on my way as I'm headed to the courthouse." Mr. Quimby tipped his hat and continued down the street.

Aunt Myrtle glowered at Aunt Fern. "You placed the hat on my head backwards. Such a bothersome sister you are at times."

"I do believe you've set your cap for Mr. Quimby."

"Pshaw." But Aunt Myrtle didn't deny it.

Aunt Fern shook her head. "I've always found Mr. Quimby to be a kindly gentleman. It's unfortunate he'll soon meet his demise."

Aunt Myrtle's eyes widened. "Whatever do you mean?"

"Once you bake him some huckleberry pie, it will be the end of him."

Charlotte giggled at Aunt Fern's exaggeration. She'd heard the story numerous times from Ma about the huckleberry pie during the aunts' first visit to Willow Falls.

"Don't believe a word she says about my baking," insisted Aunt Myrtle. "You don't win ribbons at the fair for inferior baking skills."

They continued down the main street. "Oh, look, there's the blacksmith shop," said Aunt Fern, pointing to the building on the right.

"The new smithy is such an extraordinary and upright young man. He's been here all of a few weeks, yet when the wheel on the buggy broke last week, he came to our rescue. Say, Fern, we still haven't invited him for supper like we promised."

The aunts passed a knowing glance and a niggle of suspicion arose in Charlotte. "Are you two planning something?" The aunts were obviously inept at disguising their schemes. And while the smithy may be an extraordinary and upright man, Charlotte was most certainly not interested in matchmaking ploys. Not after Cyrus.

"Yes."

"No."

"Well, we are planning something," said Aunt Fern. "Planning to have that nice young man over for supper. He has no family here, poor dear. He lives at the boardinghouse over on Second Street. The food there is most atrocious from what I've heard. Yes, Myrt, I believe we shall make those plans."

Aunt Myrtle, who Ma warned rarely agreed with her sister on anything—and vice versa—added, "I'm a planner, but Fern, not so much. She likes to wait until the very last minute. A procrastinator is among us."

They continued to argue, all the while traveling the short distance to the Peabody home they'd inherited after the passing of their charges.

And as she watched the passing scenery of her temporary home, Charlotte smiled to herself. Yes, Ma was right. Time with her two feisty aunts would heal her melancholy. And when they invited the smithy to the house, Charlotte would firmly, but kindly, remind them she was of no mindset to fall in love again.

Not that she didn't see the good in Cyrus breaking off their engagement and marrying Violet. Not now that she saw what kind of man he really was.

But her heart still ached for being so naïve, for giving her heart to him, and for wasting time courting someone who never loved her in the first place.

CHAPTER TWO

CHARLOTTE PULLED HER LONG blonde hair into a tight coil atop her head like she'd seen women do on the pages of *The Utmost of Fashion Ladies Magazine* at Morton's Mercantile in Willow Falls. While she had no intention of considering the aunts' matchmaking machinations when it came to the new smithy, Charlotte did prefer to at least look presentable. She pinched her cheeks to encourage color and smoothed her skirt.

Aunt Myrtle referred to the smithy as "an extraordinary and upright young man." At their ages, they likely believed anyone younger than sixty to be young. Just as Pa referred to any male younger than him as "son". Rather, the smithy was likely a great deal older than Charlotte with already-graying hair at the temples—perhaps he was balding. Mr. Gormon, the barber Aunt Fern referenced on the way to the house, flashed in her mind. She giggled.

Ma had warned her of the aunts' propensity to engage in shenanigans.

And even if the smithy wasn't old and instead was young and dapper, Charlotte would never be interested for he could very well be just like Cyrus.

Charlotte tidied her meager belongings then left the room to assist the aunts with meal preparation. She removed a huckleberry pie from the oven. The dessert's aroma was heavenly, but details were important. She needed to find out who baked it. "The pie looks delicious."

"That's because it is," Aunt Myrtle beamed.

Aunt Fern snorted a most unladylike snort. "Your Aunt Myrtle made the pie. As they say, looks can be deceiving. Her huckleberry pies remind me of Mr. Wilkins. All attractive on the outside and abhorrent on the inside. Rotten character, but a nice outward appearance."

"Of all things to say!" Aunt Myrtle placed her hands firmly on her ample hips. "That my pies remind you of Mr. Wilkins—that is indeed the most horrendous of insults. My huckleberry pie is award…"

"Yes, yes, award-winning. We know. Although the judge at the fair was at least one hundred and fifty years old and had long lost his sense of taste. I rather like Charlotte and the smithy and don't wish for either of them to meet their demise anytime soon."

"No one has met their untimely demise eating my huckleberry pies," snapped Aunt Myrtle.

"Just a shortened lifespan. Look at Solomon. Poor, poor man. Can you imagine if he had keeled over after eating your pies that first time in Willow Falls? Where would we be then? No Solomon. No Lydie finding her one true love, no Caleb, John Mark, and Charlotte. No great-great-nieces and great-great nephew. It would be devastating to say the least."

"Such a dramatic sort you are, Fern. Nearly everyone loves my huckleberry pies. I'm sorry you have poor taste when it comes to such things."

Aunt Fern harrumphed. "Remember that poor Mr. Opalinski who ate a huge piece of your huckleberry pie at the Prune Creek County Fair last fall? They had to fetch Doc because we thought we were going to lose him."

"Well, I never! Doc was fetched for Mr. Opalinski because he had indigestion from inhaling the huckleberry pie a little too hastily because it was so scrumptious."

The aunts continued their squabbling, and Charlotte recalled what Ma had said about their witty comebacks. They indeed had developed a penchant for arguing. Speaking of Ma, Charlotte suddenly had more sympathy for all the times Ma had to endure her and John Mark's frequent quarreling all those years.

"Shall I put the stew and biscuits on the table?" Charlotte asked when she could get a word in edgewise.

Both aunts ceased their chatter and gaped at her with wide eyes and slack jaws. And Charlotte could again see the family resemblance.

Ma's words echoed in her mind. *"Never insinuate the aunts favor each other. I speak from experience."*

"Well..." Aunt Fern finally muttered. "Yes, dear, please do. The smithy will be here any minute. I sure wish I could remember his name. Do you remember his name, Myrt?"

"No, I do not. Did he even tell us?"

"Perhaps not. I'll fetch the butter."

No sooner had they completely prepared the table when there was a knock at the door. "Would you please get that, Charlotte, dear?" Aunt Myrtle asked and winked, not so discreetly, at Aunt Fern.

The aunts were so obvious in their agenda. "Yes, ma'am," she answered and walked slowly toward the door, uneager to see the man whom the aunts decided would be in her future. In her mind, she weaved a condensed version of the story she'd already imagined earlier. The balding man, older than Pa, hunched with his filthy, wrinkled plaid shirt and spectacles with smudges on them, would still be wearing his blackened blacksmith apron. He would have forgotten to bathe before attending this all-important meal at the aunts' home in gratitude for his assistance. The smithy would chew with his mouth open, creating an abhorrent and detestable smacking sound as the food was tossed to and fro between the gaping space between his front teeth and the missing ones on the bottom. Not one to patiently listen as others spoke, he frequently interrupted, never swallowing his food before he spoke.

She nearly gagged at the image planted in her mind.

Surely the aunts would realize that, while Charlotte placed much more emphasis on character than appearance, the smithy would never be one she would consider for courtship. Besides, she still mourned her broken heart.

"Charlotte? Is everything quite all right?" called Aunt Fern. "You need only take a few more steps to reach the door."

Charlotte jolted from her daydream. "Yes, I'm quite all right, thank you, Aunt Fern." She took the remaining steps, held her breath, and opened the door.

She needn't see her reflection to know her eyes bulged and her mouth fell open. Surely she was still exhausted from her journey and wasn't seeing clearly. Charlotte closed the door, rubbed her eyes, and reopened the door a few seconds later.

Sure enough, he still remained standing on Aunt Fern and Aunt Myrtle's porch.

"Tobias Hallman?"

"Charlotte Eliason?"

"You two know each other? What a grand occurrence!" Aunt Fern clasped her hands together. "How did you meet?"

For the first time in what may be her entire life, Charlotte was temporarily speechless.

"Aren't you going to invite me in?" Tobias asked.

Finally her vocal cords functioned again. "Might I ask why you are here?" She peeked around him. "We are expecting the smithy for supper."

"I *am* the smithy."

Tobias Hallman was the smithy?

"And why are you here, Charlotte? Don't you still live in Willow Falls?"

"Well, goodnesses," interrupted Aunt Myrtle. "Do invite the young man in. You two can carry on your conversation in the parlor or at the supper table."

Charlotte stepped aside and Tobias Hallman strutted in. Still the same overly-confident irritant she remembered from not so long ago. He smirked at her, the dimple in his left cheek becoming more pronounced as he did so. "Good to see you, Charlotte."

She'd concede to the fact that Tobias had always been a handsome sort with his broad shoulders, strong arms, engaging smile, and his golden-brown eyes. He was the exact opposite in appearance from the man she imagined would be arriving for supper.

She did her best to overcome her shock. Never had she imagined she'd see her adversary in Prune Creek. Hadn't

Charlotte determined the best way to heal from Cyrus's betrayal was to *escape* to Prune Creek? Apparently Tobias had escaped to Prune Creek as well.

"Charlotte, dear," said Aunt Fern, "Why do you look like you've just eaten some of Aunt Myrtle's cooking?"

"I—"

Aunt Myrtle straightened her posture. "If she'd just eaten some of my cooking, she'd be smiling and requesting seconds."

"Not sure about that. More like asking why she was being punished to have to partake in such a meal."

"Pshaw." Aunt Myrtle glowered. "You've always been jealous of my talent for making appetizing and New York restaurant-worthy meals."

Aunt Fern ignored her sister and instead turned to Tobias. "Do have a seat," she gushed as she gestured toward the chair across from Charlotte. "Supper is ready to be served. I do hope you like stew and biscuits." Aunt Fern paused for a moment and thumbed her heart. "I made both."

For which Charlotte was grateful.

"Now do tell us again your name. Myrtle and I apologize that we didn't ask it the day you rescued us during the buggy incident."

"Tobias. Tobias Hallman. Pleasure to meet you." He nodded and acted as though he were the most gentlemanly man this side of the Mississippi.

But Charlotte knew better. She narrowed her eyes at him, and he feigned innocence.

"Nice to meet you, Tobias. May we call you Tobias?"

"Yes, ma'am."

Aunt Fern took a seat beside him. "And you may call us Aunt Fern and Aunt Myrtle. Now, do tell us how you and Charlotte know each other. Did you meet on the train?"

"We know each other from Willow Falls." Charlotte thought her voice sounded distraught in her own ears.

Aunt Myrtle's bright smile did nothing to alleviate the disturbance Charlotte felt. "You two were friends from Willow Falls? How absolutely splendid!"

Tobias cleared his throat. "No offense, ma'am—Aunt Fern—"

"I'm Aunt Myrtle."

"Sorry. Aunt Myrtle. No offense, but we were not friends. More like, uh, foes."

"This isn't the man who broke your heart is it?" Aunt Fern turned a tempestuous gaze upon Tobias. "For if you are the one, you are not welcome at our table."

Aunt Fern and Aunt Myrtle may have their faults, but their loyalty endeared them to Charlotte. "No, Aunt Fern. That is someone else." She noticed Tobias quirk an eyebrow at her, and she bet he'd like to know just who had broken her heart. Well, he would just have to hear it from someone else.

"Good. We'll not have any such cads at this house."

Aunt Myrtle nodded in agreement. "Most certainly not. Now, then isn't it quite something you both are from Willow Falls and are now living in Prune Creek? It's..."

"Unfortunate," both Charlotte and Tobias chorused.

"Oh!" squealed Aunt Myrtle. "What's that saying, that birds of a feather..."

"Flock together," finished Aunt Fern.

Aunt Myrtle nodded. "Yes, that's it. Both of you knowing exactly what the other would say."

Charlotte didn't believe in coincidences. Except maybe this once.

"It's probably because 'unfortunate' was one of our vocabulary words. Annie was our teacher for a time," Tobias said, "and she made sure we used all sorts of words in sentences."

"Oh, my, but yes. Annie is a smart one. We do adore her," declared Aunt Myrtle. "Well, I'm just so impressed that you both already know each other. Fern and I were telling Charlotte what an extraordinary and upright young man you are. We were so grateful you fixed our buggy."

Tobias sat straighter in his chair. "Yes, ma'am. I aim only to be extraordinary and upright. Chivalrous, obliging, and of good character too. It's how my ma and pa taught me."

It was Charlotte's turn to smirk. "Your ma and pa may have attempted to teach you to be chivalrous, obliging, and of good character, but they failed miserably."

"Ah, Charlotte, I see you're still holding a grudge against me for tying your braids in knots because they were resting on my desk."

"No. I'm still holding a grudge from the time you brought Slithers to school and the time my doll *somehow* landed in the pond."

Tobias shrugged. "It was a hot day. Thought she'd like to go for a swim. And that wasn't just me. Two others were in on that prank. I was only an accomplice. Besides, you've always exaggerated something fierce."

"And you've always been a vexatious cad, Tobias Hallman."

"Surprised you still don't use my middle name every time too."

The encouragement was all Charlotte needed. "All right, then, Tobias Edgar Hallman."

Tobias groaned.

And Charlotte figured she'd won this round.

A suspicious "psst" drew Charlotte's attention from Tobias and to the two dubious women whispering amongst themselves.

"Are you thinking what I'm thinking?" Aunt Myrtle asked.

"In most cases no, but in this case, yes."

Charlotte could only imagine what they were plotting. If she could hazard a guess, she sensed it had something to do with her and Tobias.

And it likely wasn't good.

She tried her best to put on her "Ma" face, the one that her mother used when Charlotte and John Mark incessantly argued during their younger years.

Aunt Myrtle averted her gaze to the floor. Aunt Fern stared without blinking.

"Just what are you two pondering?" Charlotte asked.

"Pondering? Us?" Aunt Fern's brow creased. "We don't often ponder, do we, Myrtle?"

"No, not us. Why do you ask?"

"You two look like you've been up to mischief, and I believe I heard you scheming something just a moment ago."

Aunt Myrtle wrung her hands, and Aunt Fern's unblinking stare included a dart of her eyes toward Tobias, then back to Charlotte.

Just as I thought!

Aunt Myrtle cleared her throat. "Now, now, you two. Fern and I heard you arguing about past transgressions on the part of our guest. This is a splendorous evening, and arguing is so unbecoming. Let's say grace, and then we'll eat."

Tobias sniggered at Charlotte before pleasantly agreeing with Aunt Myrtle. "My apologies. I can't wait to partake in this delicious meal. Thank you for inviting me."

Aunt Fern beamed and appeared to recover from her unblinking state. "You are most welcome. And I daresay you'll enjoy the stew and biscuits."

Tobias led them in saying grace, and for the next few minutes, all was calm. But Charlotte still reeled in shock at realizing Tobias now resided in Prune Creek. That *he* was the new smithy. That she would likely see him more often than necessary due to the aunts' fondness for him.

After they'd finished supper, Aunt Myrtle prattled for several minutes about her huckleberry pie and the awards she'd won. To her credit, Aunt Fern wasn't contrary.

Aunt Myrtle scooped a most generous piece of pie on a plate for Tobias, then asked if Aunt Fern or Charlotte would like a piece as well.

"I couldn't eat another thing," said Charlotte.

"Nor could I," agreed Aunt Fern. "Although thank you just the same."

"Well, that is a loss for both of you. Tobias and I shall partake in the pie then." She took a generous bite and closed her eyes as if to savor the taste. "I see why this recipe has won prizes."

Aunt Fern tossed Charlotte a knowing look .

"Do try it, Tobias. I'm sure you'll find it to your liking."

"It smells wonderful, Aunt Myrtle. I sure do appreciate you and Aunt Fern going to all this work."

"Yes, well, we sure do appreciate you rescuing us from the buggy fiasco." Aunt Myrtle waved a hand at the piece of pie. "Do enjoy the pie."

Tobias forked a piece and slid it into his mouth. His eyes enlarged and he made a throaty sound before reaching for his cup of milk. He guzzled it for several seconds before returning his cup to the table. That's when Charlotte realized his eyes were watering.

Aunt Myrtle leaned forward and fixed her gaze on him. "What do you think?"

"I—uh..."

"Yes, that's the response I most often receive from those who try my famous huckleberry pie. You're at a loss for words, and I completely understand why. The pie is so delectable it makes it difficult for one to describe just how savory it is."

"Indeed," agreed Aunt Fern.

"Aunt Myrtle, you and Aunt Fern are so appreciative of all that Tobias did for you regarding the buggy. Perhaps he'd like to take the entire remainder of huckleberry pie home with him," suggested Charlotte. "After all, I've heard the boardinghouse food can be less than palatable." Ma would be pleased Charlotte was being so generous toward her foe.

Tobias, finally having recovered from his horrific experience, shook his head. "I couldn't do that. I was raised to be generous. It would be selfish of me to take the entire pie for myself."

"Nonsense!" admonished Aunt Myrtle. "Charlotte is right. You shall take the entire pie home with you when you go. It's the least we can do in return for your assistance with the buggy."

Charlotte fought the urge to be smug, but it was a rewarding experience to gain a point in the now ongoing battle between her and Tobias Hallman.

Tobias held the pie carefully while he rode his horse into town after the supper. He wasn't sure he could stomach another bite of the acidic and sour pie, but he hadn't wanted to hurt Aunt Myrtle's feelings.

The ride back to the boardinghouse was slower than usual due to him attempting not to drop the pie, but it gave him time to think.

Time to think about all that had transpired in the last hour and a half.

Charlotte Eliason. When was the last time he'd seen her? He'd visited Willow Falls briefly when his brother, Chester, his wife, Paulina, and their daughter, Lanie, moved there from Cheyenne, but Tobias hadn't seen Charlotte during those times.

She was still annoying, although she was pretty. But then, Charlotte always had been beautiful with her long hair, expressive eyes, and slender figure. But he hadn't missed her at all. He couldn't even begin to count how many times she'd gotten him into trouble during their school days. She was a tattletale and never passed up the opportunity to make sure the teachers knew of Tobias's pranks.

He chuckled. They were adults now. Years had passed since those days of having to be in her presence more than necessary, due largely in part to her brother, John Mark, being his best friend. Yet even though they were in their early twenties, he two years older than she, they remained at odds.

Not that it mattered. What mattered was ensuring his blacksmith shop was successful enough for him to carve a future for himself. Tobias never cared about being wealthy, but had aspired to owning his own place someday. And maybe getting married and having children like his brother. But it was doubtful he'd find any suitable young women in Prune Creek as the offerings were scarce. So far, he'd met two eligible women, neither of whom Tobias cared to court.

But that time would come, if the Lord willed it. And if not, Tobias would immerse himself in his work, church, and the new friendships he was forming in Prune Creek.

His thoughts returned to Charlotte. It was strange seeing her again. But it was also something familiar in this new town he aimed to call home. He'd never imagined she'd be related to the two elderly women he'd assisted that day.

CHAPTER THREE

CHARLOTTE OPENED THE DOOR of the ornate hutch and returned the supper dishes to their rightful place.

Aunt Fern finished wiping the table then faced Charlotte, a mischievous glint in her eyes. Eyes that darted about the kitchen. She shifted her feet and clasped, then unclasped her hands.

Something about Aunt Fern's demeanor warranted suspicion. Charlotte had to wait only three seconds before the mystery of her shifty behavior was solved.

"Don't you think that young man is a handsome fellow?"

Charlotte knew full well where Aunt Fern was going with this line of inquiry. She and Aunt Myrtle alternated their insinuations that Tobias Hallman was just the man Charlotte ought to consider for courtship. But Charlotte would have none of it.

"On the contrary, Aunt Fern. He's a rather homely man." But even as she said the words, Charlotte turned away from Aunt Fern's perusal lest her aunt see Charlotte's true feelings about Tobias's appearance. Heat climbed her cheeks. Tobias was no more homely than Aunt Myrtle was a world-renowned chef.

"What's this we're discussing about the young Tobias?" Aunt Myrtle entered the kitchen and stored the broom in the corner of the room.

Charlotte held her breath. Once the aunts started on a topic, it would be next Christmas before they switched the subject.

"I was just asking our dear Charlotte if she finds the smithy to be a handsome fellow."

How long could one peruse the mismatched pieces of china in the hutch that the aunts had brought with them all those years ago from Minnesota? How long could one inspect the lines etched in the dishes from years of use? Charlotte could stare for hours, if need be. She pressed the wrinkles in her apron and slowly closed the door to the hutch. Her reflection greeted her.

The reflection of a woman who did, in fact, think Tobias Hallman a dapper man.

Dapper, but vexing. And for certain no one she would ever find interest in courting, not only because of who he was, but also because she would never allow her heart to be broken again.

Never.

No, from now on, Charlotte would appreciate the romantic lives of those in the dime novels, rather than seek to find a true love of her own.

Aunt Myrtle interrupted Charlotte's introspections. "Tobias would be a fine catch," she declared.

A fine catch? No. Most certainly, most assuredly, most absolutely not!

Charlotte spun around. "My dearest aunts, I do not find Tobias Hallman to be a handsome fellow, nor do I find him to be a fine catch." But even as she uttered the words, they sounded suspiciously fallacious in her own ears. "I have known him for years, and he's the same exasperating man he's always been. I do not consider him a suitable one with whom to pursue courtship, nor would I ever. Besides, I will never entertain the thought of falling in love again after that loathsome Cyrus Keller broke my heart into two million pieces."

"I understand completely," said Aunt Fern. "I felt the same way after that reprehensible Mr. Wilkins broke my heart into two million pieces. It's perfectly fine to be a spinster."

Aunt Myrtle must have decided it was a good time to start an argument with her sister. "Oh, you'll fall in love someday, Fern. Just wait."

"To the contrary. There is no true love for me."

Aunt Fern's voice sounded somewhat whiny and pouty as if she herself were a character in one of the dime novels Charlotte so frequently read. But she was just grateful the topic had switched from her and Tobias to Aunt Fern's refusal to fall in love.

Aunt Myrtle's one pointy eyebrow became more pronounced. "What about Mr. Gormon?"

Aunt Fern's eyes bulged. "A despicable thought indeed. That man is brash, obnoxious, and has a faulty memory. He asks me day after day if I'd like a haircut. No, there will be no interest on the part of Fern L. Beauchamp when it comes to Mr. Gormon."

While the aunts continued their discord, something Aunt Fern mentioned planted itself in Charlotte's mind. *"It's perfectly fine to be a spinster."*

And while Charlotte was content with the life the Lord had blessed her with, a niggling feeling stuck deep in her belly, competing with the bland biscuits she'd eaten for supper.

"This is our pew," said Aunt Myrtle, gesturing toward the pew five from the front at church that Sunday. "There's Mr. Quimby. I think I shall invite him to sit with us. Shall I invite Mr. Gormon too?"

"Absolutely not. That man has his own pew."

"To the contrary. He has no family in town, nor does Mr. Quimby." Aunt Myrtle peered around the church. "There's that kindly young smithy. He doesn't have any family here either. Perhaps we shall invite him to sit in our pew too."

The words tumbled from Charlotte's mouth. "Perhaps not, Aunt Myrtle. After all, I'm sure he would rather sit with some friends he's made in Prune Creek."

But Aunt Myrtle was on a mission and hadn't heard Charlotte's suggestion. She motioned toward the pew to first Mr. Quimby, then Mr. Gorman, and finally Tobias.

"I think there might be room in the Joneses' pew," muttered Aunt Fern. "Perhaps I shall sit there." Instead, she took a seat next to Charlotte just as Mr. Gormon plopped down beside her.

"Did you do something different with your hair, Fern?" Mr. Gormon asked, "It looks fashionable like those city ladies."

Aunt Fern crowded Charlotte, likely to escape Mr. Gormon's nearness on her other side. "You know full well I haven't done anything different with my hair. I've worn it this way since the seventies."

Mr. Gormon chuckled. "Ah, Fern Beauchamp. Such a spitfire."

Aunt Myrtle beamed as Mr. Quimby took a seat on her left at the edge of the pew. "Charlotte, have I introduced you to Mr. Quimby?" she asked, her face brightening to a deep red.

"Yes, you have. Nice to see you again, Mr. Quimby."

"You as well, Miss Eliason. And please, everyone, do call me Quimby."

"Oh," tittered Aunt Myrtle. "Quimby rather than your given first name of Clifford?"

Quimby nodded. "My family started calling me that when I was just a young'un. Pretty soon everyone was referring to me by that name, and I do like it better than the name 'Clifford', although I'd never tell my ma that as she and Pa named me after my maternal grandfather."

"Quimby it is, then. And you must call me Myrtle, and all of us by our given names."

"Indeed I will."

Charlotte watched as Aunt Myrtle dipped her head. Could what Aunt Fern said be true? Had Aunt Myrtle set her cap for the attorney?

"I'm Stanley Gormon," Mr. Gormon said, introducing himself to Charlotte.

"This is our niece, Charlotte Eliason from Willow Falls." Aunt Fern continued staring straight ahead.

"Nice to meet you, Mr. Gormon."

"And you as well. And you all must call me Stanley."

Charlotte smiled at the bald man with the contagious smile. Deep embedded wrinkles indicated he was a jovial one who grinned often, and his green eyes flashed with a mischievous glint.

"And may I call you Fern?" he asked Aunt Fern.

"No, you absolutely may not. You may refer to me as Miss Beauchamp."

Stanley remained undeterred by Aunt Fern's abrupt response. "All right, Miss *Fern* Beauchamp."

Aunt Fern pressed her lips together.

"And look, here's that kindly young smithy," announced Aunt Myrtle, drawing her attention from Quimby for the briefest of moments. "I'm so glad you could join us in our pew, Thomas. There's a seat at the end right there next to our lovely and enchanting Charlotte."

"Oh, he..."

"Ma'am, it's Tobias, and yes, I'd be thrilled to sit by your lovely and enchanting niece." Tobias squeezed into the spot on the very end on Charlotte's right.

"Hello, Charlotte."

"Tobias Hallman."

"Fancy sitting in the same pew as you."

Tobias's suspicious expression made Stanley's mischievous one paltry in comparison. So many people in the pew was a cramped situation, and were it not that they were in the Lord's House and respect was of utmost importance, Charlotte may have moved to the pew in front of them with a family she hadn't yet met.

He was still staring at her, likely expecting a witty response. Their gazes connected. He was clean shaven and had combed his black hair. His dimple was prominent, as was the scar on the left side of his chin from the time he, John Mark, and Russell had decided it was a wise idea to have a sword fight with sticks during recess. His brown eyes crinkled at the corners with his broad smile.

And Charlotte realized she had her nemesis' appearance memorized. With the exception of his face being thinner and two horizontal lines beginning to form on his forehead, Tobias Hallman looked exactly as he had during the days he tormented her in Willow Falls.

"Are you staring at me, Charlotte?" he whispered, a glint catching his sparkling eyes once again.

"You have some nerve to even suggest such a thing, Tobias Edgar Hallman."

Thankfully, Reverend Lloyd began to speak, and Charlotte was spared any more of Tobias's nonsense. Staring at him? But goodness. Some women may find Tobias handsome, but handsome or not, he was just as irritating now as he had been years ago.

"It's a pleasure to see you all here today. Shall we begin with some hymns? Please turn to page forty to "Great is Thy Faithfulness". My lovely wife will be providing the music on the new church organ donated by the Peabody family last year."

Charlotte loved all of the hymns, especially "Great is Thy Faithfulness" and "It is Well", and having been raised with a father who was a pastor, she knew the words to every one of the beloved hymns found within the pages of the worn hymnal. She lifted her voice to the Lord as she sang:

Great is Thy faithfulness!
Great is Thy faithfulness!

Morning by morning new mercies I see;
All I have needed Thy hand hath provided:
Great is Thy faithfulness, Lord, unto me!

Her eyes misted as she thought of her family. They would be in church this very moment also, Pa preparing his sermon, Ma likely holding one of her granddaughters, and Caleb fulfilling his duties as an elder, the position to which he'd been appointed last year.

Ma would turn and smile at Charlotte, and they would rejoice in singing to their Lord together. Charlotte was close to both of her parents, but she was especially close to Ma.

After church, the entire family would return to Ma and Pa's house for the noonday meal. Charlotte would assist Ma with preparing the food, which always consisted of a delicious dessert.

Her sweet little nieces would run around and play in the yard while Charlotte, Ma, and Annie would visit. Pa and Caleb would talk of cattle prices. Sunday afternoons were perfect, with the exception of Charlotte missing John Mark. But John Mark had reassured Ma that once the baby was born, he, Hannah, Ambrose, and the baby would be visiting Willow Falls again.

Only this time Charlotte wouldn't be there to see them.

Disappointment embedded itself in her thoughts, and with effort, she shoved it aside. Aunt Myrtle and Aunt Fern were delighted to have her for a visit, and Charlotte would do her best to enjoy the time with her beloved aunts. In time, she'd return home to the family she missed so much.

After three more hymns, Reverend Lloyd began his sermon.

"Today we will spend some time in Psalm 121. Will you all please stand as we read from God's Word?"

Charlotte stood, her shoulder connecting with Tobias's. He took a step to the right, nearly colliding with the wall.

She joined in the chorus of voices as she mouthed the treasured words from her Bible.

"I will lift up mine eyes unto the hills, from whence cometh my help. My help cometh from the Lord, which made heaven and earth..."

Tobias's voice was strong and clear as he did the same. He had closed his eyes, the memorized verses likely flowing from somewhere deep within him.

His parents had passed away in the last several years. Had he thought of this verse as he now navigated through his life as an orphan?

When they finished reading, everyone took their seats. Reverend Lloyd was a gifted preacher, but he couldn't compare to Pa and his preaching. No one could.

"We'll first look at the context of the verses in the chapter, and later we'll discuss how God is ready and able to help us with whatever difficulty we may face."

CHAPTER FOUR

TOBIAS LEFT THE BLACKSMITH shop to fix one of the spindles on the porch railing the aunts had asked him to mend and hopefully return in time to finish the sizable project he'd acquired yesterday. He whistled as he climbed the gentle slope of a hill to the Peabody house. As he neared, he ceased his whistling and wandered up the three steps to the front door. Thinking he heard something in the backyard, he traipsed around to the side of the house.

That's when he saw her.

Charlotte sat on a blanket on the ground beneath the towering elm tree, her back to him and her posture hunched. Her head bobbed up and down.

He stared, unable to pull his eyes away.

And then she spoke. "No! You must go after her, Ferdinand! She is your one true love!" Charlotte sat up straighter and shook her head. "Why must you be such a chucklehead? Go, Ferdinand! Catch her before she boards the stagecoach and rides out of your life forever."

Tobias stifled a chuckle and covered his mouth with his hand. Charlotte Eliason had always been dramatic, but as far as he knew, she'd never spoken to herself or to what sounded like a book.

"Aunt Myrtle? Aunt Fern?" Charlotte peered over her shoulder to the left, and Tobias hid behind the side of the house. It wouldn't do for her to catch him eavesdropping.

Likely satisfied any noise she heard was only a figment of her overactive imagination, Charlotte returned to the book.

And Tobias waited.

He peered again around the side of the house. Charlotte's head bobbed and shook from side to side. The sound of pages turning echoed in the peaceful afternoon.

Should he wait until she put the book down? Walk towards her? Make a commotion so as not to scare her?

Continue to wait?

In school, Charlotte was a studious scholar, as Miss Ledbetter, now Annie Eliason, had often mentioned. Charlotte had always finished her book-reading faster than anyone else in class. Tobias liked to absorb each word and take his time perusing the book, although some of that might have been due to his lack of motivation on some of the assigned topics.

Careful so as to avoid being seen, Tobias edged out further away from the house. From his standpoint, he could see her profile. Charlotte suddenly closed the book and held it to her heart. She closed her eyes.

And Tobias ignored a thought that entered his mind unannounced.

That Charlotte Eliason was indeed a beautiful woman.

"Well done, Ferdinand. Well done. It took you some time to come to your senses, ten pages to be exact, but you succeeded in stopping the stagecoach and declaring your undying love." Charlotte sighed and swooned. "Such a remarkable story."

Tobias snickered, unable to contain his amusement any longer.

Charlotte jolted and whipped around to face him. "Tobias Hallman, what are you doing?"

He snorted, the chortling emerging from him before he could give it a second thought. "I just stopped by to fix something for the aunts when I came upon a woman having a conversation with herself."

"I was not having a conversation with myself. I was reading one of the best books I've read in a long time. One I found in the parlor that Mrs. Peabody left behind."

"Reading a book? And talking to the characters?" Tobias raised his voice, closed his eyes, and gestured toward one of the trees. "Oh, Ferdinand, you must stop the stagecoach. Don't let your true love get away! Must you be a chucklehead?" He slapped his knee and laughed again.

"I do declare, Tobias, must you always make such a nuisance of yourself?"

When he'd finally stopped laughing for a few seconds, he asked, "How many times have you read that book?"

"Well..."

"How many times, Charlotte? Fifteen? Twenty?"

"Hardly. I have read it four times and..."

"Four times and you're still concerned that Ferdinand will not realize she is his true love?" Tobias could not understand women. Such oddities.

Charlotte stood and narrowed her eyes at him. "And what would you know about true love?"

"Nothing. I know nothing about such absurd topics. I do know, however, that if I read a book once I can be assured it will end the same way should I read it a second time. Now on the fourth time, the ending might change."

"It's not that I don't *know* how the book will end, it's just that..." Charlotte regarded him. "It's just that the characters are so well-written that I feel as though I am right alongside them going through their happy moments and their distressing ones as well. I don't expect someone such as yourself to understand the plight of a bibliophile."

Tobias shrugged. "Not only do I *not* care to understand since I would never read a dime novel, but I also could never understand you, Charlotte. You should have joined one of those theaters and been an actress."

"Theaters?"

"Yes, they had melodramas all the time in the theater in Cheyenne. I recently lived there when I was a blacksmith apprentice and heard about the theatrical productions. You would do well on stage being your usual dramatic self."

Her blue eyes flashed and he tamped down the thought that he'd always been drawn to her spirited personality.

"I would not do well as an actress in a melodrama, Tobias Hallman, no more than you would do well as a librarian."

Tobias threw his head back and chuckled. "You're right, I would never be a librarian. I read the Bible and I read the newspaper at the boardinghouse from time to time. But dime novels? Why would anyone read such drivel?"

"Some are drivel. But this collection of stories is delightfully wonderful. Clean, wholesome, faith-filled, and always with a happy ending."

"I have a question for you, Charlotte."

She lifted her chin. "And what would that be?"

"Why do you always call me 'Tobias Hallman' and never just 'Tobias?'"

Charlotte chewed on her bottom lip. Had he stumped her with his question?

"It's not like there are several others by the same name in Wyoming. Matter of fact, I've never even met another 'Tobias' let alone a 'Tobias Hallman'."

"I don't rightly know. I suppose it has more effect than just saying your first name."

He regarded her for a moment. Today she wore a green skirt with a green and pink plaid blouse. Wisps of hair had slipped from her bun and framed her face.

It was unfortunate she was so annoying.

He blinked, lest she think he was staring. "I...uh, are the aunts around? I should fix the broken railing on the porch and be on my way back to work. I...uh...I have a large project to finish there."

"They went to town for a brief visit with some friends. They should be back soon. You're welcome to fix the railing. I was just about to remove the clothes from the clothesline."

"All right." But his feet remained where they were. Tobias watched as Charlotte walked toward the clothesline. She removed a skirt from the line, then hung it up again.

"Not quite dry," she said to herself, more than to him.

"Oh."

Why all of a sudden were things awkward between them? When he attended school with Charlotte when they were youngsters, Tobias never lacked for words in sparring with her. Now, standing near her and watching the breeze blow the wisps of hair from her face, he found himself slightly mesmerized.

Mesmerized. Miss Ledbetter would have been proud he recalled one of their vocabulary words. Although back then when he'd been the one called on to use the word in a sentence, it hadn't described Charlotte. *"I was mesmerized by the size of the trout I caught when Pa and I went fishing the other day."*

He shook his head and dug his hands into his trouser pockets. What was wrong with him? He wasn't mesmerized by her any more than he was mesmerized by prairie dogs perched on rock piles.

Tobias needed to remind himself numerous times that this was the same irritating know-it-all Charlotte Eliason he'd known all his life.

Tobias stepped outside the blacksmith shop and arched his back and rolled his shoulders. He perused the bustling boardwalk when he saw Charlotte walking with a basket. "Hello, Charlotte," he said as she neared.

"Hello, Tobias Hallman."

"Doing some errands?"

"Yes."

They stood for a moment facing each other in silence. Then the words popped from his mouth before he gave them thought. "Was it true you really courted Cyrus?"

Charlotte's eyes widened. "What makes you ask?"

"Just something I heard and was wondering if it was true."

Charlotte took a deep breath, then stiffened her shoulders. "Yes, it is true."

"Cyrus Keller?"

"There's only one 'Cyrus' to my knowledge."

"Yes, but..." Tobias scratched his head. "Why would you court Cyrus? And how did John Mark feel about that?"

Something flashed in her eyes, but it wasn't the usual spark of agitation when Tobias said something that irritated her. It was more of a...sadness?

"I'd prefer not to discuss Cyrus." She fingered her purple necklace. "Besides, didn't I hear you were fond of Violet during our school years? Something about you finding her lovely?"

"No. I was never fond of Violet, and I for sure did not find her lovely. At all. Now, that is someone who would make a fine woman for Cyrus."

Charlotte peered off into the distance. Whenever she was in deep thought, she twisted her mouth to one side.

And Tobias admonished himself for noticing her habits.

"Say, do you recall that teacher we had before Annie...what was her name? Miss Barry?"

"Yes."

Tobias began to chuckle. "Do you remember how she wore her hair? That tall bun thing? It kept hitting the top of the doorway, and then before the school day was over, it was nearly sideways on her head. Remember that?"

"Yes, but pray tell what made you think of Miss Barry's coiffure?"

"Your hair..."

"My hair?" She reached up and patted her head.

"Yes, your hair."

Charlotte lifted her chin. "My hair is *nothing* like Miss Barry's."

"It does somewhat resemble...a tall mound."

"I beg your pardon. My hair does *not* resemble a tall mound. I'll have you know it's one of the latest fashions. A lovely coiffure with a sweeping, loose, and fluffy pompadour like one of the hairstyles in *The Utmost of Fashion Ladies Magazine.*"

"I know nothing about style, and even less about pompadours. Besides, this isn't some fancy city back East. This is Prune Creek, Wyoming."

Charlotte signed. "My dearest, Tobias, that is why you'll never be considered fashionable. Just because you live in a small Wild West town doesn't mean you ought to dress or maintain your hair in a dreadfully ghastly way."

It was Tobias's turn to reach up and pat his dark hair that had long since been plastered to his head from sweat caused by the stifling heat in the shop. "Men don't care about fashion or pompadours or looking dreadfully ghastly. We just don't."

"Yes, well..."

Not that he wanted Charlotte to find him dapper, but he secretly hoped she didn't find his appearance ghastly.

Her expression made him chuckle again, and he realized he missed bantering with her.

He cleared his throat. This necessitated a change of topic. "So..." He kicked at a pebble that had found itself on the boardwalk. "The weather is nice today."

"Yes, it is. Aunt Fern says it'll rain tonight. She said she feels it in her bones."

The aunts were such cards. Tobias had never known any of his relatives outside of his parents, brother, and later, his sister-in-law, Paulina, and niece, Lanie. He'd have to be careful or he might just "adopt" the aunts as his own. "I've heard that before," he said. "But then, I think I recall Aunt Fern mentioning she had arthritis."

"Yes. It's difficult to believe she's in anything but optimal health, with a few instances of gastrointestinal disturbances from eating Aunt Myrtle's food."

Tobias rubbed his stomach and groaned. "Speaking of gastrointestinal disturbances, as you put it...I didn't feel so well after eating Aunt Myrtle's huckleberry pie. I noticed you were quick to make sure I took the remainder of it home."

Charlotte giggled as a glint of something mischievous touched her eyes. "I believe full well in being a generous sort. Ma and Pa always instilled in me the importance of feeding the needy."

"I'm hardly needy enough to eat Aunt Myrtle's huckleberry pie. That stuff was awful." Tobias recalled the tart and powdery taste and how difficult it had been to swallow. He'd attempted a second piece the next day as he didn't want to be wasteful. It tasted no different and caused him to gag.

"I believe Aunt Fern mentioned something about Aunt Myrtle adding too much baking powder or some such thing." Charlotte shrugged. "Aunt Myrtle does have her own way of cooking."

"Did you inherit her cooking skills?"

"I most certainly did not."

Tobias chuckled at her thinly pressed lips and widened eyes. "One thing about you that has never changed is that anyone can see exactly what your thoughts are on a matter just from your expression."

"Well then you can ascertain from my expression that I am appalled that you would think my cooking skills would be anything like Aunt Myrtle's. I'm fortunate my pa survived when he first sampled her baking all those years ago in Willow Falls. Ma always warned us never to eat too much of it. Of course, Pa didn't realize it then. He told us he nearly died an early death that day. Ma didn't cotton much to him back in those days before they fell in love." Charlotte took a pause to swoon. "Such a romantic notion of how they fell in love, but I digress."

He wanted to ask about the story of Mrs. Eliason and Reverend Solomon, but Tobias didn't want Charlotte to think men cared about such ridiculous things. So instead, he asked about John Mark. "I hear John Mark got married."

"Yes. Hannah is just the sweetest woman. They have a son named Ambrose and another child soon to be born."

"Well, I'll be." He had missed seeing John Mark while he'd been in Cheyenne during his apprenticeship. "Just doesn't seem like it could be true that he's already married and a pa." Memories of his times with his best friend entered his mind. Tobias had always wanted his own family like Chester and John Mark now had. To find a godly wife, settle down, raise a family, and work for an honest wage to provide for that family. He'd never admitted it to anyone, not even John Mark or their other friend, Russell, but his own family was something Tobias longed for.

"Time moves on. Most of our classmates are married, and many live in Willow Falls."

"I heard what happened to Russell."

"Yes, and I'm so sorry you and John Mark lost your friend to a senseless murder. Russell was a godly and kind man who never deserved what they did to him. He had a fiancée named Amaya. I met her at the funeral. Awful to think they were so close to being married. They were planning their wedding and dreaming of their future together."

Tobias sobered at the thought of Russell's bereaved fiancée. Ma and Pa had been taken together when they passed. His brother, Chester, entered his thoughts. What would he do if he lost Paulina? "Couldn't be easy for her."

"No, I couldn't imagine it. John Mark says it's been difficult for Amaya, and understandably so." She paused. "How are Chester, Paulina, and Lanie? It's been a while since I've seen them.

"Doing well. Of course, Lanie is growing like a weed, but you have probably seen her more recently than I have."

"True. She spends a lot of time at Caleb and Annie's house since she and my nieces are close. As a matter of fact, she's taken to calling me 'Aunt Charlotte' because she hears them say it so often. I'm honored. She's a sweetheart."

Tobias nodded. "That she is. I saw them more often when we all lived in Cheyenne." All of them moving to the northern part of the state in closer proximity had been a good thing, but it also meant that Tobias didn't get to see his family as often since they moved back to Willow Falls and he'd purchased the blacksmith shop in Prune Creek. He made a note to himself to take some time and visit them. There was no excuse now that the train went all the way to Nelsonville, and a short stagecoach ride to Willow Falls meant a fairly easy trip. "Well, I best get back to work."

"Yes."

His stomach rumbled.

"I hear Aunt Myrtle is contemplating making some of her famous meatloaf for the noonday meal. Shall I have some delivered to you?"

41

"No thanks. I'd have to be starving for days before trying any more of her cooking."

Charlotte appeared thoughtful, her mouth twisting to the side. "What happened to the remainder of the huckleberry pie, if I might ask?"

"It went to a worthwhile cause."

"Really?"

"Yes, I donated it for dessert at the boardinghouse." Tobias shook his head. "You should have seen how excited the boarders were when they first saw the pie. They didn't seem to mind one bit that there was a sizable chunk taken from it. I'm not sure two of them could eat their meals fast enough before scooping heaping pieces onto their plates. It was all I could do not to laugh." Tobias started to chuckle then, and Charlotte joined in his amusement.

They paused, then laughed together again. "You should have seen their faces... One man, his name is Mr. Ruegge, a grouchy elderly man, his expression was the best. Wish I had a tintype of it to remember the occasion by."

"Oh, dear. Poor man." Charlotte held her stomach as she laughed again.

A sweet, joyous laugh. Tobias stopped long enough just to listen to it all by its lonesome without his own laughter interfering.

"Did anyone have to fetch the doctor?"

"No, but Mr. Ruegge asked Mrs. White, the proprietress of the boardinghouse, if she was the one who'd made the pie in retaliation for the residents having done something to anger her. I reckon he was thinking of maybe finding somewhere else to live after eating that huckleberry pie." Tobias grimaced as he recalled the taste.

"Oh, dear. Mr. Ruegge thought Mrs. White was angry at the residents and the huckleberry pie was her way of revenge?"

"Something like that. Mr. Ruegge is a peculiar sort. Always thinking the worst of others with his suspicious nature."

They continued in easy camaraderie for several seconds. "Well, I guess I better return to work," Tobias said again.

"Yes. It is getting rather late, and I still have errands to complete."

But they stood there awkwardly, no one speaking another word before Charlotte continued on her way down the boardwalk.

And as he watched her go, Tobias realized just how much of the same history they shared. They knew each other's family and friends and hailed from the same town. They were older now and more mature, but also much the same, even though time had passed.

And she was pretty, even with her mounded hair.

Tobias raked his fingers through his own hair. What were the odds that Charlotte Eliason was the great-niece of Fern and Myrtle Beauchamp? What were the odds she'd be here in Prune Creek, the place he now called home?

Chapter Five

After supper, Charlotte retrieved a piece of stationery from the weathered chest of drawers in the parlor. While the Peabody home, a pleasant whitewashed two-story with a porch, had been a generous gift to the aunts, there wasn't much in the way of furnishings.

Not that she was complaining. She loved the home with its cheery atmosphere, spacious porch, and well-landscaped yard with numerous flowers, trees, and a garden. According to the aunts, the Peabodys had a hired hand who kept up with the constant work of the yard. Now, the aunts, without sufficient funds, did what they could, and Charlotte was thrilled to assist them, especially with tending to the flowers and garden.

Charlotte returned to the kitchen and perched at the table to pen a letter to Ma. The room was quiet, save for the mantle clock ticking as the time passed and the low rumble of one of the aunts—presumably Aunt Myrtle—snoring.

She put pencil to paper:

Dear Ma,

I hope this finds you and Pa doing well. You will never believe who also resides in Prune Creek. Tobias Hallman! The aunts didn't realize we knew each other. I must admit it is a profound disappointment to discover he is the new blacksmith here. While I miss Willow Falls dreadfully, I don't miss some of the residents, namely Cyrus, Violet, and Tobias. Needless to say, that while I haven't seen him in some time, Tobias remains the same challenging individual he was all those years ago.

The aunts are doing well. You were right when you said they are quite the comical duo. I believe Aunt Myrtle might be fond of an attorney in town named Mr. Quimby. As for Aunt Fern, she declares she will never fall in love again.

How are Caleb, Annie, and the girls? I must admit I am rather homesick. Yes, you were correct in that time away from Willow Falls will do me good in light of Cyrus's betrayal. However, I do miss my family and am looking forward to the time when I can make a return trip home for a visit.

Charlotte paused and held her pencil midair. She didn't wish for Ma to fret. She again began to write:

But although I am homesick, I am enjoying Prune Creek and spending time with the aunts. The garden is lovely, and we are seeing the beginnings of green beans, corn, and peas. I do wish the growing season was longer in Wyoming as I would like to expand the garden.

The church service on Sunday included an excellent sermon, but do tell Pa there really is no one who can share the Word of God the way he can.

I think you would be amazed at how much Prune Creek has grown since we last visited. The depot seems much busier, there is a second bank, and a brand-new millinery. I've gazed into the window, and I dare say the fashions are quite exquisite, especially for Wyoming.

The aunts have a sizable bookcase left behind by the Peabodys that houses dozens of books. Apparently Mrs. Peabody was an avid reader because most of the books on the shelf are dime novels. Clean and wholesome, mind you, and I found one to be especially engaging. I've already read it four times in my tenure here.

Please tell everyone hello and that I love and miss them.

Much love,

Charlotte

Charlotte folded and tucked the letter into an envelope and addressed it to Ma. Tomorrow she would walk to town and mail it when she took the eggs to sell at the mercantile.

Minutes later, she rested her head on her pillow and attempted to fall asleep. But her mind raced.

Missing her family.

Tobias Hallman in Prune Creek.

Cyrus marrying Violet after he'd professed his love for Charlotte.

The latter filled her mind, and she thought once again of how she'd been caught unawares that Cyrus fancied Violet. John Mark had told her he'd suspected *after* Charlotte broke her engagement with Cyrus. The pain had been significant for some time afterwards, especially given Charlotte had planned every detail of the wedding and had even contemplated their new home on the Keller Ranch. She envisioned herself a mother, caring diligently for their children and their family sitting around the supper table discussing their day as her own family had done during her growing-up years.

A tear slid down her cheek and landed on her pillow.

Cyrus would lead their family in the Lord, just as Pa did. He would be a godly young man like her brothers, serving in the church as Caleb and John Mark often did. Cyrus would love her and cherish her as Pa loved Ma. They would grow old together and reminisce about their younger years while reveling in the joy of spending time with their grandchildren.

Charlotte had imagined being a part of the Willow Falls Ladies Society at church, able to give plentiful contributions to the missions society and to purchase items for the needy. She would sit on the porch of her and Cyrus's home and sew clothes for their children and the children in town who were lacking, just as Ma did.

Yes, she could still assist the needy and sew clothes for less fortunate children whether she married Cyrus or not, but in her mind, it had been planned so perfectly.

She, Cyrus, and their children would visit Ma, Pa, Caleb, and Annie often. The cousins would play and grow up together. Then, several times a year, they would visit John Mark, Hannah, and little Ambrose in Poplar Springs. In her imagination, John Mark and Cyrus had even become friends.

Charlotte would seek mothering advice from Ma as they sat sipping hot chocolate as the children ice skated on the pond where each member of her family had learned to skate.

It had all been such a fanciful dream.

And while Charlotte was determined to be happy without those things, a piece of her shattered when she realized it was not to be. When she discovered Cyrus hadn't been faithful to her and that he instead fancied Violet.

There was a certain amount of grief and mourning that followed a broken heart.

But deep inside, she knew John Mark had been right about Cyrus. He wasn't the godly, charming, and affable man Charlotte thought him to be. John Mark's words rang in her ears: "*There's a man out there somewhere who will appreciate you, be faithful to you, and love you the way God intends. The funny, charismatic, kind, beautiful, and somewhat-dramatic woman you are.*"

Perhaps there was a man who would love her the way God intended a man love his wife. Or perhaps Charlotte would become like Aunt Fern and never fall in love again. Or like Aunt Myrtle, who through loyalty to her sister, had decided to also be a spinster. It wasn't a new thought, for Charlotte had contemplated it many times, even as recently as a few nights ago after she'd learned the aunts were scheming a plan for her and Tobias.

For now, her focus would be on anything but the dream that once occupied her heart and her mind.

Lord, I know Cyrus wasn't the one You had planned for me. I know I was blinded by the thought of being in love, of marrying, and having a family. I pray, Lord, for whatever Your will is for me in that regard. Thank You that I didn't marry someone who didn't truly love me. And more importantly, that I didn't marry someone who didn't really love You. Father, give me wisdom, guide me, and help me to be a blessing to the aunts. Show me the path You have for my future. I surrender it to You.

Charlotte wiped the tears with the back of her hand. Tomorrow was a new day, and thankfully, the Lord knew what was to come.

In that knowledge, she would rest in Him.

CHAPTER SIX

AFTER DELIVERING THE EGGS to sell at the mercantile and posting her letter to Ma, Charlotte continued down the boardwalk toward home. She swung the now empty brown basket and reveled in the pleasant early summer day. So enthralled by the gentle breeze and the sunshine, Charlotte nearly ran plumb into someone exiting the barbershop at the same time she traversed by.

"Oh!"

"Hello, Charlotte."

Charlotte quickly recovered from nearly causing a collision and glanced up, attention honing in on one Tobias Hallman standing with Mr. Gormon outside the barbershop.

For a brief moment, she forgot that Tobias was who he was. He stood in front of her, strong and handsome with thick dark hair that had recently been cut and a cleanly-shaven face. Her heart stuttered and she fumbled the basket, attempting to right it before it fell from her hand.

How could it be that such a dapper man could be such a bothersome individual?

"What's the matter? Cat got your tongue as the saying goes?" Tobias asked.

Heat crawled up Charlotte's face. "No," she said, regretting her voice emerged as a squeak. "I was just daydreaming about the pleasant day, or the formerly pleasant day."

"Before you and I crossed paths?" A teasing glint shone in Tobias's eyes, and Charlotte removed her attention from him and instead focused on Mr. Gormon.

"Mr. Gormon, how are you today?"

"Hello, Miss Charlotte. Do call me Stanley."

"Stanley." The older man's weathered face almost seemed creased into a permanent smile. He was a likable fellow to all but Aunt Fern.

Stanley nodded toward Tobias. "I was just yapping a moment here with the young Tobias. We thought we'd gotten all caught up during his time in the barber chair, but reckon there's more to discuss. Did you know he did his apprenticeship way down in Cheyenne?"

Tobias straightened his posture and puffed out his chest. "True, and not only did I do my apprenticeship in Cheyenne, but I learned under one of the best blacksmiths."

"It shows. I have heard nothing but good things about your work. It's always been amazing to me how someone can turn a piece of metal into something useful." Stanley patted Tobias on the back. "This here gentleman is also becoming a pillar of our town. As I said to Quimby the other day, it's always nice to have fine folks move in."

Tobias lifted his chin and held his shoulders back. "I'm pleased to be an outstanding addition to this town."

"Well," said Charlotte, "as much as I'd love to sit and chat about the young Tobias, I best be on my way. The aunts will be expecting me."

Stanley shifted his weight and tugged at his collar. "Just one question, if I could."

"Certainly."

"I was wondering, if by chance, you might have some sage advice to impart about how I might woo Fern. You know, win her heart. I'm drawn to her wit, and she's the comeliest woman I've ever laid eyes on."

Charlotte covered her mouth in surprise. Of all things, she was not expecting that to be the barber's inquiry. "Oh, yes, she is witty, and she is lovely."

Tobias snorted. "You're asking Charlotte for advice on this type of matter?"

"Matters of the heart are my specialty," said Charlotte.

"Your specialty?" Tobias shook his head. "Because you read dime novels about Ferdinand?"

Charlotte ignored Tobias's comment. "Now, I do have to warn you, Stanley, that Aunt Fern won't relinquish her heart easily."

Stanley scratched his bald head. "That I can see. I've attempted to yap with her at church and here on the board-walk, but she seems...disinterested."

The disappointment etched in Stanley's small round eyes encouraged Charlotte to at least attempt to assist the elderly gent, although she wouldn't share with him that Aunt Fern's disinterest likely had more to do with the broken heart Mr. Wilkins caused rather than Stanley himself. "There are many things you don't know about Aunt Fern, things I'm not at liberty to share, but I will say this—she does appreciate a man of his word."

Stanley tucked his fingers through his suspenders. "I am a man of my word."

Tobias looked from Charlotte to Stanley, then to Charlotte again as if awaiting her answer.

"Tobias, this probably isn't a matter that would interest you."

"Have to disagree with you. I'd like to hear how one goes about winning a woman's heart."

Stanley's eyes widened. "Do you have a fondness for that Rita woman? She'd be a fine catch."

A peculiar niggle of dismay fluttered through Charlotte's mind before she brushed it aside. Why should she be concerned if Tobias had a fondness for Rita, whoever she may be?

"She might be a fine catch," said Tobias, not once removing his gaze from Charlotte. "I don't know her real well."

Charlotte shrugged. "I've never met her, but far be it from me to know who is and who isn't a fine catch for Tobias. Although surely there are other prospects for Rita. As far as Aunt Fern," Charlotte tapped on her chin, "I do believe she and Aunt Myrtle are planning to invite Quimby for supper Thursday evening. Perhaps you'd care to join us."

Stanley's forehead creased. "Would you recommend that? Attending supper? Will Fern be agreeable?"

"I'm sure all will be well. The aunts have the gift of hospitality and love entertaining friends. I'll let them know I invited you."

"Could you invite me too?" Tobias asked.

Charlotte turned to face him. "Sorry, but no. I know you miss Aunt Myrtle's huckleberry pie, but I think it's unbecoming of you to insist on an invitation."

"Just like the company is all, well, most of it."

Stanley chuckled. "Aunt Myrtle is a nice woman once you get to know her."

Charlotte wanted to tell Stanley Aunt Myrtle wasn't whom Tobias spoke of in regards to liking most in attendance at the aunts' house, but she refrained. "Supper will be served at seven o'clock."

"I'll be there," said Tobias.

Such an incorrigible man. She would do her best to ignore him, although it was rather difficult with him standing so close and nosing in on the conversation.

"What kind of flowers are Fern's favorite?" Stanley asked and elbowed Tobias. "If there's one thing I do know, a way to a woman's heart is through flowers. Women love them. Keep that in mind when you decide to woo Rita."

What was Aunt Fern's favorite type of flower? As far as Charlotte knew, there wasn't a flower her aunt *didn't* appreciate. "I know she loves the purple lupines that are so prevalent this time of year in the meadows."

"I know just where to find those. I'll bring some when I come for supper."

And Charlotte hoped—really hoped—that Aunt Fern would be amenable to Stanley's thoughtful gesture.

Sunday at church, Tobias plopped beside Charlotte. If nothing else, her expression provided amusement. "Do you know if Aunt Myrtle is doing the cooking Thursday night?" he asked. He might have to eat at the boardinghouse first depending on Charlotte's answer.

"It's a strong possibility."

Sitting this close to her, Tobias caught a hint of Charlotte's flowery perfume, and he inhaled. Today, she had fixed her hair in a braid that wrapped around the back of her head, not that he noticed her hair.

All right, he did.

He noticed a lot about her. Always had. He'd always liked it when she braided her hair, even when he'd tied her braids together in school. Tobias figured Charlotte preferred he *didn't* come to supper, but why would he miss an opportunity to banter with her? Besides, if Aunt Fern or even Charlotte did the cooking, it far surpassed anything he'd be served at the boardinghouse. And Quimby and Stanley were quickly becoming his friends, even though they were older than his pa.

"There might be some huckleberry pie left over again," she said when he didn't answer.

"Glad to know, although I'm not sure the residents at the boardinghouse would appreciate me bringing more of it to share."

Charlotte laughed, and he brushed aside the thought that he liked the tinkling sound.

The aunts finished their conversations and took their seats in the pew, Aunt Myrtle sitting between Quimby and Aunt Fern. Stanley took his place between Aunt Fern and Charlotte. "You sure do look mighty fine today, Fern," he said.

Tobias watched with amusement as Aunt Fern brushed his comment aside. She was a feisty woman, and Stanley had a lot of work ahead of him if he was to "win her heart" as he'd mentioned.

The following day, the aunts were far too excited about something. Definitely antsy aunts. And that something made Charlotte nervous. They'd barely been able to eat their breakfast, and Aunt Myrtle had paced the parlor for a good fifteen minutes. Perhaps it was just because they were on the planning committee for the special Founder's Day Celebration. "We best get to the meeting," urged Aunt Myrtle. "It would be imprudent for the president and vice president of the Prune Creek Ladies Society to be late."

"Which of you is the president and who is the vice president?" Charlotte asked as the horse clopped down the dirt road toward town.

Aunt Fern jabbed a thumb toward herself. "I was nominated as the president."

"Only because you have somehow coerced Judith into believing the treats you bring to the meetings are far superior to mine." Aunt Myrtle's expression turned sour.

"That's because it's true."

Aunt Myrtle tilted her chin upward. "Mine are unrivaled. I don't know you did it, Fern, but I suspect there's an element of dishonesty involved."

"Not so, Myrt. We should survey the fine folks of Prune Creek and ask them their thoughts. Your baking or mine?"

"I know someone who would vote for mine." Aunt Myrtle's face brightened, and her downturned mouth became a smile.

"If you're speaking of Quimby, then yes, he will vote for your baking; however, that is because of one of two reasons."

55

"Which are?"

Aunt Fern held up her hand and ticked off the two reasons. "Number one, his ability to taste failed long ago, and..."

"Fern Lydie Beauchamp! That is a bold untruth!"

"And second, he is smitten with you."

"Now that isn't a bold untruth, at least I hope it's not, but your former statement..."

And on it went until they arrived in town several minutes later and parked the buggy beyond an area where several people had gathered between the church and the school.

"Attention! May I have your attention?" Quimby's voice carried through the crowd, and the townsfolk quieted.

Tobias sidled alongside Charlotte and whispered, "Appears the aunts are scheming something."

Charlotte peered over at Aunt Myrtle and Aunt Fern who stood not far from Quimby with a sheet of stationery in Aunt Myrtle's hand. The two carried on a conversation and pointed toward the audience. "They are extremely suspicious," said Charlotte.

"That they are."

She wanted to comment on the previously unimaginable happenstance that she and Tobias actually agreed on something, but just then Quimby began to speak.

"It's that wonderful time of year again in Prune Creek, and as the chairman of the Prune Creek Founder's Day Committee, I'm pleased to announce that we are only five days away from our celebration on Saturday."

The townsfolk cheered, and Quimby continued. "We have many events, including a bake sale, sewing contest, pie eating contest, a parade, singing by our pupils in the children's choir, and a shooting tournament. We'll conclude the event with a potluck."

Murmurs echoed throughout the crowd, and a twinge of homesickness filled Charlotte's heart. Every year in Willow Falls, the town held an ice cream social. This would be the first year she wasn't there to partake.

"The Prune Creek Ladies Society will be procuring a list of folks with an expressed interest in helping with the festivities. They will be meeting at the table outside of the mercantile to take names of those eager to assist in making this the best Prune Creek Founder's Day Celebration thus far."

After the crowd dispersed, Charlotte stood in line at the table. Perhaps she could be of some assistance, maybe aiding the teacher with the children's choir. Aunt Myrtle and Aunt Fern sat behind the worn table jotting names on the stationery.

"Oh, yes, there you two are," gushed Aunt Fern when Charlotte reached the front of the line.

Charlotte turned around and nearly bumped into Tobias. "Oh!" Why was it she was forever bumping into him?

Tobias smirked. "Hello again, Charlotte."

Charlotte bit her lip. Perhaps she should have forgone visiting Prune Creek. There were so many people and things she was missing in Willow Falls. "I'd like to sign up to volunteer as well," she told the aunts.

"We've already addressed that matter." Aunt Fern tapped her pencil on the table. "Charlotte, you and Tobias will be in charge of the bake sale."

"The bake sale?" Tobias wrinkled his nose. "Won't the Ladies Society be in charge of that? I was thinking more of helping with the shooting tournament."

"Look at this way, Tobias. You'll be able to *compete* in the shooting tournament if you aren't a volunteer for it," suggested Aunt Fern.

Tobias nodded. "That's true. But still, isn't this a position better suited for the Ladies Society?"

"I agree," said Charlotte. "Won't you two be in charge of the bake sale?"

Tobias leaned toward her. "Did you notice we just agreed on something?"

Aunt Fern's eyes grew large. "That thought didn't escape *my* attention. Now, in answer to your question about Myrtle and I being in charge of the bake sale...we are hoping to train someone else for the position as we are contemplating retiring from it. Besides, we, along with Judith and the reverend's wife, will be overseeing the pie eating contest."

"Indeed," chirped Aunt Myrtle. "After all, I'm providing some of the pies for the contest."

Aunt Fern lifted her chin. "And Doc has already agreed to stand nearby and be ready to provide medical services should anyone fall dead away from eating Myrtle's huckleberry pies."

CHAPTER SEVEN

AFTER THE MEETING, AUNT Myrtle linked arms with Charlotte and Aunt Fern, and together they walked to the buggy. The aunts' voices entwined in perfect harmony as they sang, "While Strolling Through the Park One Day".

Only Charlotte wasn't in a very jovial mood. As a matter of fact, she was slightly miffed at the aunts for their matchmaking shenanigans and assuming she would want to volunteer to oversee the bake sale with Tobias Hallman.

Nothing could be further from the truth.

After they'd crowded into the buggy, the aunts continued their merrymaking as Aunt Myrtle steered the buggy around the corner and up the hill toward home.

Charlotte peered to the side at the scenery.

"My, but you're a quiet one this afternoon," remarked Aunt Fern.

Aunt Myrtle leaned forward and peered at her. "Are you not feeling well, dear?"

"I'm fine," Charlotte answered, her voice sounding more impatient than she intended.

Aunt Myrtle and Aunt Fern exchanged glances, likely sharing some secret code between them about Charlotte's peculiar behavior.

When they reached the house, Charlotte was the first to disembark from the buggy.

"Do wait a moment, please, Charlotte," said Aunt Myrtle.

Charlotte stopped and waited for Aunt Myrtle to continue.

Aunt Fern rested a hand on her arm. "Please do tell us what is the matter."

Charlotte looked from one aunt to the other. Such dear, precious women. How could she tell them in a kind way that she neither needed nor wanted their matchmaking assistance?

She prayed for guidance, took a deep breath, then proceeded as gently as she could. "It's a matchmaking shenanigan if there ever was one." She sighed. "Aunt Myrtle and Aunt Fern, I appreciate that you are fond of Tobias. However, I am not so fond of him. Would you please kindly refrain from arranging things such as overseeing the bake sale wherein we are volunteers together?"

Aunt Fern's mouth fell open. Aunt Myrtle's eyes bulged.

"My, but we are dreadfully sorry for the imposition," gasped Aunt Myrtle.

"Dreadfully sorry," warbled Aunt Fern.

"I don't wish to upset you with my request, it's just that..."

Each aunt wrapped an arm around her. "No need to explain," said Aunt Myrtle. "We understand, don't we, Fern?"

"Yes, we do."

Remorse was written in Aunt Myrtle's eyes. "I am sorry for my role in this entire ordeal."

"As am I," added Aunt Fern.

An awkward silence surrounded them before Aunt Myrtle declared she best see to unhitching the horse. Aunt Fern remained standing next to Charlotte. "Would you care to sit on the porch for a spell?" she asked.

Charlotte followed her aunt to the porch and took a seat in one of the rocking chairs.

"I'm sorry we arranged for you and Tobias to oversee the bake sale. If you'd like, I would be happy to talk to Myrtle about an alternative arrangement."

"No, I don't want to cause an imposition. It's just that..." Charlotte picked at a loose thread on her dress.

Aunt Fern placed a wrinkled hand on her arm. "Yes?"

"It's just—you wouldn't appreciate it if we arranged for you and Stanley to supervise the bake sale together." The words tumbled from her mouth before she had the wherewithal to stop them.

"You're right, I wouldn't."

They sat for a few silent moments before Charlotte spoke again. "Aunt Fern, I'm sorry. I shouldn't have said that."

"No, you should absolutely have said it. You're right."

"Cyrus broke my heart when he was unfaithful during our courtship. I used to dream of a life being married to him. Now I see clearly that marrying him would have been unwise, but the hurt is there all the same. Even though it's been nearly a year, I have vowed not to fall in love again. Especially not with someone like Tobias Hallman. He's been a nuisance since the first day I met him when I was six and he was eight."

"But goodness. You've known him that long?"

"I have. His family moved to Willow Falls, and of course, he became best friends with John Mark. Those two, along with their other friend, Russell, caused all kinds of mischief during our school years. Many of those pranks involved me, my braids, my dolls, and snakes."

Aunt Fern inhaled a sharp breath. "I had no idea. I can see why you wouldn't want a thing to do with him. And to think Myrtle and I thought him to be such a nice young man."

"He is thoughtful and does care about others; he's just vexing."

"Charlotte, are you familiar with the story about Mr. Wilkins?"

Charlotte nodded. "Yes. He's the one who broke your heart when you, Aunt Myrtle, and Ma moved here from Minnesota. He broke off your courtship."

"Indeed. My heart was shattered into a million pieces, and I decided never to fall in love again. Now, I was much older than your twenty-two years." Aunt Fern sat back against the frame of the rocking chair. "Mind you, I don't regret the life God chose for me. Myrtle and I raised your ma after our brother and sister-in-law passed. It was a good life, the three of us. Lydie was and is such a blessing to us. Once she married your pa, whom she did not like at first..." Aunt Fern tossed Charlotte a knowing glance, "we remained in Prune Creek and cared for the Peabodys. God has been gracious to us in that we are in relatively good health, with the exception of a few aches and pains and some arthritis. No, I don't regret the life God chose for me. What I do regret is the bitterness."

"Bitterness?"

"Yes. After Mr. Wilkins broke my heart, I allowed the bitterness to take root in my heart. I believed all men were just the same as the one who lied to me. That clearly is not the case. Examples of godly men are all around me—your pa, your brothers, the reverend here, Quimby, and the list goes on. As the verse in Ephesians says, we are to put bitterness away from us. Sadly I have not done that."

Aunt Fern's eyes glistened with unshed tears, and Charlotte reached over and rested her head on her aunt's shoulder. "I don't think you're bitter, Aunt Fern. I think you were just hurt and it took a while to recover."

"Bless your heart, child, but it shouldn't take over twenty years to recover. It shouldn't take me that long to forgive someone, even if his name is Mr. Wilkins." Aunt Fern sniffled. "But I spent some time with the Good Lord last night and repented for my unforgiveness. He's shown me a lot of grace and has forgiven me for much. I ought to learn from His example no matter the transgression against me."

"Thank you for sharing that with me, Aunt Fern."

"You're welcome. And there is a point I'm slowly coming to with this story. You see, Charlotte, you're young. You have your entire life ahead of you. Don't believe that every man is like Cyrus and that your heart will get broken if you allow it to love again. Don't be like I've been. Forgive, move on, and await with anticipation the life God has planned for you. Be like Aunt Myrtle, who I daresay has opened her heart to Quimby."

Charlotte swallowed the lump that had formed in her throat. "I will, Aunt Fern. I've already forgiven Cyrus, but the pain does linger."

"Of course it does, and that's to be expected. Now, I do promise you that your ornerier aunt and I will no longer be attempting to arrange for you and Tobias to someday court. Yes, that was our intention, but no longer. Will you please forgive us?"

"Yes, I absolutely do forgive you both."

"Splendid. Now, shall we go inside and see what we can find for the noonday meal? I hear Myrtle in there making all kinds of noise in the kitchen. It's likely she's preparing to bake something. We wouldn't want that now, would we?"

Charlotte giggled. "No, I think *we* should offer to cook today."

"I agree."

"Aunt Fern?"

"Yes?"

"Thank you. For everything. For you and Aunt Myrtle raising Ma, for allowing me to stay here with you, and for loving me. You two are the best."

Aunt Fern embraced her. "That's a sweet thing to say. Be sure you tell Aunt Myrtle that too. She'll appreciate it."

"Oh, and Aunt Fern?"

"Yes?"

"Since we're being honest, I might as well share something with you." Charlotte took a deep breath. "I may have invited Stanley to supper tomorrow night."

"You might have or you did?"

"I did."

Aunt Fern tilted her head to the side. "Why, might I ask, would you do such a thing? That man is such a strange bird."

"It's a long story, but Quimby was invited, Tobias invited himself..."

"Tobias invited himself?"

"Indeed. So it was only fitting that I invite Stanley as well. Is he really so bad, Aunt Fern?"

Was it Charlotte's imagination or did a bit of pink touch Aunt Fern's cheeks?

"Now who's scheming matchmaking shenanigans?"
They shared a laugh as they walked into the house.
And Charlotte felt lighter than she had in some time.

CHAPTER EIGHT

CHARLOTTE FINISHED HANGING THE laundry on the clothesline, tending to the garden, and whipping up a batch of gingerbread cookies before heading to her room to change for supper.

Hopefully all went well tonight. What would Aunt Fern think about Stanley bringing her flowers? Would Tobias be his typical annoying self? Would anyone develop a stomachache from eating Aunt Myrtle's lumpy cookies?

The aroma of gingerbread cookies, Aunt Myrtle's sugar cookies, and Aunt Fern's stew and biscuits all merged together to cause Charlotte's stomach to rumble. She planned on partaking in all of the offerings, except Aunt Myrtle's cookies, of course.

Bless her heart, Aunt Myrtle tried hard to make delicious meals and desserts, but cooking and baking were clearly not her gift. The cookie dough for sugar cookies was typically light, soft, and cohesive. Aunt Myrtle's was heavy, hard, and clumped together. Charlotte hadn't said a word when they prepared the treats side by side, but instead rolled her own gingerbread cookies—Ma's recipe—and placed them in the oven.

"I wondered if I accidentally added too much flour," Aunt Myrtle had muttered.

Now, minutes later, Charlotte dashed down the stairs and assisted the aunts with setting the table. The mismatched dishes, ones that the aunts had since their days in Minnesota, made a charming addition to the new tablecloth Aunt Myrtle had sewn. "Do you think Quimby will like the new tablecloth?" she asked, stepping back to peruse it from a short distance.

Aunt Fern added the pitcher of milk to the table. "Something tells me you're growing fond of that man."

"He is a respectable and kindly man, and I do appreciate his delightful sense of humor. So, yes, Fern, as much as I hate to admit you might be right about something, you *could* be right that I am growing fond of Quimby."

"More like besotted," murmured Aunt Fern.

Aunt Myrtle didn't argue with her sister, but instead hummed a tune while she bustled about finishing necessary chores before supper.

A thought popped into Charlotte's head. What would Aunt Fern do if Aunt Myrtle someday married Quimby? The two sisters had lived together for all their lives. Would Aunt Fern adjust to life without her sister always there?

"Don't borrow worries." Ma's voice entered Charlotte's mind. She wouldn't borrow worries, but the thought of Aunt Fern being all alone did concern her. Perhaps she would plan to stay in Prune Creek longer than anticipated if Aunt Myrtle did, in fact, marry Quimby. After all, Quimby did own a tidy house not far from his law office. It wouldn't do for Aunt Fern to have to live in the Peabody house all by herself.

"My, but aren't you the woolgathering sort," quipped Aunt Fern. "Whenever you're deep in thought, you bunch your mouth over to the side, just like our ma did. Do you remember that, Myrtle? Doesn't Charlotte make that same expression?"

Aunt Myrtle's head jerked up from the task of buttering the biscuits, and she ceased her humming. "Pardon me?"

"Just as I thought. You've been busy daydreaming about Quimby." Aunt Fern pursed her lips. "As I was saying, doesn't Charlotte make the same expression when she's deep in thought that Ma did all those years ago?"

"Yes, now that you mention it, she does. However, I've always thought Charlotte more favors her pa with his coloring, rather than our side of the family."

Charlotte listened as the conversation continued about who looked like whom in the family.

A knock on the door interrupted the aunts' musings.

Aunt Fern checked the mantle clock. "Someone is early."

"Wait! Before you answer it, let's hazard a guess on who is the first to arrive," suggested Aunt Myrtle. "I vote for Quimby."

"Of course you do. I vote that it's Tobias. What do you say, Charlotte?"

Charlotte had no idea which man would arrive at the house first, but since the other choices were taken, she guessed Stanley.

"Oh, yes, Stanley Gormon." Aunt Myrtle elbowed her sister. "Now you be nice to him, Fern."

"Pshaw. I'm always nice to him. I just hope he doesn't ask me if I need a haircut. The answer will always be no."

The knock sounded again, and Charlotte opened the door. "Hello, Stanley."

Stanley stood before her, right hand behind his back. "Hello, Miss Charlotte."

"Do come in. You're the first to arrive."

"Well, I could say I smelled the delicious food cooking all the way to town." His spectacles fell slightly down the bridge of his nose, and he righted them with his free hand.

"Hello, Stanley," greeted Aunt Myrtle. "Did you by chance see Quimby on your way here?"

"Didn't see him, Myrtle, but I know he's planning to come. We discussed the matter earlier today when he came in for a haircut."

Stanley meandered toward Aunt Fern, his right hand still behind his back. "Hello, Fern," he said.

It was then that Charlotte noticed Aunt Fern had put on her special dangly earrings that she usually only wore to church. Aunt Fern glanced up from her task. "Mr. Gormon."

"I brought these for you." Stanley produced a bouquet of vibrant purple flowers from behind his back.

Aunt Fern gasped. "Oh!"

"They're pretty just like you are."

"Now, I must say, the purple lupines are the most beautiful wildflowers in my humble opinion, but you, Mr. Gorman, have old and tired eyes if you think I'm as pretty as a lupine."

Red crept up Stanley's wrinkled cheeks. "To me you are as pretty as lupine. Prettier, in fact."

Aunt Fern patted her gray bun. "I—well—" it was her turn to blush, and she quickly turned away from Stanley and put the flowers in a vase with some water. "I best go retrieve the stew off the stove."

"Already been done," said Aunt Myrtle. "Why don't you and Stanley take a seat on the porch and await the arrival of the others while Charlotte and I finish setting the table?"

Aunt Fern narrowed her eyes at her sister. "Why don't you go wait on the porch since you're anticipating Quimby's arrival?"

"Actually, Fern, I'd like to talk to you about something anyhow." Stanley stood next to her, his short stature barely making him as tall as Aunt Fern. "You see, I need to pick out a buggy. I've needed one for some time. Yes, I have a pair of strong horses and a decent wagon, but a buggy is more to my liking. I thought I'd ask your opinion."

"I'm hardly the one to talk to about buggies. Perhaps Quimby or Tobias would be better equipped to answer your questions."

Aunt Myrtle gently patted her sister on the back. "Off with the two of you to the porch. Let us know when everyone has arrived. And, Stanley? You are making a wise choice when it comes to asking Fern about buggies. She has a vast knowledge about all sorts of matters."

"Here's something I know a lot about. Irritating sisters." But rather than argue further, Aunt Fern followed Stanley to the door. He opened it, and the two stepped outside.

"Perhaps I shouldn't chide her so," said Aunt Myrtle. "But don't you think they make a handsome pair?"

Charlotte saw their heads through the window. Stanley's mouth was moving, but Aunt Fern stared straight ahead. It appeared Stanley was sincere in his intentions. Would Aunt Fern allow herself a second chance at love?

Tobias greeted Aunt Fern and Stanley on the porch when he arrived. Stanley prattled on about the history of barbershops while Aunt Fern stared straight ahead and nodded at appropriate times. Quimby and Aunt Myrtle were in deep conversation in the parlor.

Tobias inhaled the aroma of gingerbread mixed with biscuits and followed his nose to the kitchen where he found Charlotte tending to the baking. She opened the oven door and retrieved a pan of golden-brown cookies and placed them beside another pan of smaller round white cookies.

"Did I miss something? Is it Christmas?" His words caused Charlotte to startle, and she whipped around and held a hand to her heart. He immediately regretted catching her unawares. "Sorry. I didn't mean to scare you."

He inhaled the delicious scent all over again. An aroma that took him back to the days of holiday celebrations when he was a young'un. Loneliness crept into his heart at missing his parents, and Tobias did his best to shove it aside. "Not sure about gingerbread as it's months before Christmas, but what are those other cookies?" He pointed to the unrecognizable and less-than-cohesive white cookies.

"It's never too early for gingerbread, and this is Ma's famous recipe."

"Like Aunt Myrtle's famous recipe?"

Charlotte set the potholders she'd used to retrieve the cookies to the side. "No, not like Aunt Myrtle's. For as often as you were always making yourself a nuisance during suppertime at the Eliason home, you should know my ma's baking is some of the best in Willow Falls."

"Yes, but that was your ma's baking. This is you." Tobias shrugged for added effect. "Who knows if you are a baker like your ma or more like Aunt Myrtle."

She narrowed her eyes at him. "You don't have to have any gingerbread if you're apprehensive. Incidentally, my baking is much like Ma's." She lowered her voice. "And nothing like Aunt Myrtle's."

Tobias chuckled, enjoying once again the banter between them. "Well, I do recall eating at the Eliason home many times as a young'un, and your ma's cooking was tasty. If you'll remember, John Mark was no stranger to the Hallman home."

"True. I recall him mentioning that he sometimes ate supper twice—once at our house and then at your house or vice versa."

"That happened often. He could always outeat both Russell and me, but I did come in second place."

"Something to be proud of, to be sure." A glint lit her eyes, drawing him to her.

Tobias returned her smile, not really intending to, but that was the thing about Charlotte. Her vivacious personality was contagious—when she wasn't irritated with him. She looked away first, and Tobias discovered a fingernail he needed to pick at. "So, uh, what kind of cookies are the white ones? Sugar cookies?" The ones on the tray were more rounded than he'd usually seen in contrast to the flatter, more pancake-like ones, and some pieces of each cookie strayed off by itself.

"Yes."

His stomach rumbled and he patted it. "Are they any good?"

"Only one way to find out." Charlotte used the spatula to remove one and positioned it on a nearby plate. "Careful. It's still hot."

Tobias appreciated her concern for him. His hunger since he hadn't eaten since the tasteless mush Mrs. White served at the boardinghouse that morning had gotten the best of him. He pinched the edge of the sugar cookie, noting how it crumbled easily, and popped it in his mouth, preparing himself for the heat.

What he hadn't anticipated was the taste.

"Pleh!" He covered his mouth, and with the best manners he could contrive at such short notice, he spit the cookie into his hand. He scanned the area for the water pitcher.

Charlotte giggled. "Was it too hot?"

"No, it wasn't that." Tobias willed his taste buds to forget the repugnant taste.

"Were they not cooked enough? I could bake them for longer if need be."

"No, it's not that." The taste seemed to linger inside of his mouth. "Say, is there some water?"

Charlotte walked past him and wound her way through the kitchen and toward the table where she retrieved the water pitcher. She poured him a cup and handed it to him.

"Thank you." Tobias guzzled the water, begging it to wash away the chalky taste of the cookies. "Did you make those cookies?"

Charlotte laughed again. "No, Aunt Myrtle did. I made the gingerbread cookies. Would you care for one?"

"If you're sure she didn't make those, then yes."

"I'm sure." Charlotte removed a gingerbread cookie and put it on his plate.

Even if the gingerbread cookies were bland, they couldn't be anywhere as bad as the sugar cookie sample he'd just endured. He took a bite and allowed the dessert to melt on his tongue. The flavorful taste took him back several years to the days at the Eliason home when he, John Mark, and Russell would sneak cookies while Mrs. Eliason tended to other duties.

"Well? Is it better than the sugar cookie?"

"Much." He took another bite. He could easily ruin his supper devouring too many of these.

"Even though gingerbread cookies should only be made at Christmas?"

"All I have to say is that I'm mighty glad your cooking is nothing like Aunt Myrtle's!"

CHAPTER NINE

CHARLOTTE STOOD NEXT TO Tobias behind the bake sale table at the Founder's Day Celebration. The turnout for the event was impressive, and already, Charlotte had met several Prune Creek residents for the first time. Tobias appeared less than thrilled to be facilitating with her, but excelled at prattling on with the townsfolk when his attention wasn't focused on the men setting up for the shooting tournament. "Wonder if they need assistance," he said, tossing a wistful nod toward Stanley, Sheriff Rettig, Hugh, Reverend Lloyd, and several other men.

"I'm sure they're capable. Just think, Tobias, you'll be able to join the tournament after you sell some more pies, cakes, and cookies."

He offered a sideways smile. "Thanks, Charlotte."

A rotund man with a thick middle, slim arms, and trousers hiked up higher than his waist, approached the table. "Why are you working the bake sale table?" he asked Tobias.

"Good morning, Mr. Ruegge, fancy seeing you here. This is Charlotte Eliason."

Mr. Ruegge offered an obligatory half-smile that never reached his eyes before his expression returned to that of a scowl. "Hello, Miss Eliason."

"Mr. Ruegge."

The man perused the wide variety of desserts on the table before pointing to Aunt Myrtle's huckleberry pie. "Is that the same type of pie you brought to the boardinghouse that one time?"

A grin danced on Tobias's lips. "It is. Would you care to purchase it? It's all for a good cause seeing as how we're raising funds for new hymnals this year."

"Don't care what you're raising the funds for, young man. That pie was absolutely atrocious. Mrs. White still hasn't forgiven me for blaming her for baking it." Mr. Ruegge's tone was nasally and whiny, a trait that fit well with his appearance and personality.

"I'm sorry for that, Mr. Ruegge," said Charlotte. "Perhaps we might interest you in some of our other delectable offerings."

Mr. Ruegge rested his folded hands across his expansive girth. "What about those apple fritters, or perhaps the gingerbread cookies?"

"Uh, the gingerbread cookies are sold." Tobias reached for the plate and placed it beneath the table.

"I'll take the apple fritters." Mr. Ruegge produced a dime from his pocket, and Charlotte dropped it into the coin box.

"Have a good day, sir," Tobias said.

The elderly man said nothing, but took his plate of goodies and plodded toward the next table.

Charlotte faced Tobias and firmed her hands on her hips. "Why did you put the gingerbread cookies beneath the table? We could have sold those to Mr. Ruegge as well."

Tobias plucked a dime from his pocket and handed it to Charlotte. His fingers lightly touched her palm, and a shiver zipped up her arm. She attempted to ignore it.

"Thought I'd help out with the purchase of the new hymnals this year." He lifted a gingerbread cookie from the plate and savored a bite.

"Well, thank you."

Tobias offered her a cookie. "Care for one? They make me think of Christmas."

Against her better judgment since she'd eaten far too many while baking the cookies, Charlotte acquired a cookie from the top of the pile. "Mr. Ruegge certainly wasn't too fond of Aunt Myrtle's huckleberry pie."

"No, he's a cantankerous man." Tobias took a bite of his second cookie. "Surprised he purchased anything at all since he's a miserly sort. He's always disputing the charge for rent with Mrs. White although he's been a boarder for years."

"Sounds like a pleasant fellow."

Tobias chuckled, the sound of his laugh reminding her how she'd grown accustomed to it over the years.

Several other customers arrived to purchase the desserts, including Doc, Mrs. White, Hugh, who of course purchased his wife, Judith's cake, and Sheriff Rettig after he finished setting up for the shooting tournament.

Soon there were two items left—Aunt Myrtle's huckleberry pie and Aunt Fern's apple pie. Charlotte was astonished that no one had claimed the apple pie as Aunt Fern was a decent cook. Not as skilled as Ma, but no one had acquired indigestion, stomach disturbances, or frequent trips to the privy because of it.

Mr. Opalinkski, the man whom Aunt Fern spoke of needing a doctor after consuming Aunt Myrtle's huckleberry pie, arrived next. His pale face rivaled snow on a Wyoming winter day. For being such a thin and frail man, his resonant voice boomed as he inquired about the remaining offerings. He pointed a gnarled finger at Aunt Myrtle's huckleberry pie. "Who made that?"

"Aunt Myrtle," answered Tobias.

Mr. Opalinski retched. "No fond memories from the last time I ate something that woman made. How 'bout that other pie?"

"Aunt Fern," Tobias said. "We can offer you the huckleberry pie at a special half-off price of a nickel rather than a dime."

Mr. Opalinski shook his head so fast his white hair flapped in the breeze. "No thank you and no thank you." He pointed to Aunt Fern's apple pie. "Is her cooking anything like her sister's?"

Both Charlotte and Tobias chorused a hearty "no."

"I'll take it."

Charlotte giggled at Mr. Opalinski's swift response and attempted to disregard the fact that she and Tobias made a stellar team. "Well, we have one more item. I wonder who will purchase Aunt Myrtle's huckleberry pie? That was a magnificent idea to offer it at half price."

Tobias bowed. "Prune Creek's top salesman at your service."

"Except it didn't sell."

"True. But look, there's Quimby heading this way."

Quimby stood in front of their table seconds later. "I've been so busy arranging things for the celebration that I nearly missed the opportunity to make a purchase." He retrieved a quarter from his pocket. "I'll take that huckleberry pie." He licked his lips. "I can almost taste it now."

"Aunt Myrtle will be so pleased you purchased it," said Charlotte.

"I was worried someone else may have bought it already." Quimby pinched a piece of crust from the side of the pie plate and popped it into his mouth. "I may not need any food at the potluck seeing as how this could be my noonday meal."

Tobias stood beside six other men preparing for the shooting contest. He wiped his hands on his trousers and rolled his shoulders. Why was he nervous? He'd practically been born with a rifle in his hands. He scanned the crowd that gathered behind the contestants. Charlotte's face outshone the rest. He wanted to impress her with his skill, even though she'd witnessed him at numerous target practices during their growing up years with John Mark, Russell, and Reverend Solomon. Some of those target practices she partook in herself. She already knew his skill or lack thereof.

He averted his attention to Quimby, the official announcer for everything related to Founder's Day.

"Ladies and gentlemen! We will now commence our shooting contest. This year, we have seven men vying for the Prune Creek Sharpshooter Award. As you all know, Mr. H.R. Prune, the founder of our town, was an avid rifleman. Some might even say he was on par with the likes of Adam Bogardus and Doc Carver in his skills. He was a sharpshooter, an accomplished trapshooter, and assisted former sheriffs of this town in apprehending many an outlaw. He went on to win numerous awards, even traveling as far as England to trumpet his abilities. Today, these men will compete in his honor, and the fine folks of Prune Creek will witness whether Deputy Shelton retains the Prune Creek Sharpshooter Award or if he passes the notoriety to another."

The crowd cheered as Quimby continued. "There will be a rifle contest with clay pigeons followed by a quickdraw revolver competition in which contestants will be judged on the quickness of their draw as well as the accuracy of their aim. Men, if there are no questions, we will begin." He took several steps behind the men and ushered the crowd to do so as well.

When it was his turn, Tobias took aim with his 1887 lever action Winchester, hoping to hit several of the twenty-five clay pigeons as they were randomly released. In the end, Tobias hit seventeen of them, while Shelton hit fifteen.

Quimby announced that Tobias was now in first place, while Deputy Shelton was in second.

Next was the revolver quickdraw and best aim competition. For this, Quimby, Stanley and Hugh arranged tin cans at fifteen paces. Tobias took a deep breath. If he was able to beat the deputy at this round, he would win the entire competition. That is if no one else won this one. Tobias again peered at the crowd. Charlotte offered him a smile. Or at least it was a smile in his direction. Maybe not necessarily directed toward him, but regardless, Tobias preferred to see it as an encouragement.

The seven competitors lined up several feet apart in a straight horizontal line each facing their own tin can targets. At Quimby's call they all drew, and smoke filled the air as those with the quickest draws in Prune Creek and surrounding towns tested their aim and speed while firing six shots. When the tally was complete, Deputy Shelton had won, but just barely. Tobias came in second place.

"Ladies and gentlemen, because we have a tie with Tobias Hallman winning the clay pigeon competition and Deputy Shelton winning the quickdraw round, we will now have one final round to see who is the 1895 Prune Creek Sharpshooter Award winner.

Sweat trickled down his back. He'd always come in second place when competing with John Mark and Russell. Could he possibly win against Shelton?

Tobias shook Shelton's hand, then took his place for the final competition, a quickdraw round with only one shot. Only one chance to gain notoriety in his new town.

And impress Charlotte.

Charlotte veered her gaze around a tall man in her line of vision. Tobias's broad shoulders strained his shirt as he prepared to aim. She wanted him to win and knew he could. She'd seen the way he could shoot from all the times she'd practiced with him, John Mark, Russell, and Pa. Tobias had impeccable aim and lightning-fast reflexes.

The crowd hushed as they awaited the final round. Would Tobias and Deputy Shelton tie again?

Finally, Quimby announced for them to take their aim and fire. In a matter of a few seconds, the competition ended, and Tobias was announced the winner.

Charlotte made her way towards him and stood in line to congratulate the new Prune Creek Sharpshooter.

"Ever thought about being a deputy?" Sheriff Rettig was asking Tobias when she approached him.

"I used to ride with the posse in Willow Falls," said Tobias.

"Well, I'd recruit you in a second if you think you'd be interested."

"I'm happy to be deputized and ride with the posse whenever you need me, but while I'm honored, I'll have to decline your offer of being a permanent deputy."

Sheriff Rettig clapped him on the shoulder. "We in Prune Creek need you as our blacksmith. But I have to say I'm impressed by your aim and speed. Your clay pigeon shooting was impressive as well."

"Thank you, sir."

Charlotte caught his eye, and he walked toward her. "Congratulations!"

He grinned at her and her heart did a flip flop in her chest.

Quimby announced in his booming voice, "Will all the winners of all the competitions please come forward so we can applaud you?"

Tobias took a place next to her on her left while all the winners who'd placed first through third in the various contests lined up in a row. "How did you do in the sewing challenge?" he whispered.

She appreciated his inquiry and momentarily forgot he was the annoying classmate of her youth. "I won first place."

An expression of admiration crossed his face. "Congratulations, Charlotte." Peculiar how they were acting so amiable towards each other as of late.

"I never thought I had a chance at winning having had to sew the tablecloth on such short notice. I fretted needlessly about the seams," she whispered back as Quimby began to announce who had won each competition. Charlotte thought of the blue ribbon attached to her calico tablecloth. Ma would be proud.

"You always were a talented seamstress," Tobias whispered back.

As they stood facing the admiring crowd and answered a few questions from the Prune Creek Weekly newspaper reporter, Charlotte marveled at the fact that maybe residing in the same town as Tobias Hallman wasn't so bothersome after all.

Chapter Ten

CHARLOTTE LEFT THE POST office, letter in hand. She stopped on the boardwalk and opened the envelope. Ma's flowing, elegant, and precise handwriting filled the page, and a yearning for home filled Charlotte's heart as she read the words.

> *Dearest Charlotte,*
>
> *How are things in Prune Creek? How are the aunts? I pray you are all doing well.*
>
> *I apologize for not responding to your letter sooner. The influenza swept through Willow Falls last month, and our entire family fell ill, save one. We are so grateful Baby Evangeline avoided becoming sick. I was quite worried about your pa as he was the sickest of us all. Thankfully, the Lord has seen fit to heal us, and we are doing much better. However, the same cannot be said for many of the members of our town. We lost five of our dear friends to this dreaded illness.*
>
> *Please do write and let us know how you fare. We miss you so.*
> *With much love,*
> *Ma*

Charlotte clutched the letter to her chest. She'd had no idea her family was ill. If only she'd been home so she could have taken care of them. And to hear five of the townsfolk succumbing to the illness? She wondered who they were, realizing Ma would likely want to share the specifics in person. Those who lost someone would be immediately added to her prayer list.

Charlotte swallowed the lump in her throat and fingered her necklace. Her family could have been among those.

Her eyes misted. *Lord, thank You for Your mercy in allowing my family to recover fully from this dreadful sickness. Thank You for not allowing us to lose Pa and for keeping Baby Evangeline healthy. I lift up the families of those who lost someone. Please be their comfort.*

It was at times like these that Charlotte faced the ever-burdening guilt of leaving home. But the guilt was hers and hers alone. Ma and Pa had encouraged her to travel to Prune Creek and assist the aunts. But what if one of her precious family members had perished?

Charlotte took a deep breath. The Lord was faithful and He had protected her loved ones.

She folded the letter and placed it back inside the envelope. If only Prune Creek had entered modern times and had a telephone exchange. Charlotte read an article in a newspaper Quimby brought to supper one evening about how Cheyenne boasted a telephone exchange since 1881. Laramie also had telephone service. While both cities were a great distance from Prune Creek, Charlotte hoped the town she was quickly coming to love would soon make a decision to offer such a modern amenity. And, oh what a wonderful thing that would be! Charlotte could place a call to Willow Falls and speak with Ma directly. No more waiting for the mail service to deliver a letter.

She would have known sooner about her family's illness and would have been able to pray for them.

Charlotte entered the mercantile next, eager to complete her tasks and return home. Perhaps she could make a plan to visit Willow Falls to see her family, check on their wellbeing, and quell some of her homesickness, at least temporarily.

The mercantile, owned by Judith and her husband, Hugh, bustled with patrons.

Charlotte located the lavender spool of thread Aunt Fern had requested to finish her mending and was about to add a bag of sugar to her purchases when she whirled around and nearly ran plumb into Tobias Hallman.

"Pardon me, Tobias, I didn't see you there."

"Excuse me, Charlotte."

A witty statement entered her mind as it oftentimes did when in Tobias's presence. "Quimby is coming for supper this evening. Would you care to join us? Aunt Myrtle is baking one of her famous huckleberry pies." Charlotte did her best to contain the smirk that threatened to erupt. She recalled Tobias's thoughts about Aunt Myrtle's baking.

But rather than one of his typical sharp-witted comebacks, Tobias answered in a monotone voice, "I can't come." His gaze failed to connect fully with hers, but rather a vacant stare filled his eyes.

Should she ask him if something was wrong? But before she could give it a second thought, he turned on his heel and trudged toward the counter, paid Judith for his purchase, and left the mercantile.

Leaving Charlotte to ponder his slumped shoulders, plodding footsteps, and downturned facial features.

Tobias needed to prepare for his trip to Willow Falls the day after tomorrow. He'd been unable to eat anything at the supper table that evening with his lack of appetite. Regret burdened him, settling in his heart with the weight of an anvil.

First Ma and Pa. Now his brother, sister-in-law, and niece.

He unfolded the telegram and re-read the haphazard penmanship.

Tobias Hallman, Prune Creek. Stop.
Willow Falls deaths in family. Stop.

He dropped to his knees beside the chair and dropped his head into his hands. His shoulders quaked and his eyes burned as he fought the sorrow rising in his throat.

For grown men didn't cry.

Not even in the privacy of their own bedrooms at the boardinghouse.

"Lord, let there be a mistake. Please."

The rest of the words he needed to pray were caught in his throat. Stifled.

A verse came to his mind from his Bible reading last week. *"Likewise the Spirit also helpeth our infirmities: for we know not what we should pray for as we ought: but the Spirit itself maketh intercession for us with groanings which cannot be uttered."*

The Holy Spirit would express the words he so desperately needed to pray.

The hard floor pressed into his knees, and Tobias hunched further over the chair, the emotion strangling him. "Please, Lord," he prayed again. Surely the telegram from Mrs. Eliason was incorrect. Surely the only remaining members of his family had not perished.

Had there been an accident?

An illness?

Had they been victims of a robbery? Willow Falls was among the safest towns in Northern Wyoming, but crime did still exist. Sheriff Townsend would attest to that.

If only there had been a train ticket available so he could board tomorrow and be on his way. If only Willow Falls was closer, he could ride there by horse and reach the town in no time.

If only I'd stayed in Willow Falls.

The words shook him. Why had the dream of owning his own blacksmith shop taken precedence over employment on a ranch with his brother? Why couldn't he find contentment working with cattle as a cowboy while employed by Pa and Chester's boss in Willow Falls? Why had his desire to be a craftsman and work with metal surged to the forefront of his plans for his future?

The questions crowded his mind and the regret smothered him.

After receiving the telegram, he'd sent one back to Mrs. Eliason, hoping for a response. Yet, there had been none before the post office closed. In the meantime, Tobias hadn't wasted another second of daylight and instead walked to the depot posthaste in hopes of securing a ticket. Whatever had happened, he knew he must travel back to Willow Falls. He purchased the ticket to board the train the day after tomorrow.

Not as soon as he would have preferred, but it was the best the apologetic stationmaster could offer.

A noise from downstairs caused him to flinch, and Tobias rose, a tingling and prickly sensation in his right leg. He shook it, hoping to alleviate the discomfort. With heavy steps, he collapsed in bed, his body and mind numb.

Tobias stared at the ceiling and again attempted to pray.

His trip to Willow Falls could not come soon enough.

CHAPTER ELEVEN

CHARLOTTE PAID FOR THE thread and started toward home. When she set out earlier to do Aunt Fern's bidding and purchase the thread, the sun was shining brightly and nary a cloud was in the sky. Now, all these hours later after the lengthy walk to town, a visit with some townsfolk, and the trip to the post office and mercantile, the voyage through town and up the hill to home now proved insurmountable. Especially after the letter from Ma. How Charlotte wished now that she had instead ridden the horse to town.

Seeing Tobias in the mercantile, so downtrodden, permeated her thoughts over the next several minutes. It wasn't like their interactions to not include sparring between them.

Folks waved their greetings as she made her way down the boardwalk. Stanley and another older gentleman nodded at her as she passed. "Say, Charlotte, would you do me the favor of saying 'hello' to Fern for me?"

Charlotte smiled at Stanley. The man for certain fancied her aunt, although Aunt Fern's feelings for the barber were not mutual. "Yes, I shall."

"Ask her if she'd like to come to town for a haircut tomorrow. Should she care to make an appointment, I'm fairly sure I could arrange for one in the afternoon." Stanley's eyes shone.

"I'll be sure to extend the invitation."

"Thank you." Stanley bowed slightly before returning to his conversation with the other gentleman.

Charlotte continued toward home, her family again on her mind. *Lord, Pa always reminds us that when we ask for wisdom, You will surely provide it. Might I ask for wisdom in the decision of whether or not to embark on a trip to Willow Falls? I want to do nothing hastily, or without thoughtful judgment.*

She would discuss the matter with the aunts and seek their advice as well. The house came into view fairly quickly, and Charlotte hastened her steps towards the outskirts of Prune Creek.

Nearly twenty minutes later, she arrived home. Charlotte could hear Aunt Myrtle's and Aunt Fern's voices from the porch. Apparently they were having a "discussion" about who did a more thorough job sweeping the floor.

For a brief moment, her concern for her family in Willow Falls edged to the peripheral of her mind as she listened to the aunts and their persistent bickering.

"Now, Myrtle, you know that Ma always said I was most adept at sweeping the floor."

Myrtle snorted a most unladylike guffaw. "While Ma was a wonderful woman, one did have to wonder about her failing eyesight."

"Not when it came to the upkeep of the cabin, and you know it, Myrt."

That started an entirely new argument for Aunt Myrtle detested being referred to as "Myrt."

Charlotte pressed herself against the wall of the house, but even without seeing her aunts, she could imagine Aunt Myrtle, hands on her hips, eyes bulging, and posture erect. "Perhaps I should shorten your name. Would you like to be called 'Fer'?"

"Pshaw, *Myrt*, you're just being addlebrained and muddleheaded. No one calls anyone 'Fer.' That's not even a name, and that's *fer* certain!" Likely Aunt Fern was proud of her wit.

"Now, Fer, or shall I call you 'Fernie' since you don't appreciate that much either? As much as I would delight in quarreling with you until our next birthdays, I have more pressing matters to tend to, what with Quimby joining us this evening."

"Oh, yes, how can we forget the dashing Clifford Quimby? You must ensure he is nothing like Mr. Wilkins. Remember him?"

Aunt Myrtle released a two-minute sigh. "How could any of us forget Mr. Wilkins? You were in a deep melancholy state for two decades over that insidious and odious man. But, need I remind you, my dear sister, not all men are like Mr. Wilkins. Some are..." Aunt Myrtle paused and Charlotte imagined her holding a hand to her bosom and swooning. "Some are dashing and considerate and witty and intellectual with nice hair and an upright posture."

"And you're about as syrupy as a pancake drenched in maple syrup when it comes to describing Quimby." Aunt Fern cleared her throat. "Here lies Clifford Quimby—dashing, considerate, witty, intellectual, nice-haired, and with an upright posture. Mr. Quimby succumbed to his untimely demise five minutes after consuming Myrtle Beauchamp's supper. Witnesses attest to the fact that Mr. Quimby was in perfect health before partaking in a meal two nights ago."

That started an argument about Aunt Myrtle's cooking and how Aunt Fern just didn't appreciate the skill of an award-winning chef.

Charlotte opened the door to the house and stepped inside. As she did so, both aunts commenced to halting their discord and pasted broad smiles on their faces. "Hello, Charlotte, dear. Did you retrieve the spool of thread?"

"Yes, Aunt Fern."

One couldn't miss the snide glances between the two sisters before Aunt Myrtle finally said, "Quimby is coming over for supper tonight. I thought I would bake a huckleberry pie seeing as how he has cultured taste and *appreciates* my baking, unlike some in our presence."

"Cultured taste, hmmf!"

Before they could begin another round of disagreements, Charlotte placed the thread on the table and clasped her hands behind her back. "I was wondering if I might speak to you both about something distressing."

"Yes, dear, have a seat." Aunt Fern gestured to a chair at the table, and she and Aunt Myrtle sat down as well.

"I received a letter from Ma. It seems there was an outbreak of the influenza in Willow Falls, and five of our townsfolk have succumbed to the illness." Gratitude that her family had been spared again entered Charlotte's mind. "Everyone is recovering, but Pa had it the worst. I..." Charlotte bit her lip. "I need to see my family."

Both aunts stood and wrapped an arm around her shoulders. "Of course, you do, dear, and go, you must," said Aunt

Myrtle. She kissed the top of Charlotte's head. "I trust every-one is well enough so as to no longer be contagious?"

"Yes, I believe so."

Aunt Fern squeezed her arm gently. "Then you must leave posthaste."

"And we have some egg money saved for a train ticket," added Aunt Myrtle.

"Oh, I couldn't..." The aunts didn't have much in the way of funds.

Aunt Myrtle shook her head. "You can and you must take the money. Hopefully it will be enough for the ticket."

"I just worry about what if something had happened to them and I wasn't there?"

"Life is precious and fleeting, and you are right to visit your family. We are so grateful they are healing. Aunt Myrtle and I will do whatever is necessary to see that you board that train within the next few days."

The reassuring words from the aunts were all Charlotte needed to commence with her plan of traveling to Willow Falls. Now if there was only a train ticket available for her journey.

Tobias packed his Bible, a comb, shaving items, his pock-etknife, lye soap, a toothbrush, and a tin of tooth powder in Pa's haversack.

He ran his hand along the top of the black leather bag Pa was issued as a Union soldier in the War Between the States. Pa would tell of how he carried the necessary items, including ammunition, rations, and personal items in the bag and had secured his rolled blanket over the top of it. Embossed scrolls decorated the top of the haversack, and a snap with a latch secured its closure.

Pa had been a hero and had saved the life of a fellow soldier.

A hero God took Home too soon.

And now Tobias had lost the remainder of his family. He wavered between anger and grief. Sleep had been difficult to obtain last night as he tossed and turned on the thin mattress. Bleary-eyed, he'd awoken, a prayer on his lips and a searing pain in his heart.

Even though Tobias was nearly an adult when he became an orphan, he couldn't fathom a life without his older brother. They clung together, knowing they were all each other had. They and Chester's wife, Paulina and their daughter, Lanie. Tobias was an integral part of Chester's life and Chester an integral part of his. Now Chester was gone.

Tobias rolled up a pair of trousers and a shirt and attached them to the top of the haversack. He slid his revolver into its holster on his belt and placed his hat atop his head. If he wanted to make the train, he best be on his way.

Yet his feet struggled to obey Tobias's command to walk. If only the post office was open, he could ask the postmaster if Mrs. Eliason had sent another telegram with further details.

The other boarders had already eaten breakfast and left for their various occupations. The aroma of the fresh-ly-cooked food filled the air. Mrs. White, the owner, brought him a plate of eggs and bacon and a cup of milk. He was surprised she still served him breakfast with her strict rule of not serving meals late. While Mrs. White was a generous landlord, she was persnickety and uncompromising regarding her dictums.

"Thank you, ma'am. Much obliged."

"Yes, well, you know the rules, but seeing as how you're leaving today, I bent them slightly for you."

"Thank you, Mrs. White. I appreciate that. I do." He regarded his landlord, a woman of about sixty, with severely-parted gray hair and a rigid demeanor. When he moved to Prune Creek, Tobias had been fortunate to find a vacancy at Mrs. White's boardinghouse.

Mrs. White left for a moment and returned with a plate with two slices of bread. "Will you be needing a sandwich for your trip?" She pursed her lips and awaited his answer.

"No, ma'am, I'll be fine."

"All right, then. I'll see you when you return."

The proprietress shuffled toward the kitchen, leaving Tobias to ponder whether or not he could consume the meal she prepared. While the food was somewhat appealing, Tobias had no appetite.

He swirled the mound of eggs in a circle and took a bite of the bacon. The train ride to Nelsonville, followed by a short stagecoach ride to Willow Falls would be a lengthy trip. Ma's voice rang through his mind. *"Son, you need your nourishment."* She always worried he didn't eat enough, although no one would describe him as scrawny. Ma worried even when he was on his second or third helping, attempting to see who could eat more—him or Chester.

Because of his talent for shoveling food into his mouth at an impressive rate of speed, Tobias nearly always won.

But now he'd never race Chester again, whether by eating or on foot to the schoolhouse. And while it had been many years since they were young'uns, the thought of never seeing his brother again this side of Heaven grieved him.

And what of his sister-in-law, Paulina, and his sweet niece, Lanie?

Tobias forced himself to eat the eggs, one of the slices of burnt bacon, and one piece of bread. The food was tasteless in the wake of his sorrow.

He stood and pushed his chair to the table. Clutching the plate, he delivered it to Mrs. White in the kitchen. "Thank you for the meal."

"You didn't eat much." Mrs. White put her hands on her ample hips and blew a hair that had fallen over her eyes. "Are you all right?"

"Yes, ma'am. Just need to get to Willow Falls is all."

Mrs. White took the plates and cup from him. "Have a safe journey and Godspeed."

CHAPTER TWELVE

CHARLOTTE CLUTCHED HER CARPETBAG and boarded the train. She'd been fortunate to secure the last ticket available for today's departure to Nelsonville. There, she would board the stage and continue the short distance to Willow Falls.

As she started down the aisle, she noticed a familiar face on the right, three rows from the front. She took a second glance, and sure enough, it was him. She stopped and gaped.

"Tobias?"

His eyes widened. "Charlotte? What are you doing on the train?"

Someone from behind her cleared his throat. "Excuse me, miss, but could you continue on?"

"Yes, but of course." Charlotte continued down the aisle, twice directing her gaze to Tobias. Something in his countenance caused concern, although she couldn't explain exactly what. Charlotte took a seat four rows from Tobias's and pondered why he would be on the train.

As she prepared for the train's departure, a man about her father's age in a buttoned jacket with a stiffened collar and a black top hat paused by her seat. "Pardon me, miss."

"Yes?"

"My seat was near the gent at the front of the train with whom you briefly spoke. If you would care to have that seat, I could trade you."

Should she trade seats? If she did, perhaps she could ask Tobias what was wrong. "Thank you kindly, sir."

Charlotte shuffled past the other passengers and hesitated by Tobias's seat.

His eyes met hers, and he stood and gestured for her to sit on the inside of the seat near the window.

"Surprised you'd want to sit by me, Charlotte."

Should she return to her former seat? Would the man who traded her seats be amenable to trading once again? Charlotte chastised herself for not mulling it over before making such a hasty decision. She struggled to concoct a witty response, but the lack of sleep last night left her mind somewhat dulled. The scenery slowly rolled by, and Charlotte waved at the aunts on the boardwalk outside the depot. She watched as they disappeared from her vision, and she folded her hands in her lap and once again prayed for her family's full recovery and for safe travels.

Passengers carried on conversations around them, and Charlotte reached into her carpetbag for her book. Tobias reclined against the seat, his eyes focused in front of them. She'd always known him to be clean-shaven, but a day's growth of dark whiskers peppered his chin and upper lip. "Is everything all right?" she asked.

"Yes. No."

She waited patiently for him to elaborate. Instead of doing so, he asked, "Are you going to Willow Falls?"

"Yes. My family was ill during the influenza outbreak."

"I'm sorry to hear that. Are they feeling better now?"

"They are. In my ma's letter, she mentioned that Pa suffered the worst, and thankfully, Baby Evangeline, Caleb and Annie's youngest, avoided the illness altogether."

"Sorry to hear your pa suffered the worst, but grateful Evangeline stayed well."

How many times had she thanked the Lord for those very things? "Ma sent me a letter, and I knew I needed to visit. If only I'd known beforehand of their illnesses, I could have prayed. And if only I'd been there, I could have tended to them when they took ill." Charlotte placed the book in her lap and folded her hands atop it.

An unreadable expression crossed Tobias's face. "Yes, well, regrets are just that."

"Are you traveling to Willow Falls as well?" she asked for the second time.

"Yes."

"What are the odds you and I both are going to Willow Falls at the same time on the same day and sitting in the same seat?" Would her attempt to liven the conversation be successful?

The answer arrived quickly and added to her list of compunctions.

"I'm going to Willow Falls because I received a telegram from your ma that there had been deaths in my family."

Charlotte gasped and instinctively placed a hand on his arm. "Tobias, I am so sorry." She'd had no idea the ones who lost their lives were those in his family.

She realized her hand still rested on his arm, and she hastily removed it.

"It was a shock, and I immediately sent a telegram to her asking for clarification. None came. Reckon it would have been better to have received a letter as you did, rather than the curt method in which a telegram arrives."

"I am curious why she didn't send a letter or a second telegram in answer to your inquiries. Perhaps something prevented her from being able to do so." Charlotte imagined Ma had a great deal of extra duties heaped upon her due to caring for Pa and possibly other townsfolk. But excuses would do Tobias no good in his grief. She searched for words to say to help alleviate his pain.

None came.

Several conversations took place around them, likely from people who hadn't just discovered they lost loved ones. "Tobias, I am so sorry about your family. Did they all succumb to the illness?"

"Your ma didn't say. Just that there had been deaths in my family. I..." he cleared his throat and his shoulders slumped.

"Tobias, I don't know what to say."

"I should have been there. I should have stayed in Willow Falls and worked as a hired hand at the ranch with Chester. I should have taken care of them when they got sick. Perhaps if I hadn't decided I needed to be a smithy—if I had instead been content to be a hired hand—none of this would have happened."

"You can't..."

"Oh, I can blame myself and I'm quite adept at it. They were all I have left of my family. And Lanie, she was so young."

Growing up in Willow Falls, Charlotte knew Tobias's parents and brother well. They attended the church where Pa preached, and she had attended Chester and Paulina's wedding. Lanie called her "Aunt Charlotte" because that's how Esther, Lena, and Lola referred to her. And Charlotte hadn't minded that the sweet little girl with long blonde braids and the classic Hallman smile adopted her as an aunt. Tears blurred her vision. Chester, with his devoted love for his family; Paulina, with her gentle and humble personality; and adorable and spirited Lanie...

How could she tell him that his being in Willow Falls rather than Prune Creek was no guarantee his family would have survived the horrific outbreak? Hadn't she felt much the same when her family fell ill? "You can't blame yourself."

"Oh, but I can. Now, instead of going to Willow Falls to visit my family, I'll be planning their funerals."

In all the years she'd known Tobias, Charlotte had never seen this side of him. Always somewhat arrogant, quick-witted, intelligent, and ambitious, she'd not yet seen him wrestle with grief. When his parents had died, she'd attended their funerals and, with her family, came alongside Tobias and Chester in their time of mourning. And while she was certain Tobias struggled then just as he was struggling now, she'd not been privy to that struggle. She prayed for the Lord's peace and comfort for Tobias.

"I'm so sorry. I had no idea that when my ma mentioned some townsfolk had died from the influenza outbreak that it would be your family." Her heart broke for him.

"I never even had the chance to say goodbye." He stared straight ahead, but she could see the emotion so close to the surface.

"They knew you loved them, Tobias. You were a loyal and loving brother to Chester, was the brother Paulina never had, and there wasn't an uncle who loved and doted on his niece more than you did with Lanie."

"Thank you, Charlotte. That means a lot. I'm hoping to have the opportunity to speak with your pa while I'm in Willow Falls. He always gives wise counsel."

"That he does, although I may be a bit partial." She paused. "If there is anything..."

"Thank you."

They rode in silence for some time, the sounds of the other passengers all around them, combined with the click-clack of the train on the rails and the gentle swaying motion as it chugged along.

Charlotte reached for her carpetbag and retrieved two gingerbread cookies from a cookie tin. She handed one to Tobias. "Don't worry. Aunt Myrtle didn't make these."

Tobias offered the slightest smile. "Did Aunt Fern?"

"On the contrary. I made them."

He handed the cookie back to her. "Suddenly, I have no appetite." A mischievous glint lit his brown eyes in the midst of his sorrow.

"Very funny, Tobias."

Charlotte handed the cookie back to him, and he took a bite and closed his eyes.

"These are delicious, and here I thought I had my fill at the Founder's Day Celebration a couple of weeks ago."

His compliment lifted her countenance. "I appreciate you supporting a good cause." And oddly, she cared about whether or not he found her cookies tasty like something his own ma would have baked, rather than detestable like Aunt Myrtle's.

"You know, you haven't once called me 'Tobias Hallman' yet. Are you feeling all right?"

"Don't worry, the day isn't over yet."

"No, we still have a ways to go even before we reach Nelsonville. That cookie was good. Do you have another?"

Charlotte handed him a second cookie. "Did I hear you give me a compliment? Perhaps a kind word that I did not inherit Aunt Myrtle's baking skills?"

He turned to face her, his ornery expression reminiscent of the Tobias she'd always known. "Well, I *did* buy an entire plate of your gingerbread cookies at the celebration, and I *did* devour them all in one day, with the exception of the one you ate."

"Perhaps you were famished." Hopefully her attempt to lighten the situation would prove beneficial to temporarily taking his mind off his grief.

"I was famished after having to mind the bake sale for a good portion of my life." His amusement danced on his face. "As far as the gingerbread cookies—you are Aunt Myrtle's great-niece, so there is definitely some likeness in the baking skills, but I'm not retching like I did after I ate her huckleberry pie."

"Or her buttermilk biscuits?"

Tobias laughed, but the humor failed to reach his eyes. "I've never tasted biscuits so burnt."

"And, yet, she won awards at the fair. Who would have known?"

"Your aunts are amusing, especially the way they bicker."

Charlotte nodded. "Constant quarreling. I think they agree on two things, and that's their love for the Lord and their family." She handed Tobias a third cookie and ate another as well. "I do have some snickerdoodles Aunt Myrtle made and packed for me, but I'm saving them in case I'm in danger of suffering from starvation."

Tobias chuckled a hearty laugh that caused Charlotte to join in his amusement. "Not sure I'd eat one of Aunt Myrtle's snickerdoodles, even if I'm starving."

Charlotte rummaged through her carpetbag and once again withdrew the cookie tin. She stared at the lid, decorated with a cheerful Christmas scene with several children, wrapped presents, holly berries, and a tree. When she opened the lid, the aroma of the two remaining gingerbread cookies filled the air. Beside them, packed with meticulous love and care, were four snickerdoodles. "My ma makes the best snickerdoodles, Aunt Myrtle on the other hand..." Charlotte pilfered through the pile and produced a rock-hard cookie. "This could be a weapon." She handed it to Tobias.

He squeezed it between his forefinger and thumb. "I think I've seen rocks that were softer." He handed the cookie back to her. "Hopefully we'll never be that hungry."

Charlotte placed the cookie back in the tin and the tin back into her carpetbag. A perusal out the window indicated they were in a lower valley area. Meadows and clearings dotted the landscape with the exception of a random grove of aspens or pines. She attempted to dismiss the concern that the trestle portion of the journey was forthcoming.

Tobias interrupted her thoughts. "I've been thinking about John Mark. Sure wish I could have made it to his wedding. I still can't believe he's married with young'uns."

"He and Hannah married in Poplar Springs, so we had a get-together soon after at my parents' home. There wasn't a whole lot of time for planning as Ma decided at the last minute." She avoided giving the details of the urgency of John Mark and Hannah's marriage.

"Ah, I didn't realize that. Still seems strange how fast the years have passed. It seems just yesterday we were playing baseball in the school yard."

"I remember those days. You had the best arm in the school and could easily out-throw any of our classmates."

A smirk crossed his face. "I was hoping to be asked to join the Boston Reds. And as I recall, Charlotte, you weren't too bad of a player yourself."

"The Boston Reds would have recruited you in a moment had the distance between Massachusetts and the Wyoming Territory been less substantial. And thank you for that compliment. Those were fond memories, and I did rather enjoy hitting the ball across the schoolyard."

"You really think they would have recruited me?" He puffed up his chest.

Charlotte giggled. "Yes, I do."

"Well, thanks, Charlotte." He paused for a moment as if to savor her statement. "The Boston Reds. Hmm." He nodded his head as if to mull over the prospect of playing for such a prestigious team. "Remember John Mark always stubbornly having to have the ash bat Mr. Morton ordered from back East rather than the maple one everyone else used?"

"He's still as stubborn and ornery as ever while upholding justice in Poplar Springs."

Tobias crossed an ankle over his knee. "He always was the most stubborn of the three of us."

"Well..."

"You're right. Russell was the most stubborn."

They were both silent for a moment, likely both recalling the horrific events surrounding Russell's untimely death.

Finally, Charlotte spoke again. "Actually, Tobias—Tobias Hallman—I do believe you are the most stubborn and ornery of the three of you."

Although he laughed, Charlotte could clearly see the pain from all he'd lost just below the surface. "And you, Charlotte Eliason, are the most featherheaded woman I know."

"Featherheaded? I'll kindly take that cookie back." She reached for the half-eaten gingerbread cookie in his hand, and he moved it just out of her reach. They tussled for the cookie, Tobias winning because of his ability to transfer the cookie to his other hand and toward the aisle.

Finally after a few seconds, Tobias turned his head, and in an expedient moment, inhaled the remainder of the gingerbread cookie. When he faced forward again, his cheeks bulged and he chewed slowly, attempting to devour the far-too-large-for-one-bite cookie.

She laughed at the sight of him. "You remind me of a chipmunk attempting to store his entire winter provisions in his mouth all at once."

Tobias's eyes watered and he swallowed the cookie with an exaggerated gulp. "Can't say as I tasted much of that cookie, but I think I won this debate with the infamous Charlotte Eliason."

"Perhaps this one, but there are always more to come."

"Reckon those are the truest words ever spoken. How many years have we quarreled over a variety of things?"

Charlotte put a finger to her mouth. "On the contrary, Mr. Hallman. You've quarreled, and I've done my utmost best to ignore your infuriating buffoonery."

"Infuriating buffoonery?"

"Oh, yes. Do you remember when our spelling words were 'flibbertigibbet,' 'wool-gathering,' 'muddleheaded,' 'austere,' 'accolades,' and 'armadillo?' And we were to use all of the words in a sentence?"

Before he even confirmed his remembrance of that assignment, Charlotte could see the recognition in the way his eyes darted around and he shook his knee in a nervous manner. "Oh, I remember all right. I remember having to clean the chalkboard for a week after that one."

"Let's see, it was something such as, 'Accolades were presented to the most featherbrained flibbertigibbet in all of the Wyoming Territory—a girl named Charlotte Eliason, who sits around all day woolgathering and being muddleheaded with her austere armadillo.'"

"You memorized it?"

"How could I not remember your ridiculous sentence? Not only had you written it on a piece of paper, you read it aloud in class when Annie called on you, but you also wrote it on the chalkboard for the entire class to see when we came in from recess."

"But the part of the austere armadillo notwithstanding, there was truth to the sentence."

Charlotte nudged him. "No truth whatsoever. I am neither featherbrained nor a flibbertigibbet, nor do I woolgather or consider myself muddleheaded, and I for certain do not have an austere armadillo for a pet."

They laughed for several more seconds before Tobias sobered. "Thank you for listening today."

"You're welcome."

And on that day as they rode the train to Nelsonville, something changed between the two nemeses.

CHAPTER THIRTEEN

SOMETHING HAD CHANGED BETWEEN him and Charlotte. She was still annoying and dramatic, but perhaps less so. And he was grateful for her attempts to temporarily distract him from the overwhelming thoughts of losing the remainder of his family.

Tobias leaned back against the uncomfortable seat and fiddled with his hat. He dreaded this lengthy commute to Willow Falls and what awaited him.

In days past when he would return home, Ma, Pa, and Chester would be there to greet him. Time assisting Pa with the chores, fishing, attending church on Sunday, and talking with Ma highlighted his time spent in Willow Falls.

Now none of that would happen. He would plan the funerals, collect any important items Chester, Paulina, and Lanie had left behind, and return to Prune Creek. He swallowed hard as grief and regret again threatened to consume him.

Charlotte flipped open her dime novel. Her head tilted from side to side, her mouth dropped open, and her eyes enlarged. How many times had she read this particular book? Yet, she still proceeded to be in awe of the words. Charlotte held the book closer to her face before rapidly flipping to the next page.

Her reading theatrics amused him, and he couldn't stop himself from staring. In the days of their youth, he'd done all he could to present himself as an aggravating annoyance. From Charlotte's reactions, he'd succeeded. Tying her hair in braids and offering witty responses to her statements had been a few of the shenanigans Tobias prided himself in achieving.

While John Mark and Russell insinuated Tobias fancied Charlotte, he'd denied it all those years and still would if they broached the matter again.

Another regret filled his thoughts. He should have made more time for his friends from his school days. He, John Mark, and Russell had been inseparable during those years. Now Russell was gone.

He was just about to lament it further when Charlotte clutched his arm.

Tobias jolted from his thoughts and gaped at Charlotte, who sat frozen in her seat, book open in her lap. She'd squeezed her eyes closed and her face paled.

The woman had a firm grip, and Tobias wondered how long it would be before he lost feeling in his forearm.

"Charlotte?"

"Yes?" He barely heard her strained response.

The train slowed as it headed up another hill. They were climbing, and the trees below became smaller and smaller. She clutched the necklace she always wore with her free hand.

"Are you all right?"

"I detest this part of the voyage."

Voyage?

Charlotte whispered the words, and he inclined toward her. Her fingers dug into the skin on his forearm. "What part?"

"This part. With the…" Tobias heard a tremor in her voice, and she squeezed her eyes tighter and stiffened her shoulders. Her hold on his arm remained steadfast.

"The climb?" The train whistled and struggled up the mountain. Was she worried it didn't have enough power to scale the hill? Tobias had never really given much thought to that possibility.

A black plume flitted past the window as the odor of smoke waffled through the air.

Charlotte shuddered.

"Is it the climb?" he asked again, keeping his own voice low so as not to attract attention from the other passengers. The last thing he wished was to embarrass Charlotte.

She shook her head, eyes remaining closed. Her chin trembled. "The trestle."

It wasn't the answer Tobias expected. At that moment, they began to cross the thin wooden trestle. If he angled himself just right, Tobias could see the rushing water beneath them as the train trudged across the bridge. "We're almost across," he said, carefully attempting to remove the penetrating grip she had on his arm. His hand enfolded hers. She flinched, and he half expected her to pull her hand from his grasp.

But Charlotte's hand remained in his, scarcely moving. The strict posture in her shoulders relented, and the tension drained from her. She blew out a breath, and her eyes fluttered open.

Tobias pondered the thought that holding her hand almost felt natural.

Of course it does. She's frightened and you're comforting her.

"I don't like trestles."

If he could drive the train and meander around the trestle, he surely would—for her. "We're across it now."

Charlotte blinked. "I...thank you." Her attention rested on his hand holding hers, and her eyes grew large. "Oh."

Tobias released her hand. "I...sorry."

Her gaze met his, and her brow furrowed. The pallid coloring in her cheeks was replaced with a deep red hue. If he was honest, he'd have to admit he'd always found her to be beautiful.

Charlotte was the first to look away. She folded her hands in her lap. "I'm so extremely embarrassed."

"It's nothing, Charlotte. We all have fears."

"Of trestles?"

A wisp of hair fell from her bun and rested on her cheek. Without a thought, he reached up and tucked it behind her ear, then busied his own hands with idly resting in his lap. "Even trestles," he finally answered. "It's nothing to be ashamed of or embarrassed about."

Tobias had never known Charlotte to be anything but confident. She was smart—the smartest girl, if not student—in school. She was plucky, spirited, animated, self-assured, and vivacious. Never fearful or worried or consumed by fright.

"Well, thank you for allowing me to squeeze your arm to its death."

He chuckled. "You're welcome."

"I don't know what it is about trestles, but I'm grateful there are only two on this journey, and the other one is far less intimidating than the one we just crossed. I don't know if it's the height of them or the seemingly flimsy construction, or..." her voice trailed.

"The trestles are high in the air, but I imagine they're constructed better than we think."

"Foolish, I know, to be worried about something so trivial. After all, trains cross over trestles often."

"They do. But, Charlotte, we all have fears, and it's nothing to be ashamed of or embarrassed by," he reiterated, hoping to assuage her concerns.

"Do you have fears?"

"I do."

She waited for him to elaborate, and he attempted to swallow the knot of pride. "I worry about being a successful blacksmith. Before that, I feared losing my family."

Charlotte clasped a hand over her mouth. "Oh, Tobias, I'm sorry. Losing those we love is a legitimate fear, and you've just lost yours."

Tobias cleared his throat. "Yes. But we all do have fears, probably multiple ones."

"As far as being a blacksmith, I think you're doing an admirable job. You have an outstanding reputation in Prune Creek, and the townsfolk have come to trust you. It seems you're busy."

"Yes, almost too busy. I may have to hire someone."

"That's good news."

"It is." He paused. "Anytime you need to clutch my arm, feel free to do so."

She blushed again, the color making her blue eyes more vibrant. "There is one more trestle."

Tobias leaned back in his seat again, and although Charlotte had settled now and had resumed her reading, Tobias's mind remained on her and all that had transpired in their short journey so far.

CHAPTER FOURTEEN

CHARLOTTE MEANDERED AROUND TO the back of the depot where regular usage in the area between the depot and the outhouse created a thin trail. She forged farther ahead toward a clearing, mindful to stay within earshot of the train.

The sun's warmth beat down on her, and she closed her eyes for a moment and tilted her face toward the sky. A bird chirped in the distance, and she could hear the muffled voices of passengers interacting while they waited to again embark.

Charlotte opened her eyes and perused the view before her. Magnificent, breathtaking, and extraordinary were three words that crossed her mind as she viewed from the hill the expansive tops of pines clustered with aspens dotting the plush wildflower-laden meadow below. She'd never been beyond Wyoming's borders, but doubted God had created anywhere as beautiful as the state she called home.

She'd never wandered behind or beyond the depot in times past, but a short walk to stretch her legs before re-boarding was a welcome reprieve from the lengthy train ride—and preparation for the remaining prolonged distance to come before they reached Nelsonville.

It also gave her a chance to revisit all that had transpired between her and Tobias on the first portion of the trip. She bowed her head and again prayed for him. While it was likely their conversations helped pass the time, thoughts of all he'd endured and the grief Tobias would suffer anew once they reached Willow Falls caused her to wish she could do something to help alleviate the pain. She, along with her family, would endeavor to be there for him in this time of profound loss.

She thanked the Lord again for His protection over her own family, that they had not perished from the influenza, and that she would soon be reunited with them.

Charlotte ended her prayer and began to walk farther on the worn path. She thought of Tobias's kindness about her fear of trestles, their camaraderie, and their recollections of the past.

She realized they shared a history, one of their youth, and now were beginning to build a friendship all these years later. She was beginning to consider him as a friend rather than a foe.

Charlotte reached up to grasp her necklace as she often did, when she realized it was no longer there. Panic swept through her, and she turned around and retraced her steps. Where had she lost her treasured possession? She'd had it on the train. It was still around her neck five minutes ago, but where was it now?

Her gaze darted from the tall weeds that lined the pathway, to the dirt trail in front, and to the area she'd just walked through. Finally, just up ahead she saw her necklace, its amethyst heart shimmering in the sun.

A stout man beat her to the piece of jewelry. "Looking for this?" It swung from side to side in his hand, briefly mesmerizing her as she neared him.

"Thank you for finding that."

"Not so fast," he sneered, his mismatched eyes protruding as he flipped it into the palm of his fleshy hand.

Her heart thudded as two other men emerged from behind the outhouse and surrounded her.

It was nearly time to board the train.

Where was Charlotte?

Tobias asked several of the passengers as well as the conductor and porter, but none had seen her since they arrived at the depot.

Where had she gone?

He scanned the far end of the depot and in the opposite direction. He boarded the train, called her name, then exited once more. He stalked past the weathered bench and up the stairs into the depot, which was about the size of his room at the boardinghouse. The meager waiting area housed one isolated solid bench, its appearance much like a pew from church. A family of six piled on it, crammed from edge to edge with a baby atop his ma's lap.

Tobias walked toward a makeshift ticket counter, much more rustic than the one in Prune Creek. "Sir, I'm looking for a Miss Eliason. She's twenty-two years of age, slender with blonde hair and blue eyes."

"I have not seen her, but then there have been a lot of folks in and out of here."

Tobias stood on the porch and gazed in each direction. He then wandered around the back side of the depot. She couldn't have gone far. The closest town was nearly a mile walk, and as far as he knew, Charlotte wouldn't have any need to go to the town, especially since they weren't staying for longer than fifteen minutes at the depot.

Perhaps she was in the outhouse, but when a young boy emerged seconds later, his hopes of her being safely tucked in the privy diminished.

Tobias followed a worn path past the outhouse. In a clump of pines, Tobias saw a few men in a circle. Maybe they had seen her. As he approached to ask, a disturbing site awaited him.

Charlotte stood in the middle of the circle.

He hurried toward them. "Charlotte?"

"Tobias!"

Tobias rushed to her, but not before one of the men, a stout one with a long beard and a high forehead marred by a raised scar, blocked his path.

"Whaddya think you're doin'?"

Tobias ignored the man and instead spoke directly to Charlotte. "The train is leaving."

The man narrowed his eyes and put his face near Tobias's. "If it's time to go, then get on yer way."

"Not without her." Tobias pointed toward Charlotte.

A scruffy man with long hair and one eye smaller than the other chortled. "Maybe the pretty lady wants to stay." He leered at Charlotte, his gaze traveling from the top of her head to her feet. He reached a fingertip toward her cheek, and Charlotte flinched.

Anger rose within Tobias. His heartbeat increased and sweat trickled down his back. He put a hand on the revolver on his hip. "Leave her be."

"Seems I might've found something that belongs to her."
The man with the two different-sized eyes removed something from his pocket and held it up.

Charlotte's necklace.

"Sir, I would appreciate it if you would return the necklace to the lady so we can be on our way."

"And if I don't?"

"Like I said, I'd appreciate it if you would return the necklace to the lady so we can be on our way." Tobias held his gaze on all three men, watching for any nefarious movements.

"Gonna do somethin' 'bout it if we don't, is ya?" A third man, older than the other two with heavy-lidded dark eyes, stalked toward him and shoved him hard on the shoulder, causing Tobias to stumble backwards.

"We want no trouble."

"Too late for that."

Tobias prayed for the wisdom to hold his tongue and control his temper. Anger had never been a problem for him. He had other vices. But when it came to protecting those he cared about, little would stand in his way.

He bumped his shoulder against the man and shoved his way toward Charlotte. She attempted to meet him halfway until the third man clasped her by the wrist. "We was just gettin' acquainted, wasn't we, sweetheart?"

"Please, just let me go."

The desperation in her voice was nearly his undoing. Tobias forged ahead and held out his hand to her. She grabbed it and he pulled her toward him, keeping her close by his left side. "Give us the necklace and we'll be on our way, gentlemen." He again fingered the revolver and prayed he wouldn't have to use it. While he'd prefer to leave without giving a second thought to Charlotte's jewelry, he knew how much it meant to her. Perhaps he could replace it for her if the men continued to resist his request.

The man with the scarred forehead strutted toward him, his face just inches from Tobias's. "How 'bout us a trade? The revolver for the necklace?"

No necklace was worth a method of defending yourself. Surely the man must realize this despite his obvious lack of intelligence. "Give us the necklace."

The train whistle blew. "Gonna miss your train ride," the third man sneered.

The man with the different eyes dangled the necklace again. "Wonder how much I could get for this here trinket?"

Tobias, with his stealthy reflexes, reached for the necklace at just that moment, tugging it from the man's grasp so rapidly he had no idea the jewelry disappeared from his clutches until one of the other ne'er-do-wells mentioned it.

"Hey, give that back!"

But Tobias stuffed it into his trouser pocket, and stood face to face with his adversary, doing his best not to inhale the stale breath. But he was sure to hold the man's stare as he memorized every feature. A round pitted red face, a scraggly beard to match his scraggly orange hair, hazel eyes that failed to blink, and a mouth that housed two oversized teeth on the upper row, a cracked dangling one in the center, and four decaying gray and yellow teeth along the bottom.

This man was thicker than Tobias, but not in a muscled way, and were it not for his two comrades, defeating him wouldn't be an impossible feat.

But Tobias wasn't here to fight. He wasn't here to prove anything. And he wasn't here to leave Charlotte vulnerable should something happen to him.

"We'll be on our way now," he said, leaning his head an inch closer.

"You see that you are." The man spit to the side, snorted, then spit again. "You ain't seen the last of us. Now take yer woman and git."

Tobias put his arm around Charlotte, and she collapsed against him. He backed slowly away from the men and hurried back to the train just in time to board before it continued on its way to Nelsonville.

As they again took their seats, a rush of emotion flooded him. Charlotte sat beside him, trembling, and he longed to hold her in his arms. To reassure her and to vow to protect her.

But another emotion also ripped through him. She was far too independent. Far too foolish. What if he hadn't been there? Hadn't found her when he went searching for her? What if he *hadn't* searched for her? What if instead he boarded the train only to find her not there as the train departed?

What if he hadn't been on the train at all and she'd succumbed to a fate he didn't even want to entertain? If there had been *no one* to save her?

What if he'd lost her forever to the clutches of men bent on doing her harm and worse?

Charlotte willed her legs to stop shaking and her heartbeat to slow. Her shallow breathing continued to come in gasps, and her mind replayed over and over the scenario she'd just found herself in.

Why had she been so foolish to wander off?

What if Tobias hadn't been there?

What if the men had kidnapped her?

Thoughts of her family crowded her mind, and tears rolled down her face. They would never have known what happened to her in those few minutes of stopping at the depot in a desolate place in the mountains halfway between Prune Creek and Nelsonville.

Through bleary eyes, she cast a side glance at Tobias. A vein throbbed in his jaw as he kept his focus on the seat in front of them. Since they'd boarded, he hadn't said a word.

And he had every right to be infuriated with her. At the very least, they could have lost the opportunity to board the train. At the very most, she could have been whisked away never to be seen again.

Another chill riveted through her. The woman in the seat behind them tapped on her shoulder and asked if she was all right. Charlotte mutely nodded, but it would be some time before her fear would no longer threaten to consume her.

She closed her eyes and prayed for the words to apologize. Charlotte knew Tobias well enough to know that waiting a few minutes would be her best course as he, like herself, was one who experienced emotions strongly.

It was one of a few ways they were alike.

Sounds mingled through the train of conversation, a baby whimpering towards the back of the train car, a woman humming, and a man coughing. The wheels clacked on the rails and the whistle blew at intermittent times.

The seconds and minutes passed slowly.

Finally, she dabbed at her eyes and adjusted her posture in the seat. "Tobias," she whispered, her mouth dry.

He said nothing but turned to face her.

"I'm sorry," she breathed.

"What were you thinking, Charlotte?"

"I needed to stretch my—my legs and to—to think about things, and then I—I lost my necklace. The men—they came from nowhere."

Her excuses sounded flimsy in her own ears.

Charlotte had bantered with Tobias, had recently experienced what she considered a friendship with him, even a closeness, but never in all these years had she exacted his ire. Until now.

"I'm sorry. I'm so sorry," she repeated.

"When I couldn't find you, and then I saw you with those men around you, and I wasn't sure I could..." Tobias paused and took a deep breath. His brow furrowed and his gaze held hers. He lowered his voice to a whisper. "Please don't ever do something like that again."

"I won't. I promise."

"Not to stretch your legs, not to find your necklace. Unless I'm with you. You could have been hurt."

The emotion in his tender eyes enhanced her regret at causing him undue worry when he was already struggling with losing his family. Regret at her doltishness and the folly of her ways. Guilt at her foolish decision to wander off alone when she was so certain she was a capable and intelligent woman. Anger at her own pride for thinking so.

"I promise." Her voice quivered.

"All right, then. All is forgiven." Tobias patted her hand with his, and she welcomed the brief warmth of it.

"Thank you."

He nodded, then leaned against the seat once again, hands folded in his lap.

And Charlotte thanked the Lord at least another dozen times in the next minute for His Providence over her.

CHAPTER FIFTEEN

THANKFULLY, THE STAGECOACH RIDE from Nelsonville to Willow Falls passed without incident. It was six o'clock in the evening by the time she and Tobias arrived, and Charlotte wanted nothing more than to visit with her family and sleep in her own bed after the lengthy journey.

She and Tobias borrowed horses from Frederick, the mercantile owner, since the livery was already closed. Thankfully, he was home and was happy to oblige. Tobias had been silent the entire way, and she'd prayed again for him for God's very real peace and comfort, especially when Tobias entered Chester and Paulina's house for the first time since their deaths.

"Do you want me to ride with you to your house?" Tobias asked. Exhaustion tugged at his countenance. His shoulders bowed, and he continually squeezed his eyes shut, then reopened them, likely willing himself not to succumb to the sleep that beckoned.

"No, but perhaps I should accompany you so you stay on your horse."

A faint smile lit his lips. "It's not far for either of us, but if you'd rather I go with you…"

How many times had she ridden from town by her lonesome? Too many to count over the years, although she appreciated his concern for her, especially after the events of today. "Thank you, Tobias, for caring for me and for your offer. I'll be fine on the ride home." She paused. "Please know that I'm praying for you. Can I send Pa or Caleb over to Chester's house?"

"No. I don't plan to be there but to sleep. I'll ride over to your parents' house tomorrow. Good night, Charlotte." With that, he summoned his horse in the opposite direction.

Charlotte watched as he rode left toward Chester and Paulina's house, a house now void of those he loved.

After Charlotte bid Tobias goodbye at the junction, she rode toward her parents' home, her thoughts heavy. Weariness filled every limb, and she struggled to stay awake. She passed first Caleb and Annie's house, and when her own came into view, she whispered a prayer of gratitude to the One who'd delivered her safely.

Tears clouded her vision when she saw Ma sweeping the porch. She and Ma were especially close and, while Charlotte deemed herself an independent woman, she'd missed her family something awful while in Prune Creek. She barely took the time to stop the horse before dismounting. She tethered it to the fence post and bolted toward the porch, her skirt whipping around her ankles. "Ma!"

Ma stopped sweeping and gaped at Charlotte—realization likely setting in—before she dropped the broom and met Charlotte half way.

"Charlotte!" Ma embraced her, and for these brief moments, all was right in the world.

Ma, sweet and precious Ma with her petite stature and compassionate personality. Ma, the one whom Charlotte had towered over in height since she was twelve.

Charlotte took a step back, and Ma framed her face with her hands. "I had no idea you were planning a visit to Willow Falls. Are you all right?"

"Yes, everything is all right, but I was so worried about everyone after I received your letter."

"I'm so sorry I worried you. We are doing much, much better. Come inside. I imagine you are famished after your trip."

Charlotte followed Ma. While many things had changed in Charlotte's life during recent years, her home remained the same. Her refuge. Her sanctuary. The place where the people she loved most resided.

"We just ate supper, so it should still be warm." Ma set a plate of roast beef and potatoes in front of Charlotte. After blessing the meal, Charlotte took several bites, barely able to contain her hunger.

"Where's Pa?"

"He's outside in the barn. He's taken to whittling while he heals completely."

"But Doc says he'll make a full recovery, right?"

Ma placed a hand on Charlotte's. "Yes, he will make a full recovery, praise the Lord. The influenza affected him the worst and, while it's been some time since he's recovered, he's still attempting to regain his strength. He tires easily and suffers from continued aches and pains, but God is faithful, and He brought us through this illness."

"I'm so, so sorry I wasn't here to take care of you." The tears again welled in her eyes.

"Oh, Charlotte, we are grateful you *weren't* here. It's highly likely you would have become ill as well. This frightful sickness shows no bias regarding who it affects. We lost Tobias's family and three others in town. In addition, Millicent was quite ill, as was Sheriff Townsend. Lena caught it the worst of the girls, and we're ever so grateful Baby Evangeline didn't get sick."

"But I could have been here to care for you and for Pa and to help with the girls. I felt so guilty being in Prune Creek."

Ma enveloped her in another hug and patted her hair, just like she'd done when Charlotte was a young girl. "I appreciate so much your willingness to care for your family. We have missed you terribly and will enjoy your visit, although I worry about you traveling alone."

"I wasn't really alone." Charlotte sat back in her chair and took a sip of the milk Ma poured for her. "Tobias was on his way here as well." She'd not elaborate to Ma about the horrifying episode at the depot. Ma would only fret and then fret some more and would be inclined to send a chaperone to accompany Charlotte on her return trip. No one had the funds for such extravagances.

"Tobias?" A suspicious glint lit Ma's eyes. "Was he on his best behavior?"

Charlotte giggled at Ma's statement. "Yes, he was gentlemanly. I suppose at first I thought maybe it wasn't the real Tobias, but rather an imposter."

"Well, I'm thankful he was on the train as well. You know how I feel about you traveling alone." Ma sighed. "That poor man has been through a lot in recent years with the loss of his parents, and now the passing of Chester and Paulina."

"I'm worried for him. He said he'll be by tomorrow. You didn't mention Lanie—did she survive?"

Ma nodded. "She did. She was extremely ill as well but made a full recovery. She's been staying with Caleb and Annie. I also wrote a letter to Tobias that I mailed yesterday telling him about Lanie. He's her only family as far as I know. Regardless, we'll do whatever we can to help Tobias with her care."

Pa's appearance stunned Charlotte. Even with his beard, she could see how thin his face had become. He sat on the wooden bench Caleb and John Mark had built for him for Christmas a few years ago, knife in one hand and a piece of wood in the other.

"Charlotte!"

"Hello, Pa." She took a seat beside him.

"I didn't know you were planning to visit Willow Falls."

"Ma sent me a letter about how you were all so sick. I had to come."

Pa's eyes crinkled at the corners. "It's always good to see my favorite daughter."

Charlotte rested her head on Pa's shoulder. "I was so worried about everyone, and Ma said you were the sickest."

"Yes. It's the sickest I've ever been. The coughing and the sore throat were nothing compared to the constant fatigue and weakness. I'm still struggling with being tired even after a few minutes of walking."

Pa had always been so strong and so capable. Charlotte lifted her head. "I'm praying you'll be fully healed soon."

"Thank you. I've been collecting prayers, as have many of the townsfolk. Seems few remained unscathed from this illness. The little girls recovered the fastest, and thankfully Baby Evangeline stayed well."

"It looks like you've taken up a new hobby."

Pa held up the wood figurine in his hand. "Reckon I've discovered I enjoy whittling. Your ma suggested it, and I've been working on some wooden toys for Esther, Lena, Lola, and Ambrose. I'm also going to surprise your ma with a Christmas decoration. You know how she loves Christmas."

"And everything that goes along with it."

Pa chuckled. "Yes. Reckon I'm fond of that woman."

"You have been married for..." Charlotte tapped her chin, "one hundred years or so?"

"One hundred and one to be exact."

They laughed together and Charlotte praised the Lord for sparing her parents.

"I started whittling because I couldn't do much in the days following the sickness, and I was somewhat restless what with staying in bed for so many days. I'm looking forward to Sunday because I'll finally be able to preach for the first time since taking ill."

"Ma said Sheriff Townsend was sick as well so he couldn't take your place."

"Actually, Caleb has preached in my place for the past several Sundays. From what I've heard, he's done an outstanding job."

Pa's words came as no surprise. Caleb was affable, humble, and trustworthy. "I'm grateful you're feeling better, Pa."

"As am I. One thing I realized more than ever was that I was dependent on the Lord for every breath." Pa placed the wooden figurine and knife beside him on the bench. "Now tell me, how are you? How is Prune Creek? And were you able to find someone to accompany you on the journey here? You know your ma and I aren't thrilled with the prospect of you traveling so far by yourself."

Charlotte appreciated her parents' concern. "I like Prune Creek, and the aunts are a bundle of hilarity, especially when they bicker."

"They are known for quarreling. You've not been eating Aunt Myrtle's huckleberry pie, have you?" Pa wrinkled his nose and turned a bit green. "Once you've tasted that unappetizing dessert, you never forget it." For a moment, it seemed as though Pa would retch. "I've never tasted anything so awful."

Charlotte grinned at Pa's obvious, albeit exaggerated, expression. "That was even before you and Ma were courting that you had the pleasure—or shall we say, displeasure—of eating Aunt Myrtle's huckleberry pie."

"And I've never forgotten it."

She thought of Tobias and the huckleberry pie, biscuits, and sugar cookies he'd eaten at the aunts' house. He'd had much the same response. "As for me traveling here alone, Tobias was on the train as well so you needn't have worried."

"Tobias? As in Tobias Hallman, the most infuriating and vexatious boy this side of the Mississippi River?"

"He would be the one. Although he was slightly less infuriating and vexatious during the trip."

Pa chuckled, then sobered. "Did your ma tell you that he lost his brother and sister-in-law to the influenza?"

"She did. I'm worried about him, Pa. After having lost his parents and now Chester and Paulina. Ma told me Lanie survived and has been staying with Caleb and Annie."

"Annie mentioned it's been difficult for her, understandably so. At any age it's a challenge to comprehend why the Lord would take someone home, let alone grasping something like that when you're only five-years-old. I have been, and will continue to, pray for Tobias and Lanie. Your ma and I and Caleb and Annie are ready to help however we can."

Lanie would likely be coming back to Prune Creek with Tobias. "The aunts and I will assist as well."

"It's just by God's grace we didn't all go see John Mark, Hannah, and Ambrose the week we were planning to do so. That was the week we fell ill. It would have been dangerous for Hannah to get sick with the baby coming. We'll now plan to go in a few weeks once everyone has fully recovered."

Charlotte and Pa conversed for several minutes longer before she accompanied him to the house. And as she rested in her bed that night, she thanked the Lord several times over for His Providence.

Ma had gone to town, Pa was in the barn, and Charlotte was finishing cleaning up after breakfast when she heard commotion outside. She walked out to the porch and saw Caleb assisting Annie and five little girls from the wagon, one of whom was Baby Evangeline, snuggled contentedly in her mother's arms.

"Aunt Charlotte! Aunt Charlotte!" four exuberant voices chorused in unison as they ran, hand in hand, towards her.

Charlotte laughed at the line of her nieces and Lanie Hallman clutching a doll in her free hand, all dashing together, their braids flying. "Slow down, sisters!" exclaimed Lola. "I'm just a little girl and can't run that fast!"

But the older ones just giggled and continued on their way to the porch.

Annie followed with Baby Evangeline in her arms, and Charlotte kneeled down and welcomed the hugs of her nieces. "How are my favorite nieces in the whole wide world?" She asked, as she always did, when she saw Esther, Lena, and Lola.

Charlotte stood and Lena, the most affectionate of the three, grabbed Charlotte's hand and swung their joined hands. "Fine. And how are you?"

Lola began to tell a story about Baby Evangeline, while Esther, already one who loved learning, proceeded to share with Charlotte about the latest book Annie was reading to them before bedtime.

And Lanie Hallman clung to Charlotte's skirts, her face buried as she sniffled. Charlotte tenderly patted her head.

"We were berry sick, Aunt Charlotte," said Lola. She changed her tone. "My voice sounded like this. Good morning," she croaked. "We sounded like fwogs."

Lena released Charlotte's hand. "But God healed us."

"I'm so glad you are doing better."

"Yes, and we are going to go visit Uncle John Mark, Aunt Hannah, and cousin Ambrose in a couple of weeks."

"I bet you are looking forward to that."

Esther nodded. "We are. Cousin Ambrose always makes up stories, and we have a lot of fun. Except that he always has to be a sheriff." Her blonde brows creased. "Maybe someday he could be a rancher like Pa or a reverend like Grandpa."

"Not cousin Ambrose. He won't want to be anything else," declared Lena, hands on her hips.

Esther and Lena continued discussing their plans for when they visited Poplar Springs when Lola suggested they go see Grandpa in the barn. "Ma, do you and Baby Evangeline want to come with us?"

Lanie stayed behind, her face still buried in Charlotte's skirts.

"Lanie?"

She began to cry, her thin shoulders shaking.

Charlotte stooped to Lanie's height and opened her arms. Lanie fled into them and wrapped her arms around Charlotte's neck. She held the little girl close for several minutes before Lanie stepped back and rubbed at her reddened eyes. "My ma and pa went to live with Jesus, and I miss them." She gripped the doll against her chest.

"Sweetie, I am so sorry."

"God didn't heal them. They were so sick, and Pa didn't even move when I gave him a hug. And then Ma told me she loved me, but her voice was really quiet."

Charlotte prayed for the words to say that would comfort the precious child who'd lost so much so unexpectedly. She sat in the chair on the porch, and Lanie climbed into her lap.

"I'm so sorry about your ma and pa," said Charlotte. "So very sorry."

"I don't understand why they're gone." Lanie's eyes were rimmed with red, and her stifled sobs started again, causing her shoulders to cave beneath her overwhelming grief.

Charlotte pulled the child to her and rocked her in her arms. *Lord, please give me the words to say, the comfort to provide, and the love to share with this little one. I know not what to say.*

Lanie curled into a ball, her petite frame nestled against Charlotte. Charlotte kissed the top of her head and continued to hold her close.

It was only after Pa emerged from the barn, leaning on his cane, and his granddaughters giggling as he told them a story, that Lanie left Charlotte's lap.

Charlotte and Annie sat in the chairs on the porch and watched as Pa perched beneath the tree, book in hand, and read to his audience.

"Lanie has been through so much," said Annie. She bounced Evangeline on her knee and the baby turned to Charlotte, arms outstretched. "She has not allowed anyone to fix her hair or take out her braids. It's remained the way it was from the last time Paulina braided it for her."

Charlotte took the chubby baby into her arms and snuggled her. Evangeline babbled happily, amusing herself with Charlotte's necklace.

"She is such a sweet girl and to have to go through this..." Charlotte's voice trailed. "To lose your parents at such a young age would be devastating." She thought of Tobias and wondered when he would arrive at the house. He had no idea Lanie survived. Should she ride over to Chester and Paulina's and tell him? "I'm so grateful Lanie has been able to stay with you and Caleb until Tobias arrived."

Annie nodded. "Your parents offered to take her as well, but with your pa still so weak, we thought it best for us to care for her. Caleb attempted to visit Tobias last night at Chester and Paulina's house, but he wasn't there."

"He mentioned he'd stop by today. I'm not sure when he's returning to Prune Creek."

"Well, Caleb and I and your parents all are ready to help in whatever way we can with Lanie."

"And the aunts and I as well. I assume Tobias will take Lanie to Prune Creek. To my knowledge, they are the only family each other has now."

Evangeline stretched her arms out to Annie, apparently enjoying being passed between the two women. Annie settled her daughter on the porch in front of her with a doll. "I'm so thankful they have each other. Did you and Tobias travel here together?"

"Not intentionally." Charlotte explained to Annie about the trip and included the frightening part at the depot. "But please don't tell my parents. They'll only fret."

"I'm so grateful he was there," said Annie. "How terrifying!"

"I don't even want to think about what could have happened if he hadn't been there." Charlotte shivered. "We seem to have come to some type of understanding during our trip from Prune Creek."

Annie smiled. "So he's not quite as vexing as you once found him to be?"

"Perhaps slightly less."

"While a naughty pupil much of the time in school, I do know Tobias has a kind heart and is a good man."

Charlotte recalled all of Tobias's shenanigans in school. He did seem to have matured since those days in Annie's classroom.

Evangeline fussed, and Annie retreated to the house to feed her. A man on horseback rounded the corner by the trees, and soon the rider's identity became apparent.

Tobias dismounted and tethered his horse. Charlotte rose and walked toward him, and at just that moment, Lanie bolted from her place beneath the tree and ran toward Tobias. Charlotte saw the slight hesitation—disbelief—on Tobias's face as he faltered before running to meet Lanie halfway.

Charlotte stopped, unsure of whether she should remain observing the tearful moments between uncle and niece.

She averted her gaze to Pa who had rounded up the girls and was meandering slowly with the help of his cane toward the nearby pond.

"Uncle Tobias!" Lanie buried her face in Tobias's shoulder. Tobias hunched over her, his broad shoulders quaking. While he was a strong man in every sense of the word, this had shaken him, and rightfully so.

"Lanie, I'm so glad you are all right."

The two clung to each other, Lanie's sobs filling the otherwise quiet air.

"Ma and Pa..."

"I know, Lanie. I miss them too." His voice broke and he pulled slightly away from her. "I love you, Lanie, and God will help us through this. I know He will."

"But why then would he take Ma and Pa to Heaven? I prayed for them."

Tobias took both of Lanie's hands in his. "Some things are difficult to understand."

"Can I come live with you in Prune Creek?"

"Yes. And we'll ride on a stagecoach and then a train to get there."

Charlotte's eyes misted and she gently scraped at the dirt with the toe of her boot. Tobias's effort to give Lanie something to anticipate was commendable.

"A stagecoach and a train?" Lanie's voice quivered, and she tugged her hand away and rubbed her eye. "I would like to ride on a train." She peered around her. "And can Aunt Charlotte come too?"

As if noticing her for the first time, Tobias stood and his gaze met Charlotte's. "Uh, yes, Char—Aunt Charlotte—will be returning to Prune Creek as well."

Lanie's shoulders slumped a smidgeon less, but her countenance remained sorrowful. "I just want Ma and Pa. But I guess riding on a train would be a 'venture."

Charlotte's heart broke for the duo who'd lost so much in such a short amount of time.

Lord, please heal their broken hearts.

CHAPTER SIXTEEN

TOBIAS HAD ALWAYS FOUND it easy to talk to Reverend Solomon. And in the years since his own pa had passed, Tobias had sought out the reverend on more than a couple of occasions.

Today, Reverend Solomon sought him out. Tobias followed him to the barn, memories flooding his mind.

Tobias had spent a fair amount of time at the Eliason home as a young'un. He and John Mark often partook in supper at each other's homes. Times at the Eliasons' gave ample opportunity to pester Charlotte as well as spend time with the folks who had become a second family to him.

Reverend Solomon moved slowly with each laborious step, and Tobias reminded himself to consistently pray the reverend would fully regain his pre-influenza strength. He took a seat next to him on the wooden bench. It was then that Tobias noticed a stack of wood on the opposite side of the bench along with a knife and a carved wooden bird.

"I've undertaken whittling while I recover," said Reverend Solomon as though he read Tobias's thoughts. "The bird is for Lydie since that's her favorite animal. It's my third attempt at carving her one that actually resembles a bird." His mouth curved upward. "The thing is, I know my Lydie would be delighted with it no matter if it's flawed. It's just my pickiness that deems it needs to be perfect."

Tobias appreciated that Reverend Solomon loved his wife. His own pa had been the same way towards Ma. He had loved and cherished her. Someday if the Lord saw fit, Tobias hoped he would be the same kind of husband.

Reverend Solomon rested his cane on the ground. "Sure am sorry about Chester and Paulina."

"Thank you, sir. I'm still figuring I'll wake up, and it will have only been a bad dream."

"It's not easy losing those we love."

"At least Lanie survived. We're all each other has now." His voice cracked. "I should have stayed in Willow Falls. Maybe I could have nursed them back to health or..."

Reverend Solomon closed his eyes for a few seconds, likely praying before he spoke. "We all have regrets," he said. "Unfortunately we can't go back and change things."

"Sure would if I could. I'd be content in Willow Falls, not attempting to seek out a life of blacksmithing in another town. I was glad when Chester and Paulina moved back to Willow Falls from Cheyenne last year. I only wish I'd stayed instead of going to Prune Creek."

"I understand you're hurting, son, and rightfully so. But there are no guarantees that Chester and Paulina would have survived if you'd stayed here. You can't blame yourself."

Tobias took a deep breath. "For me, it's the not knowing whether or not my actions could have changed things."

"We all wonder that from time to time. Likely you being here would not have changed the outcome. For reasons we will never understand, it was God's will that He take Chester and Paulina home."

Reverend Solomon's words were soft. Kind. But the impact of his words—knowing that it *was* God's will to take Chester and Paulina home—punched Tobias square in the chest. "I know God knows best, but I don't understand why He does the things He does sometimes."

The reverend again closed his eyes for a few brief seconds. "Nor do I. We are people with limited insight and knowledge. Our God is holy, with infinite insight and knowledge. As the verse in Isaiah says, *'My thoughts are not your thoughts, neither are my ways your ways...for as the heavens are higher than the earth, so are my ways higher than your ways, and my thoughts than your thoughts.'* No one can fully comprehend—or even begin to comprehend—the ways of our Lord. Why do some live to an old age and others die young, some even before they are born? We know about death and disease entering the world through the Fall, but there is so much we will never understand this side of Heaven."

"I have so many regrets. With the train going all the way to Nelsonville now, and the stagecoach taking us to Willow Falls, I could have visited more often."

"Regrets are hard. In a way, they enable us to do our best not to make the same mistakes twice. But pondered too often and they have a way of crushing our spirit as no man can go back in time. Only forward."

Reverend Solomon's words settled into his heart and mind. "I just wish I could spend another day with them. Even an hour. My parents too. Just one more time around the supper table or even doing chores. Anything. Does it ever get easier? Will it get easier for me over the loss of my family and for Lanie over the loss of her parents?"

"Yes, it does get easier, especially when we know where our family now resides. The pain never goes away completely, and there will always be a missing place in our hearts and our lives for those we have lost. But God has a way of seeing us through these difficult times. Of never letting us go. Of holding us tight and of giving us the kind of comfort only our Heavenly Father can give. And He will place people in our lives who mourn with us and who heal with us. Lydie and I hope to be some of those people for you and Lanie."

Tobias choked on the emotion that swelled inside of him. "Yes, sir. I am grateful for you and Mrs. Eliason and your entire family."

"You've always been like a son to us, and we are here for both of you. We couldn't love Lanie more if she was our own granddaughter."

Silence consumed the barn while Tobias attempted to gather his thoughts. After several minutes, he spoke again. "I'm grateful Lanie survived." Now that Lanie was orphaned, could he be a good pa to her? Raise her in a way that honored God and would've made Chester and Paulina proud? "What if I fail with her?"

"You will make mistakes as a parent. We all do. There's no perfect father except our Lord."

"I don't know the first thing about raising a daughter, but I aim to do my best."

Reverend Solomon gripped his shoulder. "And with the Lord's help and plenty of prayer, you will succeed. And Lydie and I, Caleb and Annie, and Charlotte will all be here to help you."

Charlotte's face flashed through his mind. Lanie was fond of her. Thankfully Charlotte would be in Prune Creek as

Lanie would no doubt need a godly woman's influence after having lost her ma. And while he and Charlotte did not always get along, they both loved Lanie.

"How is Prune Creek?" Reverend Solomon asked, interrupting Tobias's thoughts.

"The blacksmithing is going well. It's all I ever wanted to do and now with having my own business..." Tobias took a deep breath. "But maybe I could have been content working for Mr. Goss on his ranch like Pa and Chester."

"Not sure if I told you or not, but I once wanted to be a preacher in South Pass City. I figured there were a lot of lost souls what with the rowdy mining conditions."

Tobias hadn't realized that about the reverend. "What made you change your mind?

Reverend Solomon grinned. "I fell in love."

"Do you ever regret not moving there?"

"Can't say as I have. God had a perfect plan for my life—a much better plan than I could have orchestrated. I rarely gave thought to South Pass City once the Lord led me to settle here with Lydie. But I do have other regrets. Things I wish I would have done differently—a relationship I wish I could have mended with my grandfather. Things such as that." Reverend Solomon stroked his beard. "But God always knows better than we do, and when we commit our lives to Him, He'll lead us exactly to where He wants us." He paused and looked thoughtful. "There's a reason why I was never able to reconcile with my grandfather, as painful as it is. I won't know the reason until I'm in the Lord's presence someday. Reckon by that time there'll only be one thing on my mind and that'll be praising the Lord for eternity."

Tobias had long appreciated the reverend's candid and humble wisdom. He crossed his ankle over his knee and focused his attention on the man who offered prudent advice—advice Tobias would no doubt be chewing on long into the night. "But if I'd stayed here..."

"Oh, you'll revisit regrets from time to time. That's part of life. You'll wish you could have changed things, just as you're wishing now. The important thing is how we live our lives from this moment forward. There's a reason you moved to Prune Creek. A reason you weren't here when the entire town fell ill. As Proverbs 16:9 says, '*A man's heart deviseth his way: but the Lord directeth his steps.*'

"A few verses earlier, we are told, '*Commit thy works unto the Lord, and thy thoughts shall be established.*' The Lord will direct your steps in raising Lanie and in all of the joy, challenges, and adventures that come with that. And yes, adventures. Lydie and I have had our share raising our three children."

"I worry about her being so young and all. When I lost my parents, I was older. I can't imagine being orphaned that young."

"I, too, lost my parents at a young age, but older than Lanie. The Lord promises to comfort us and give us peace in all circumstances. We will be lifting to the Lord our prayers for Lanie for comfort and for you. We'll also pray for wisdom as you care for Lanie."

"Thank you, sir. I appreciate that."

"We are always here for you. Now, did I hear that you accompanied our Charlotte to Willow Falls?"

"We didn't realize we were both coming to Willow Falls, but I'm glad I could see her safely here." Tobias wouldn't tell the reverend about the depot incident. If Charlotte decided to tell her father, it would be her choice.

"Thank you for doing so. Charlotte is, shall we say, a bit independent. Don't tell her I said so, but it's one of the traits she inherited from her ma's side, from the aunts to be exact. Those two have always been overly independent." Reverend Solomon shook his head. "You'll face dilemmas just as I have, wondering if it's safe to allow my daughter to travel alone on a train just a great distance. Perhaps Lanie will be easier in that manner."

Tobias hoped so as well as he wasn't sure he could allow Lanie to travel by herself after what he'd witnessed yesterday.

"Are you and Charlotte getting along better?"

"She's not quite as annoying as she once was."

Reverend Solomon chuckled. "You two and your disagreements. Well, maybe someday you'll see each other in a different way."

"Perhaps so." Tobias wouldn't mention that he already had seen Charlotte in a different way in recent weeks. "We didn't realize each other would be residing in Prune Creek either. Had I known, I should have paid to have one of those fancy photographs taken when Charlotte saw me that first time on the doorstep at the aunts' house."

"That would have been a sight to see. I'm just appreciative she's there and not married to Cyrus. Another tough decision for a father to make on whether or not to disallow a courtship. God worked that one out just perfectly without my intervention, although I hated to see my daughter's heart get broken." Reverend Solomon sighed. "You'll face all kinds of things like this with Lanie, but the Lord will guide you through it all."

Tobias pondered Charlotte's broken heart. If he ever saw Cyrus again, he might have to let him know his thoughts on the matter. For while he and Charlotte had not always been friends, he cared deeply for her. Maybe more deeply than he had ever realized.

CHAPTER SEVENTEEN

CHARLOTTE PASSED THE SHERIFF'S office after delivering the dress Ma had sewn for a customer. She stopped to peruse the various wanted posters attached to the bulletin board.

Willow Falls didn't see the crime that Poplar Springs, and even Nelsonville and Bowman saw, or the larger towns in the southern part of the state, but the mostly-peaceful town had been known to unwittingly harbor an outlaw or two.

From their appearances, the posters had been pinned some time ago, which made sense since Ma mentioned Sheriff Townsend was one of the townsfolk who'd fallen ill with the influenza. Some of the notices were smudged, their ink blurred or running, or pieces of the posters missing or obscured due to wind, rain, or mud splatters from passing horses and wagons.

Shivers ran down her spine as she attempted to apprise herself of whom she'd need to watch for in the days ahead. One poster had the haphazard words "CAPTURED" scribbled across it. Squinting, she attempted to read the next three posters. Without sketches and with half of the description being indecipherable due to smudged words, it was impossible to determine the men's appearances.

Charlotte read the remaining two wanted posters before stepping away from the postings. She was about to continue on her way when she saw Violet, who would make a good dime novel antagonist, waving at her from the opposite end of the boardwalk.

"Charlotte!"

Could she pretend she didn't see the insolent woman? Turn in the opposite direction and hasten her steps?

"Oh, Charlotte!"

Lord, please help me hold a tight rein on my tongue and grace in my heart. Knowing herself too well, Charlotte added an additional plea. *And please, Lord, I beseech thee that You please forgive me for the words that will likely emerge from my mouth should the tight rein falter.*

"Hello, Violet."

As she always did before she spoke, Violet lifted her chin and peered about the area, first in front of her, then to each side, and finally, behind her. She then placed the tip of her parasol to the ground and stood straight. She wore a pale yellow-and-green striped dress with puffy leg-of-mutton sleeves, plentiful lace appliques on the bodice, and a high collar with a pearl button. Peach accents lined the bodice and the sleeves, and a matching hat with plentiful bows and flowers completed her ensemble.

Charlotte resisted the urge to peer down at her own coral-colored skirt and plain button-up blouse, and make a comparison. While Ma stitched premium clothing, vastly superior to those found at the mercantile, and while the dresses she'd received from the aunts from Mrs. Peabody were of top fashion, Charlotte would never own the finery Violet wore. And she for certain had never owned a parasol.

She attempted not to care about such frivolities.

Violet surveyed Charlotte's appearance, her piercing, wide-set eyes failing to blink as she did so. "I hear you're still a spinster," she mocked, as if daring Charlotte to declare otherwise.

"How do you know I don't have a beau in Prune Creek?"

Violet pursed her lips, an uppity air radiating from her. "Well I declare, Charlotte Eliason. I doubt that very much. With the exception of John Mark secretly getting married to *that woman* in Poplar Springs, nothing is a secret here in Willow Falls. I would know forthwith if you were courting someone in Prune Creek."

"*That woman's* name is Hannah. And to the contrary, Violet. You might think you are the knower of all things, but you most assuredly are not." Charlotte bit the inside of her cheek even as the words flowed freely from her mouth. She silently prayed again for the Lord to rein in her tongue. Violet, with her supercilious and pompous personality, brought out the worst in Charlotte. Always had.

"The knower of all things? Really, Charlotte." Violet rolled her eyes. "Such mean-spiritedness is so unbecoming of a reverend's daughter."

Violet had uttered those words before when she and Charlotte had exchanged affronts. Charlotte's tongue had, at times, gotten the best of her while in Violet's presence, but she knew two things to be true. One, that she never wished to embarrass or tarnish her father's reputation. And, more importantly, that unkind words were never fitting of one who belonged to the Lord. She bit the inside of her cheek again. From this second on, with the Lord's help, she would endeavor to respond to Violet's insults in a more charitable way. The words of Proverbs 19:11 entered her mind for the third time since encountering the snobbish woman who had become a thorn in her side. *The discretion of a man deferreth his anger; and it is his glory to pass over a transgression.*

"I best be going," Charlotte said.

"You know," added Violet, placing her free hand on a slim hip, "you'd likely fancy someone like that incorrigible Tobias Hallman."

In the days of old, Charlotte's temper would flare plenty at the insinuation that she would ever fancy Tobias Hallman. Violet knew, as did every classmate, that Charlotte and Tobias were nemeses. But with Tobias coming to her rescue—both at the train depot and during the trestle incident and his recent loss of his family—her thoughts of him had taken a slightly different route. Violet's words no longer offended her. She considered Tobias a friend now, and even at his worst, he was nothing like what Charlotte thought of Cyrus. "Tobias Hallman is a more upstanding man than some," she said nodding toward Cyrus, who stood a short distance away discussing something with another of the townsfolk outside the livery. His robust height and build were double that of the man to whom he spoke.

"Pfft. At least Cyrus has determination and perseverance. Tobias has a severe lack of ambition. To aspire to be a blacksmith?" Violet scrunched her nose and puckered her lips as if tasting something sour.

"There is nothing wrong with being a blacksmith. It is an honorable profession and requires hard work and long hours. Has your buggy ever needed repair? Your horses shod? Your farm equipment fixed? If you answered yes to any of those questions, you could not do without a blacksmith. And you know as well as I do that the one here in Willow Falls is a valuable member of our town."

"Really, Charlotte. I care not about the repair of buggies and farm equipment and horses to be shod. That is nothing I have to worry about in the least. Besides, Cyrus says that blacksmiths will soon be obsolete due to our country's continued industrialization."

Violet would not win this argument. Charlotte was just as versed in the nation's ongoings—thanks to the local Prune Creek paper and Quimby's lending of the Denver newspaper—as Cyrus was. "To the contrary. Blacksmiths will be as valuable as ever because they will find alternate ways to assist with the ever-changing times."

"Believe what you want." Violet tucked a wisp of red hair beneath her hat. "I best go now. I'm hosting a tea at the ranch later today. I did tell you, didn't I, that Cyrus is having a magnificent house built for us?"

Charlotte did her utmost best not to grimace. "No, but congratulations."

Violet opened her parasol and sashayed away as though she were a high-society lady in Boston rather than a hoity-toity Willow Falls woman.

Several passersby greeted Charlotte as she continued down the boardwalk. All were delightful townsfolk whom she had known for most of her life. All were delightful, save one.

Cyrus Keller approached her just as Charlotte passed by the post office. "Well, hello, Charlotte."

"Cyrus."

"Now, is that any way to say the name of a former beau? It sounded more like a growl to me."

"You heard correctly." Charlotte would need to pray again for the Lord to tame her tongue. Two vexatious people in one day and in a matter of less than two minutes strained her thinning temper.

Cyrus stood in front of her, shoulders back, chest out, and legs spread wide. As if he owned the boardwalk. He smiled at her, a grin that at one time stole her breath. Today it had the completely opposite effect.

His gaze traveled over her, and she fought the urge to recoil. "You're just as beautiful as ever, Charlotte."

Tobias's image flashed through her mind, and for a brief moment, Charlotte compared the two men. One with integrity and godly character and the other a dishonest, crooked, and unscrupulous cad.

Yes, her thoughts about Tobias's character had certainly changed after the depot scare.

While Cyrus on the other hand...she thought of the time he'd sneaked a kiss without her permission. She'd almost not fled from his clutches, and she realized immediately that his kiss was not reminiscent of love but something altogether different. Charlotte should have known then that Cyrus would disrespect her.

She'd been such a fool.

"Charlotte?"

She returned to the present in the presence of a man quite opposite of Tobias. "I best be on my way. Good day, Cyrus."

He reached over and placed a warm, firm hand on her arm. "I do miss you."

Charlotte pulled away and scowled at him. "You're married to Violet now. Do you not know the meaning of faithfulness?"

Cyrus glowered at her through eyes that she saw now more as slits placed haphazardly on a spiteful face. His mustache twitched. "You never were good enough to be a Keller."

"And for that I am most grateful, although obviously the standards are not too terribly high with the choice you made." Before she uttered more words of which she'd need to repent of, Charlotte hoisted her skirts and continued on her way.

Cyrus broke her heart the day she discovered he was carrying on a dalliance with Violet. The pain and agony of knowing she would not be marrying the man she thought she loved, but rather, he would be marrying someone else, lingered for several months. But within weeks of moving to Prune Creek, her broken heart had healed.

She tilted her head to the sky. *Lord, thank You for knowing what was best for me. Thank You for Your Providence that I did not marry Cyrus Keller.*

CHAPTER EIGHTEEN

TWO DAYS LATER, CHARLOTTE held Lanie's hand as they meandered through the crowd and toward the train. The Nelsonville Depot stood out among the rest of the buildings in the town due to someone—or several someones— deciding that the drab brown paint should be replaced with a bright and cheery yellow.

As she was about to ascend the steps into the train, Charlotte noticed someone who looked familiar. Her limbs froze when she realized it was one of the men who had harassed her on the journey to Willow Falls. Was he alone or were his fellow criminals with him? Did he plan to torment passengers on the train? Was there time to alert someone? The man briefly peered her way with almost a sneer. Charlotte shrank back from his piercing perusal and once again thanked the Lord she wasn't traveling alone.

"Sir, how much time until we depart?" she asked the conductor.

"Less than five minutes."

"That gentleman over there..." Charlotte pointed in the direction she'd seen the man, but he had vanished.

"Yes?"

"I—never mind."

"Aunt Charlotte?" Lanie asked, interrupting Charlotte's thoughts.

"Yes?"

"I'm really tired."

Charlotte kneeled to Lanie's height and placed a hand on her forehead. "Are you feeling well besides that?"

Lanie nodded, her pale complexion and the red around her eyes a testament to the lengthy time she'd spent mourning the loss of her parents. While spending time with Charlotte's nieces had been a much-needed diversion, it could in no way remedy the despondency and heartbreak the young child experienced.

Charlotte gently tucked a strand of blonde hair behind Lanie's ear. "Perhaps you could sleep on the train."

"All right." Lanie again wrapped her arms around Charlotte's neck.

For as long as she lived, Charlotte would never understand why the Lord had allowed Chester and Paulina to die. They were kind, wonderful people. Young and otherwise healthy. She swallowed the emotion that threatened to come to the forefront and held Lanie to her.

Charlotte stood, lifting Lanie and clutching her in one arm and her carpetbag in the other. She spied Tobias coming toward them after briefly visiting with someone he knew. "Here, let me take her," he offered.

They entered the train, and Tobias gestured to her to take the seat closest to the window on the left-hand side five rows from the front. Lanie squeezed between them and rested her head against Charlotte. The dark circles underlining Tobias's eyes provided evidence of the weariness etched in his face.

Please Lord, allow me to be an instrument You use in helping Tobias and Lanie through this time of grief.

When his parents died, Tobias wasn't sure if his life would ever return to the way he'd grown accustomed. He mourned, not sure he would ever overcome the despair, but he'd still had family, and he'd had the town of Willow Falls. Knowing he still had Chester and Paulina made the grief more bearable.

But now...

He looked down first at Lanie, who snuggled closely next to Charlotte, her lashes wet from crying. How could he even believe he could provide a home for her? He lived in a boardinghouse that didn't allow children. He worked long hours as a blacksmith, and he barely had two pennies to rub together. He owned two fine horses, a wagon, a couple of sets of clothes, a revolver, and a few other meager possessions, but nothing of great worth, other than sentimental value. To construct the house he hoped to build, a modest cottage for he and Lanie, would cost nearly five hundred dollars, not counting the land. He was still attempting to establish his business, retain the customers the former owner had acquired, and hopefully procure more. But it hadn't been easy.

And Tobias Hallman thought he could provide for a child?

The remorse that so often resided deep within his chest settled there again, pressing against him as the accusations pricked his mind and his heart. Why hadn't he stayed in Willow Falls instead of thinking he needed to be a blacksmith? Why hadn't he been there for Chester and Paulina? Why hadn't he spent more time with them while they were alive? And the ridiculous argument he and Chester had gotten into right before Tobias left for Prune Creek. He'd apologized, as had Chester, but now, in Tobias's mind, that was more wasted time. Especially now that Chester was gone.

His eye caught Charlotte's. Her entire family had offered to help in any way possible. Reverend Solomon had already lent an ear when Tobias needed it the most. Caleb and Annie had taken care of Lanie until he could arrive in Willow Falls. And Charlotte had offered to assist in her care once they reached Prune Creek. He would need both her and the aunts' help if he was to be successful in this endeavor.

And he aimed to succeed in a way that would make the Lord, Chester, and Paulina proud.

Tobias faced forward again and rubbed his temples, attempting to ease the threatening headache.

The commotion on the train was louder than it had been on the way to Willow Falls, or maybe Tobias was just noticing it more due to the throbbing in his head. And while the railcar boasted far fewer passengers than last time, those on board were comprised mostly of women, children, and a few elderly men.

Hopefully they would arrive in Prune Creek without incident. He leaned back against the seat and closed his eyes as the exhaustion took hold.

Charlotte wasn't sure how long she'd been sleeping, but she jolted awake, short of breath.

"What's wrong?" Tobias asked.

She faced him. "One of the men who harassed me on the way to Willow Falls—I saw him in the crowd in Nelsonville as Lanie and I were preparing to board." She bit her lip, reminding herself once again of what could have happened had Tobias not been in the clearing that day.

"Why didn't you tell me?"

"I...I just, it was time to board, and I was speaking with Lanie, and..."

The sound of the door to the railcar opening drew her attention toward the back where the familiar man with orange hair and a disheveled beard entered, his gun drawn.

Several gasps replaced formerly pleasant conversation.

Charlotte sharply inhaled. "There he is," she breathed.

Tobias turned too, and Lanie stirred and murmured, "Aunt Charlotte?"

Charlotte patted her on the head. "Go back to sleep, sweetie," she whispered. Her attention reverted to the vile, unsavory man. Was he alone or were the other criminals that had been with him on their trip to Willow Falls tormenting the passengers in the other railcar? What were their ultimate plans? She cringed. Charlotte had heard of train robberies, especially in southern Wyoming, but had never expected to be involved in one.

"Now listen here. You do as I say and no one gets hurt. If not, well..." He eyed the revolver in his hand. "Let's just say if you don't, then I get to use this gun."

Murmurs and shrieks filled the railcar. A child whimpered. The man chortled at the passengers' distress before sobering. "Put all your valuables in this sack."

Charlotte swiftly removed her necklace while the man was preoccupied and placed it beneath her left leg out of sight.

"Please don't take my wife's brooch. It was a gift from her grandmother," an elderly man with thinning white hair pleaded.

The robber whacked him hard on the head with his revolver. "Shut up! I'll take what I want. Now put any jewelry or cash in the sack. Now!"

The woman sobbed, hastily put her brooch in the sack, and tended to her husband's wound. Charlotte offered a prayer heavenward for the injured man and watched as Tobias fingered his own revolver tucked in its holster.

The robber continued down the aisle, pilfering what he pleased. "Well, looky here," he said when he reached Charlotte and Tobias. "It's mighty nice to see you again." He winked the smaller of his two eyes and fixed his leering gaze on Charlotte. "Maybe I oughta just take you with me this time. No doubt you're worth more than the spoils I'll be collecting from these folks."

Tobias stiffened. "Leave her be."

"Did you not just see what happened to that man back there?" The robber held the gun on Tobias and dug the barrel into his chest, his furry face looming close. "Ain't nothing that says I can't do the same or worse to you." He sneered, his upper lip curled, exposing his few remaining rotten teeth.

The seconds ticked by in silence.

Finally the outlaw lowered his revolver. "Now, place anything of worth inside this sack. You," he nodded at Charlotte, "open your carpetbag and remove any money or jewelry."

Grateful she had previously removed the necklace, Charlotte unlatched the carpetbag's clasp as Tobias was placing a couple of coins in the sack. Would she be able to avoid giving the man the hard-earned funds Ma had given her before Charlotte left Willow Falls?

As if to read her mind, his caustic tone sounded in the railcar. "I see some cash in there. Put it in the bag," he demanded.

She removed the coins Ma had sacrificed from her egg fund so Charlotte, Tobias, and Lanie would be able to purchase food at one of the station stops for supper since the sandwiches Ma had prepared would last them for only the noonday meal. Charlotte plunked the coins into the bag, adding to the outlaw's plunder.

"And your revolver," the outlaw hissed, again steadying his own gun on Tobias's chest.

Charlotte could see the indecision in Tobias's eyes. If he relinquished his gun, how would he protect them? But if he didn't...

The outlaw pulled back the hammer. "Nice and slow. Put it in the bag."

Tobias had ridden with Pa, John Mark, Caleb, Sheriff Townsend, and the other men as a posse when hunting criminals near Willow Falls. He'd target-practiced with John Mark for hours after school and had won the Prune Creek shooting tournament just a few weeks ago. But could he out-maneuver and out-draw the robber if he chose to do so?

Prayer was again in order.

Tobias put his revolver in the bag and glared at the outlaw as he continued to make his way down the aisle to harass other passengers.

"Do we still have one of Aunt Myrtle's cookies?" he asked.

"Shut up!" the outlaw barked.

Charlotte rummaged through her carpetbag and produced all four of the rock-hard cookies Aunt Myrtle sent on the trip.

The criminal bent over a passenger three rows ahead, intimidating and forcing her to place her valuables in the bag. His back was to them, and Tobias threw the first of the hardened cookies, his impeccable aim hitting the man square in the back of the head, causing the outlaw to startle.

With the precision that rivaled a player on the Boston Reds baseball team, Tobias threw the other three cookies in rapid sequence, again hitting his target. At the same time, he leapt from his seat and rushed toward the outlaw, tackling him to the ground. The man's disorientation gave Tobias the advantage. The sack fell to the side, and one of the elderly men on board stumbled toward them in an attempt to retrieve it.

At just that time, the robber reached forward, grabbed the passenger's ankle, and sent him toppling forward, adding to the chaos. A woman in the front row aided the elderly man with his injuries, and Tobias and the outlaw continued their skirmish. Within minutes, the duel was relocated from the aisle to the back end of the railcar, and finally out the door and onto the platform. As the last railcar on the train, there was nowhere else to go.

Terrified, most of the few passengers onboard continued in their dazed confusion. Lanie remained sleeping through it all, her slight frame huddled on the seat beneath Charlotte's shawl.

Charlotte stood, and, on wobbly knees, made her way to the back of the train. Tobias, while tall, slim, and muscular, was no match for the outlaw who had an advantage due to his larger girth and odious personality. When Charlotte approached the door leading to the platform, he was on top of Tobias, his fist connecting with Tobias's face.

Lord, please...

Was there something she could do? Could someone else help her? But an efficient perusal reminded her that there were no able-bodied men. The women not tending to the injured were crouched over their children. Could she find a way to the other railcar to find help? She now understood why John Mark mentioned this railroad needing to hire agents to protect the passengers. Would this episode cause the railroad to see the necessity of doing so?

The railcar swayed, and Charlotte clutched the back of an empty seat to steady herself. As she continued to watch, Tobias miraculously gained the advantage, but his win was brief. The outlaw flipped him over and pushed Tobias's head and upper body down the stairs toward the rails.

Tobias clutched the iron railing with one arm, his muscles straining to avoid being fully thrown from the train. He'd braced his feet and used his other hand to attempt to fight back.

Charlotte gasped as time seemed to pause.

There had to be something she could do.

Where had the burlap sack gone? She discovered her answer a few seconds later when she located it beneath the last seat on the right-hand side. She rummaged through it to locate Tobias's gun. Amidst watches, jewelry, cash, and trinkets, she carefully removed the Colt revolver, clutching its dark brown grip.

For a brief moment, she was taken back in time to the target practices of several years ago. With Pa's patient instruction, she not only learned how to shoot a gun alongside her brothers, but learned how to shoot well enough to hunt. Later, John Mark, Tobias, and Russell allowed her to accompany them a few times while they practiced their aim.

The sound of the train whistle returned her to the present, but an efficient perusal out the window caused her knees to lock.

Charlotte recognized this area of the journey, for she had memorized it the times she'd traveled from Willow Falls to Prune Creek and back again. Perspiration slicked her palms as her shoulders tensed.

They were about to cross the worst trestle.

Tobias currently appreciated the upper hand, and Charlotte attempted to focus on that rather than the trestle, but her attempts failed.

Her heartbeat accelerated and her stomach twisted into tight coils. She shivered, although how could she be cold in the heat of the enclosed interior of the train? And if she couldn't contain the shivering, how could she maintain steady aim? She dared to peer outside. They were now on the trestle, high above the river below.

Why did it seem the train had slowed?

Tobias and the outlaw tussled, and the man again held Tobias's head and upper body down as he arched farther down the stairs. Much longer and the chances of Tobias losing the fight would be imminent.

Charlotte's heart hammered in her chest and her breath came in gasps, almost as though she ceased to release one full breath before the next one followed.

And if Tobias fell to his death all because of this ridiculous panic?

Move, feet, move!

But her legs remained paralyzed in place, and fear's frigid grip held steadfastly to her as the train roared along. The suffocating unease strangled her, and she pleaded with the Lord to calm her anxious countenance and begged for His peace, guidance, and the ability to do what she must do to save Tobias.

Finally, after what seemed an eternity of trembling, emitting ragged breaths, and her mind imagining the train plunging off the tracks and into the river below, Charlotte forced herself to peer out the door to where Tobias and the outlaw continued sparring. One wrong movement and he could be thrown from the train—or worse—thrown *under* the train.

Lord, please...

Her feet reluctantly obeyed her mind's mandate to move, and she stood in the entrance of the train. It was difficult to maintain her footing with the constant swaying as the train veered around a bend. Tobias was strong, but the outlaw was strong *and* cruel, and sometimes cruelty afforded an inordinate amount of extra strength.

Charlotte clutched the gun with both hands, shaking as she pulled back the hammer. Her finger edged toward the trigger. She needed a clear, steady shot. One that would maim the outlaw, but not put Tobias at risk.

She released the breath she'd been holding, raised the gun, and aimed through the open door. If the criminal maintained his advantage, Charlotte would be able to take a clean shot. But if Tobias suddenly gained control...

And if she did nothing, the man whom she'd known since childhood and who had recently become her friend could lose his life.

Willing herself to remain still and in full control, Charlotte pulled the trigger, causing a bullet to veer inches from the outlaw's head and ping off the railing.

The outlaw stilled.

It was just the opportunity Tobias needed. He hit the outlaw hard in the jaw then shoved him off. The outlaw rotated to the side, the platform stopping him from rolling off the edge. He jumped to his feet with astonishing efficiency given his rotund size, and he and Tobias circled each other in the tight area. Tobias delivered the final blow that caused the outlaw to fall backwards off the train and down the embankment below.

Tobias leaned forward, hands on his knees, shoulders heaving.

She tossed the revolver onto a seat and bolted toward him. He stood and faced her. Blood oozed from his lip, and his left cheek was swollen. A scratch marred his forehead, and his shirt was torn. Without hesitation, Charlotte put her arms around him. "I was so worried." She rested her head against his chest, attempting to recover from the thought of losing Tobias.

Charlotte could hear his heartbeat thumping loudly. What if she had been unable to compose herself long enough to shoot at and distract the outlaw? What if...

No. She'd not allow her thoughts to run amok in a frenzy. With great difficulty, Charlotte resisted the temptation to revisit what the Lord had delivered both she and Tobias from.

They stood there as the train roared down the tracks, the sound of the wheels on the rails and the breeze blowing past them. Tobias held onto the black railing with one hand to keep them steady while he circled her waist with the other. Nothing mattered but that Tobias was safe and hadn't succumbed to the future the outlaw intended for him.

Finally, after some time, Charlotte pulled back. "I was so worried," she repeated. "So scared." Her voice quaked as she searched his face.

His voice was low, intended to ease the tension of the situation even as he smirked. "Don't worry, Charlotte. You can't get rid of me that easily. Maybe *you* should have participated in the shooting tournament. That was some good aim." He paused and reached up to stroke her cheek with his thumb. "Thank you." His gaze held hers, and everything else around them ceased to exist in the gratitude of the moment.

Several minutes later, they returned to their seats amongst the clapping and cheering of the other passengers. Three thoughts filled Charlotte's mind. Thankfulness that the Lord saw fit to save Tobias; how when they arrived in Prune Creek Aunt Myrtle would be astonished and delighted, and perhaps a bit prideful, that her cookies were used to help stop a train robber; and third, the overwhelming thought and shocking realization that clouded Charlotte's mind.

She was beginning to have feelings for Tobias Hallman.

CHAPTER NINETEEN

TOBIAS AND CHARLOTTE CHECKED on the injured men, who were doing much better, then settled into their seats. Lanie was stretched out, sleeping peacefully, and he lifted her into his arms and slid into the seat, gratitude flowing through him that he hadn't succumbed to the fight with the outlaw.

He was still here to raise Lanie.

A flurry of emotions engulfed him. He could have easily lost his life during the altercation with Fraley. Had Charlotte's swift actions not distracted the outlaw, there was no telling who would have won the altercation.

Charlotte. He recalled how she'd felt in his arms. Like she belonged there. Holding her had been unexpected, but a welcome reprieve to all that happened.

"Uncle Tobias?" Lanie's groggy voice interrupted his thoughts. "Why is your face hurt?" She reached a hand toward his cheek.

"I'm all right, Lanie."

Charlotte reached over and patted Lanie's head. "Do you feel better? You must have been exhausted."

"What's 'sausted'?"

Tobias squeezed his niece's hand. "It means tired."

"Oh."

"Do you feel better rested after your nap?" Charlotte asked.

"Yes, and I can't wait to meet the aunts Grandma Lydie told me about." Lanie reached for Charlotte's hand as they rode the remainder of the way to the final depot.

Once they reached the station, a sheriff and two deputies greeted the passengers, explaining that the man who'd attempted to rob the train was Chuck "Bowlegged" Fraley, a member of a three-man gang wanted throughout Wyoming for robbery, murder, and assault. Tobias informed the sheriff of what had happened on the train before he, Charlotte, and Lanie continued on their way to Prune Creek.

It wasn't a second too soon that they arrived at the aunts' house. Charlotte and Tobias had discussed asking Aunt Myrtle and Aunt Fern if Lanie could stay with them temporarily until Tobias found somewhere other than the boardinghouse to reside.

"Oh, dear!" exclaimed Aunt Fern when she saw them arrive. "Whatever happened to your face?" She set about tending to Tobias's injuries while Aunt Myrtle hugged Charlotte, and both aunts gushed over Lanie.

Charlotte and Tobias began explaining some of the details, leaving out the part where Tobias nearly lost his life. "Apparently Fraley, the man Tobias fought, was part of a three-man gang wanted for robbing trains." She omitted the rest of the other things the notorious outlaws were wanted for to avoid unnecessary fretting for the aunts. "Aunt Myrtle, you will be thrilled to learn that Tobias bombarded Fraley with your cookies and was able to save the passengers on the train."

"You're a hero, Tobias," gushed Aunt Fern.

"A hero, indeed," agreed Aunt Myrtle. "Just a moment. You used my cookies to bombard him?" She held a hand to her chest. "Did you hear that, Fern? My cookies were used to help apprehend an outlaw. My baking skills will cause me to live in high esteem for generations to come."

"More like infamy," huffed Aunt Fern. "Besides, aren't there supposed to be agents on the train protecting the passengers?"

"On the bigger trains, yes," said Tobias. "Likely after this incident, the Driessen-Evers Railway Company, who owns the train, might begin to take safety more seriously."

"I do hope so," said Aunt Fern. "You could have been killed." She gave them each another hug.

Aunt Myrtle did the same before offering them something to eat. Everyone but Lanie declined. "While you've all been away, some rather thrilling things have happened here as well."

"Oh?" Charlotte took a sip of the milk Aunt Myrtle poured for her.

"Indeed. Your Aunt Fern is not nearly as perturbed by Stanley as she previously was. This most recent time he and Quimby came for supper, she even willingly sat by him and they shared in conversation."

"Pshaw, Myrt. I always knew Stan was a likable fellow."

"Stan?" asked Charlotte.

Aunt Myrtle guffawed. "It's what she calls him now from time to time."

"Aunt Fern, that's extraordinary news!"

"I don't know if it's extraordinary, Charlotte, but..." Color mottled Aunt Fern's cheeks. "I think he and I will get along reasonably well."

"Reasonably well," snorted Aunt Myrtle in a most unmannerly huff. "You are fond of him, Fernie."

"It's 'Fern', Myrtle. 'Fern', not 'Fernie'."

That comment ignited a whole new round of playful banter.

Tobias placed a hand on Lanie's shoulder. "Welcome to Prune Creek."

That evening on the front porch, Tobias explained to Lanie that she would be residing with the aunts.

"I have to go, but I will see you tomorrow."

"I don't want you to go. Why can't I go with you?"

"I live at the boardinghouse in a very small room. This is much better here." There was no way Mrs. White would allow a child to stay at the boardinghouse, and even if she did, it was far too cramped. Yet he knew this was only a temporary solution for Lanie to stay with the aunts. He couldn't impose on them forever. He needed to find a house and get Lanie settled permanently, especially after all she'd been through.

"But I want to stay with you."

"You like Aunt Charlotte, right?"

"Yes. I like her very much."

"She lives here. And you'll like the aunts too. They're really nice."

Lanie gestured toward the house. "But it's a big house."

"Yes, it is." Lanie would have her own room at the aunts' house while she was there. The home boasted several upstairs rooms, although not many furnishings. "You'll have a room right next to Aunt Charlotte, and I'll bring you a crate to put your things in." If Mrs. White would allow him to borrow the bureau in his room for Lanie, he'd do that, but for now, a crate would suffice.

"Will you come see me?"

"Every day, and this is only for a few days." But even as he said the words, Tobias realized he may not be able to keep his promise. "And Aunt Charlotte will bring you to see me often at the blacksmith shop, we'll see each other for supper and at church, and tomorrow we'll have a picnic."

"Please can you stay here?"

Her sorrowful gaze, combined with the desperation in her voice, tugged at Tobias. She'd lost her parents, stayed with Caleb and Annie, and now would stay with Charlotte and the aunts. Her life had been a mass of upheaval since Chester's and Paulina's deaths. And while she was well-cared for and loved at each of those places, it was still a lot to expect for a girl of five to comprehend.

Was it possible for him to stay in the parlor just for tonight? Could he impose that much on the aunts?

Yes, he could.

And he would do it for Lanie as he'd do just about anything for his niece.

"I'll ask the aunts if I can stay here in the parlor just for tonight. But I won't be able to stay beyond that as I have to return to where I live. It would just be for tonight," he reiterated.

"Just for tonight," Lanie agreed. She stood and wrapped her thin arms around Tobias's neck. "Thank you, Uncle Tobias."

"You're welcome."

Now if the aunts would agree to his plan.

After supper two hours later, Tobias knelt beside Lanie by the bed in the room next to Charlotte's to say prayers. It had been a long time since he'd prayed by his bedside, and it brought back memories of Ma and Pa kneeling beside him and Chester in their bedroom years ago. "Do you have any prayers you'd like to lift to the Lord?" he asked, just as Pa had done.

"Can we please pray my heart won't hurt so much?"

Tobias swallowed the lump in his throat at Lanie's request. He wished he could take away every ounce of pain she was feeling right now and would continue to feel for some time to come. "Yes, we can."

"And we should pray for all my cousins—Lola, Lena, Esther, Evangeline, and Ambrose."

"Yes, we should." It was endearing that Lanie considered the Eliason family her own.

"And of course Aunt Charlotte, Aunt Annie, Uncle Caleb, Grandpa Solomon, Grandma Lydie..." She ticked off the names on two hands. "Oh, and for Bunny."

Tobias wasn't familiar with Bunny. "Is that a friend from Willow Falls?"

Lanie giggled. "No, silly. Bunny is my dog."

"Your dog?" In their rush to meet the stage in Willow Falls to return to Prune Creek, had they forgotten Lanie's pet?

"Is it all right to pray that the Lord would bring a dog to me? One that I could play 'fetch and carry' with and we could have 'ventures?'"

Lanie wanted a dog? Tobias vowed to remember that once they were settled into their own home. "Did you have a dog in Willow Falls?"

Her smile quickly faded to a frown. "No. Pa was going to get me one, but..." Her voice trailed, and Tobias regretted asking.

"Yes, we can pray for that. We can bring anything to the Lord. He cares very much for us."

If He cares so much, then why did He allow your parents and Chester and Paulina to die? The niggling thought entered his mind, and with difficulty, Tobias pushed it aside. There were some things he would never understand.

Tobias saw from his peripheral that Lanie had folded her hands and bowed her head. He did the same and lifted all of her prayer requests to the Lord.

When they finished, he tucked her into bed and reminded her that Charlotte was in the room beside her and that he was downstairs. Then he stumbled down the stairs and to the parlor where he attempted to stretch out on the sofa. The small and uncomfortable blue piece of hard furniture was not conducive to a good night's sleep. It was too short to accommodate his long legs and too thin to properly accommodate his girth. He rolled over, tumbled off with a thud, and hoped he hadn't awakened anyone with his clumsiness. The straw pillow Aunt Myrtle had loaned him fell as well, and he tucked it beneath his head while stretching out on the floor.

Then he lifted his own prayers to the Lord that His Father in Heaven would give him wisdom and guidance in raising Lanie and that He would help Tobias find a home for both of them.

Charlotte awakened with a start. Confusion reigned as she attempted to decipher in her mind the origin of the whimpering. Was it coming from outside? Had it been just a dream? A figment of her imagination?

Finally, realization settled in.

Lanie.

Charlotte bolted from her bed, reached for her full-length wrap to properly cover her nightgown, and rushed to the room beside hers. Lanie thrashed in her bed, sobbing and calling out to her parents. Charlotte lit the lantern, then took a seat on the bed beside her and gently patted her arm. "Lanie?"

"Ma? Where are you? Where is Pa? Please, where are you?" Her anguished cries caused Charlotte's heart to constrict.

The flickering of the lantern cast an eerie glow in the otherwise dark room. "Lanie?" she said, again tapping lightly on Lanie's arm.

"Please, please don't die. You can't die. I'm your little girl, and I don't want you to die."

Lanie again cried out, her eyes remaining shut as the tears flowed down her cheeks.

Charlotte leaned forward, not wishing to startle Lanie, but knowing she needed to do whatever she could to extract the girl from her nightmare. "Sweetie?"

Lanie's eyes fluttered open, and for a moment, she gawked at Charlotte as if not comprehending where she was.

"Lanie, sweetie, you were having a bad dream."

"I want Ma and Pa." She sniffled, her narrow shoulders quaking.

Charlotte reached forward and pulled Lanie to her, and the girl crawled into her lap and rested her head against Charlotte's chest. She kissed the top of Lanie's head, and Lanie snuggled closer. "I want them back, Aunt Charlotte. I don't want them to be in Heaven. Did they forget they have a little girl to care for?"

Charlotte's eyes misted. It was times like these that she didn't understand the Lord's ways. She rocked Lanie back and forth, praying for a way to provide comfort.

Minutes passed, with the only noises being Lanie's muted sobs, the ticking of the clock, and somewhere down the hall, the rhythmic sound of one of the aunts snoring.

She reclined against the wall, resting her head against it while continuing to console Lanie. Finally, a hymn filled her mind, and she began to hum first before singing the lyrics.

When peace, like a river, attendeth my way,
When sorrows like sea billows roll;
Whatever my lot, Thou hast taught me to say,
It is well, it is well with my soul.
It is well with my soul,
It is well, it is well with my soul.

Tobias had been sleeping hard when the peaceful melody of singing interrupted his slumber. He opened his eyes and scrutinized the ceiling, attempting to remember where he was and why he was sleeping on the floor.

The singing continued, the words of his favorite hymn, the soothing and ethereal strains floating on the air from upstairs. He sat up and bemoaned the stiffness in every part of his body. Rising, he placed his hands on his lower back, stretched, then proceeded to climb the stairs, the draw of the voice of a songbird reeling him in.

Not completely familiar with the aunts' house, especially in the dark, Tobias groped his way toward the harmonious melody, willing that it continue.

He could recognize Charlotte's voice anywhere, even in his clouded, sleepy, and nearly incoherent mind. But Tobias was completely unprepared for the sight before him once he reached the source of the singing.

The moonlight and the lantern's dancing flame cast a soft glow on Charlotte as she sat on the bed, rocking Lanie in her arms. Her voice was intermittently interrupted by Lanie's sniffles, and he pondered entering the room and assisting in comforting his niece.

Charlotte stopped singing for a moment and bent to kiss the top of Lanie's head. Tobias immediately missed her voice. The void was filled with one of the aunt's periodic snores.

He was about to step inside the room when Charlotte continued with the next verse. Tobias remained tucked into the shadows unseen, his own heart breaking once again for Lanie's loss. But another emotion coincided with the pain.

Thoughts of Charlotte.

The sight was reminiscent of a mother comforting a child, rather than an adopted aunt comforting an orphan girl she already likely loved. Charlotte and her entire family had opened their hearts to Lanie. For that he was extremely grateful, especially since he and Lanie had no other family of their own.

Tobias quietly exhaled. He ought to return to the parlor rather than spy, but his feet remained fixed in place and his eyes focused on Charlotte. Two thoughts occurred to him—that he was ill-equipped to raise Lanie alone and that what he felt for Charlotte Eliason had begun to go far beyond friendship.

Tobias struggled to fall back asleep after he returned to the parlor. It wouldn't be long until sunrise and the start of a new day. He again stretched out on the floor and clasped his hands behind his head. Tobias knew he himself would struggle far into the future with the loss of those he loved, but he couldn't imagine the grief Lanie suffered.

He wouldn't soon forget Charlotte singing to his niece and comforting her in the middle of the night. Charlotte had always irritated him, especially with her know-it-all personality in school. True, she was intelligent and knew the answers to the questions the teacher asked and always finished her schoolwork first. When he spent time at the Eliason home, she was particularly annoying. But even through it all, Tobias admired her. Admired her intellect. Admired her beauty. And admired her tenacity and determination. She was well thought of by nearly everyone who knew her and had a compassionate and vivacious personality. No wonder that maggot, Cyrus Keller, had asked for her hand in courtship.

But Cyrus had no more deserved her than a horse deserved to live in a mansion. Tobias's shoulders tensed. He wouldn't mind pummeling Cyrus for breaking her heart. For being unfaithful with Violet. For having Charlotte believe he loved her.

Tobias rolled to one side in an effort to get comfortable. He was glad Charlotte hadn't married Cyrus, and he knew her family was as well. How John Mark didn't find a way to stop the courtship was beyond Tobias. But then, Charlotte was an independent woman and likely wouldn't have listened to her brother.

And if Charlotte *had* married Cyrus...

If she had married Cyrus, Tobias might not have had a chance to win her heart.

Tobias blew out a deep breath. It was obvious he was in need of some serious shut-eye for his mind to conjure up such ridiculous thoughts.

Charlotte checked on Lanie in her bedroom before assisting the aunts with breakfast. The petite girl sat perched on the edge of her bed, a faraway look in her eyes. "Lanie?"

"Hi, Aunt Charlotte."

Charlotte lowered herself onto the bed, and Lanie snuggled against her. "At first, I didn't know what house this was," said Lanie, her puffy eyes sorrowful and dried tear tracks lining her cheeks.

"Remember when you stayed with Aunt Annie and Uncle Caleb for a couple of weeks?"

"Yes."

"It was an adventure."

Lanie nodded. "Yes, it was. Aunt Annie let us all sleep in the same bed, except for Baby Evangeline. She's too wiggly."

"That sounds delightful."

"It was. Except did you know that Esther snores?"

Charlotte laughed. "I did not know that."

"Do you know how long I will stay here?"

"Until Uncle Tobias is able to find a different home. Right now he is staying at the boardinghouse." Charlotte twirled one of Lanie's messy braids.

Lanie pulled away. "No, Aunt Charlotte. No one can fix my hair but Ma." Tears glistened in her eyes. She scooted toward the edge of the bed. "Only Ma braids my hair."

"Oh, sweetie." Emotion welled up in Charlotte's chest. "That is fine. I was just thinking how long and beautiful your braids have gotten since the last time I saw you."

Lanie tossed her a wary glance before moving back towards Charlotte. "Do the aunts make pancakes for breakfast?" Her head was bent and her attention focused on picking at a fingernail.

"I think we could make some pancakes. Why don't you and I go downstairs and mix up some batter to surprise everyone."

A gradual smile crossed Lanie's face. "I can help you cook them too."

Chapter Twenty

TOBIAS FINISHED REPAIRING A plow, then took a break and stepped outside. He squinted at the bright sun after being inside for most of the morning. His stomach's rumbling reminded him he didn't need a clock to know it was time for the noonday meal.

He wondered how Lanie had fared after he'd left the aunts' house after breakfast. She had shuffled toward him and bid him farewell. He'd half expected her to beg him not to leave, but Charlotte whisked her to the side and promised they'd see the new flower blooms right after breakfast.

Her suggestion had worked, and Tobias was able to head to the shop without the guilt of leaving Lanie behind.

Now he looked forward to their arrival for the picnic. Tobias glanced down at his dirty apron and the dark smudges on the sleeves of his shirt. Smithing was a filthy job, and he needed to wash up a bit before they arrived.

Heading to the wash basin, he splashed the water over his face, taking care to be gentle over his wounds, wiped his face and neck, then rolled up the sleeves of his shirt. Ma's words from years ago crowded his mind: *"A man ought to always look his best when attending a function."* Tobias wasn't sure if she always said that for his benefit or Pa's or Chester's—or all three of them. Pa would dutifully wash up after time in the fields, plant a kiss on Ma's forehead, and declare he was as clean as he could be without a bath.

Tobias peered at the clock. Eleven fifty-five.

Perfect. He couldn't wait to show them the picturesque setting just on the other side of the church near the babbling waters of Prune Creek.

Tobias finished another task quicker than normal and stood in the front watching the passersby. Stanley waved at him from across the street. Judith was sweeping the boardwalk outside the mercantile. Quimby and Doc were chatting outside the new restaurant, and Sheriff Rettig strolled near the courthouse.

Prune Creek reminded him a lot of Willow Falls, only Prune Creek was twice the size and had more crime, although it was far safer than Poplar Springs and towns in other parts of the state. And while the folks in Prune Creek were friendly and welcoming, nothing could compare with Willow Falls and the camaraderie and closeness many folks in that town shared.

Seconds later, he spied Charlotte and Lanie walking toward him. Charlotte carried a basket and held Lanie's hand. He recalled her singing last night after Lanie's nightmare and the soothing and motherly way she'd tended to his niece. Not that he would expect anything else from Charlotte. Even during the times he found her to be irritating, he knew she possessed a sympathetic and compassionate heart.

"Uncle Tobias!" Lanie released Charlotte's hand and dashed toward him. He lifted her off the ground and swung her around.

"Are you ready for a picnic?"

"Yes!"

It was good to see his niece smiling again, and he set her down. "Hello, Charlotte."

"Hello."

Tobias cleared his throat and rubbed the back of his neck, and Charlotte twisted her mouth to one side. And he pondered why there were these awkward types of moments like this between them after all the years they'd known each other. He supposed for himself it was because things had changed, but he doubted that was the reason for her. As far as Tobias knew, Charlotte still found him to be aggravating, although he was attempting to be less so.

"The weather is nice," he said, squinting toward the cloudless sky. "Reckon I always appreciate a summer day."

"Indeed. If only summer in Wyoming was the state's lengthiest season."

"True. Before long, we'll be having snowstorms and blizzards and the like."

Tobias shifted his weight. He could still hear her velvety and melodious voice singing to Lanie. Sure, he'd heard it many times in church, and even when they were young'uns, Charlotte had a gift for singing. He grinned to himself when he recalled one time while practicing for the Christmas program at school how he'd laughed every time she would start singing her solo. He'd gotten in a fair amount of trouble in those days and spent an inordinate amount of time in the corner and writing, 'I will behave during school' one hundred times on the chalkboard for his repeat offenses. And then there was Pa's punishment when he arrived home.

But the worst was the punishment for laughing when she sang and being ordered to write Charlotte a note apologizing for his brash behavior. Then he had to read it in front of class. Without smirking. And with a sincere heart. Neither had been an easy task. Tobias chuckled out loud.

Charlotte raised her eyebrows. "Are you all right, Tobias?"

"Yes, I was just remembering the time at school with the Christmas carols and you singing and me..."

"Laughing? Snickering? Guffawing?" She glowered at him.

Tobias scratched his head. "All three."

"You were such an irksome sort, Tobias Hallman. It took me weeks to return to my love of singing after that."

Her words caused guilt and shame to humble him. At the time as an immature boy, he hadn't realized how detrimental his witless actions were. His choice to be rude during her singing could have caused her to never sing again. Tobias sobered at the thought. Charlotte then might not have sung to Lanie last night to console her. His thoughtless actions could have caused her not to worship the Lord with such passion, and that would have been the worst outcome of all.

Charlotte was still glowering at him, her eyes narrowed and her free hand on her hip.

Tobias cleared his throat and nodded at a passerby. "Here, let me take the basket," he said.

She handed it to him, and he set it on the ground. "Charlotte," he said.

"Yes?"

"I'm sorry for mocking your singing. It would have been a shame had you never...had you never sang again."

Lanie peered up at him, then averted her attention to Charlotte.

And Tobias hoped Charlotte could hear the sincerity in his voice.

"Well, thank you," she finally said.

"I made some stupid choices back then." He stared at the basket, its contents no doubt filled with a tasty lunch. They needed to proceed to the picnic spot before the day slipped away. But he needed to rectify the situation first. "I shouldn't have laughed. It wasn't funny then and it isn't funny now. I'm sorry, Charlotte. I really am. I'm glad you still sing. Mighty glad." He caught her eye. She blinked rapidly and twisted her mouth again to one side, and Tobias was reminded of how her face always revealed her thoughts.

Just another thing he knew about her.

"I forgive you," she finally said.

"Thank you. I think you have a velvety and melodious voice, and I'm glad my ears get to hear it." Tobias cringed at the words that flowed from his mouth before he could ponder them. "I mean, I'm just glad is all."

Miss Ledbetter, or rather Annie, would have reminded him to use more variety in his word usage if she'd heard him use the word "glad" with such repetition.

"Velvety and melodious?"

"Uh, yeah, something like that."

He was such a knucklehead.

The corners of her mouth turned upward, and she had a glint in her sparkling blue eyes.

Tobias fidgeted and wiped his palms on his trousers. Why the embarrassment all of a sudden? "I remember," he said, attempting to change the topic. "When I would come home from school in trouble yet again. Pa would have my punishments ready, and one time, Ma—I think she was tired of having to hear about my constant shenanigans—told me with all seriousness..." Tobias changed his tone to reflect his mother's. "She said, 'Tobias, I hope one day you'll have five sons just like you.' At the time, I didn't really see what could be wrong with that. My sons and I would go fishing and hunting all the time. But after I thought about it that evening, I realized it wasn't a compliment."

Charlotte laughed. "No, that wouldn't be a compliment. Quite the opposite in fact."

"I now realize that if the Good Lord ever does bless me with sons, I hope they're like their ma."

"That would be welcome for all who know you, I'm sure."

His attention remained focused on her. Bantering with Charlotte was one of his favorite pastimes.

"Uncle Tobias, can we please eat?" Lanie asked, desperation lining her features.

He knelt to her height. "I'm sorry, Lanie. Here we are talking when we should be enjoying that delicious noonday meal you and Aunt Charlotte packed. Shall we go for a walk and find a place near the creek?" Tobias lifted the basket and they began their walk down the boardwalk and toward the tree-lined area between the church and the creek.

"You know what, Uncle Tobias? Me and Aunt Charlotte went to see the pretty flowers in the garden." Lanie's eyes lit up as she described the different colors. "And after me and Aunt Charlotte do the wash, me and Aunt Myrtle are going to make dessert for supper tonight. Are you going to come to supper?"

Tobias smirked at Charlotte who had placed a hand over her mouth. He could see from the way her eyes crinkled at the corners that she was attempting to suppress a giggle.

It could be a dangerous thing to have another person with Aunt Myrtle's lack of baking skills. "Aunt Myrtle is going to teach you?"

Lanie nodded, her messy blonde braids bobbing as she did so. "Yes, and we are going to make a pie that Aunt Myrtle says wins awards. Can you come for supper tonight, Uncle Tobias? Please?"

"Or you could invite yourself," suggested Charlotte, a smile touching her lips.

"Reckon I might just do that. Yes, Lanie, I will be there for supper tonight."

Lanie clapped her hands. "And will you have some of the dessert me and Aunt Myrtle make?"

"Well..."

"As a gracious and mannerly uncle, I'm sure Uncle Tobias would love to have some of the dessert you and Aunt Myrtle make."

Lanie clasped Tobias's free hand. "Aunt Fern says if I try my most hardest, I can be a baker just like Aunt Myrtle."

"Why do I think Aunt Fern was joshing about that?" Tobias asked.

Lanie tilted her head to one side, her expression reminding Tobias of one his own ma used to make when questioning him and Chester about one of their schemes. Lanie was such a perfect blend of both a Hallman with her golden-brown eyes and round face—and Paulina with her blonde hair and fair skin. He was taken back to the day she was born and the tears he saw in Chester's eyes. Tears he'd only seen Chester shed twice—when Lanie was born and tears of grief when their parents died. *"What did I ever do to deserve such blessings?"* Chester asked the day of Lanie's birth. And Tobias had experienced a nip of envy, although now he regretted ever even allowing such an emotion to be directed toward his brother.

"Uncle Tobias?" Lanie asked, tapping him on the arm.

"I'm sorry, Lanie. I was just thinking about things."

"About supper?"

Supper maybe, but Aunt Myrtle's cooking, no.

The day was perfect for a picnic. Tobias and Lanie chatted nearly nonstop, and Charlotte was grateful Lanie was doing far better this morning than she had been last night. She'd finally fallen asleep while Charlotte was singing, and Charlotte had moseyed back to bed. She had want of rest, but the overwhelming insomnia had prevented a relaxing night. Over and over, she thought about Lanie and the tragedy of losing her parents. She thought of Tobias and how he'd become far more tolerable since their journey to Willow Falls. How he'd assisted her with her fear of the trestles and later saved her life. On the return trip to Prune Creek, he'd bested an outlaw. The thought of him succumbing to the plans the outlaw had for him caused her to shudder. Were it not for God's Providence, it could have been Tobias thrown off the train or *under* the train.

The thought of how close she'd come to losing him terrified her.

So much had occurred in such a short amount of time.

Finally, just as the sun peeked in through the curtains, Charlotte had fallen asleep. When she woke, the morning went quickly with breakfast preparation. Tobias was then on his way out the door to the shop, and the morning progressed swiftly with assisting the aunts with chores and tending to Lanie.

Not that Charlotte minded. She longed to someday be a mother, even though those hopes had been dashed by Cyrus.

Speaking of the Lord's Providence...

Each day her heart ached less from Cyrus's betrayal and more and more gratitude filled the empty spaces.

She watched Tobias and Lanie from her peripheral. He was patient with his niece, kind, caring, and jovial. Lanie was fortunate to have him.

And what of his memory about her singing? Charlotte recalled those days during the practicing of Christmas carols. Tobias had always been irksome, especially in school. When he'd told her just minutes ago that her voice was "velvety and melodious", she'd not known what to think.

His opinion mattered to her.

"Here we are." Tobias led them to a place beneath the trees just in view of the church, and Charlotte spread the blanket on the ground and set the basket atop it.

"This is a beautiful setting. I don't even think I realized such a blissful place was hidden back here." Charlotte beheld the idyllic scene with plush green meadows, trees, and the sound of the creek nearby.

"I stumbled upon it one day by accident. Usually we spend time on the other side of the church or in the front. This is a hidden gem for sure."

They prayed for their meal, and Charlotte passed out the sandwiches. "Before you ask, I prepared them."

"I live yet another day," jested Tobias.

Lanie ate her sandwich swiftly, her eyes darting around the meadow that surrounded them. "Aunt Charlotte?" she asked, barely giving herself time to swallow before speaking, "Can I go pick some dandelions?"

"You may, but you need to finish your noonday meal first. Remember, we have cookies for dessert."

"But there are just so many dandelions. Can we make jelly? Ma loves to…" Lanie paused and her lip quivered. "Ma loves to make dandelion jelly."

Charlotte held her arms open, and Lanie fell into them. "I want to make dandelion jelly with Ma," she sobbed.

Tobias patted her on her arm. "I remember your ma made the best dandelion jelly."

Lanie nodded. "She did."

"Lanie?" Charlotte asked as the child buried her face against Charlotte, "Do you remember the ingredients in the recipe your ma used?"

"What's 'gredients?" she asked, her voice muffled.

"Ingredients are the items used to make the jelly. For instance, the dandelions themselves and likely some sugar."

Lanie squirmed. "Yes, there was sugar. Lots of it. I think I 'member the 'gredients, but I was just little when we made it last time."

Charlotte glanced at Tobias, prayed for the proper words to say, then spoke again. "If you remember the recipe, would you please help me make some of your ma's famous jelly? I know Uncle Tobias would appreciate it on some toast, and the aunts love jelly."

"They do?"

"Yes, and we could even enter some in the fair later this summer. What do you think?"

Lanie sat back and brushed her hair from her eyes. "I think I'd like that."

"Do you remember how many dandelions we would need?"

"Lots upon lots. Ma had me pick bunches of them and put them in a pail."

Tobias grinned. "From the looks of it, there are an awful lot of dandelions just around here and over there by the church as well."

"Can I go pick some?"

"You sure can," said Tobias, "but stay on this side of the creek, all right?"

Lanie jumped to her feet. "Do we have a pail?"

Charlotte peered into the basket. "We could use the tin we packed the cookies in for our picnic once it's emptied."

"That won't be a problem," Tobias said, reaching for a gingerbread cookie. "I could eat about ten of these things. Wait. Who made them?"

Charlotte laughed. "Lanie and I made them this morning."

Moments later, Lanie bounded toward the meadow, tin in hand. As though a butterfly, she flitted from dandelion to dandelion, picking them and placing them in the tin.

"I wish I had something larger for her. She'll have the tin filled in no time."

Tobias reclined onto his side, resting his head in his palm. "It'll keep her busy for a while."

He stared up at Charlotte, as if wanting to say more. His lip was still swollen and the bruise still visible, although slightly less prominent. He was clean-shaven, and his ruffled thick, dark hair added to his rugged appearance.

When they were young, she'd always found Tobias to be a handsome fellow, but she'd never told a soul. A handsome nuisance is what she secretly referred to him as. Pa was forever saying how a person's character was far more important than outer appearances, and Charlotte imagined that if Tobias had a pleasing personality rather than being a pestilence, she might have considered him a fine catch.

That pesky little voice that sometimes interrupted her thoughts did so again. *But what are your thoughts about his personality now?*

Tobias took in the sight of her with her hair she'd again braided and fashioned into some sort of coiffure. He recalled when that word had been one of their vocabulary words. Why he had to know about women's hairstyles was far beyond him. But Annie had often reiterated the importance of knowing how to spell peculiar words.

He gazed for a moment at her full lips, her creamy-white skin, and her blue eyes. Her beauty, as it often did, took his breath away. If she'd not been such a tattletale, always getting him into trouble during their school years—if she hadn't been such a know-it-all bookworm who had to answer every question the teacher asked, he might have considered her as someone worth courting as they grew older. Yet, even though he hadn't admitted it back then, Tobias admired her intelligence.

But even if he did find her to be someone he might consider courting now, Tobias knew that after what Cyrus had done, it would be a while before Charlotte would entertain the idea of again courting someone.

When she did entertain the idea again, Tobias wanted to be worthy of her.

"Are you staring at me, Tobias Hallman?"

Her voice jolted him to the realization he *had* been staring at her, and for longer than necessary. "I—uh—well, yes, I was."

"I thought so."

He shook his head at her smugness. "I was thinking that you don't have your tall mounded hair that resembles Miss Barry's today."

Charlotte leaned over and pinched him on the arm. It was so sudden that Tobias hadn't been able to anticipate it. "Ouch!"

"It is *not* like Miss Barry's at all, and it's not a tall mound."

"Not today, it's not."

"Not ever."

"Today it's pretty."

She blushed, the red climbing her cheeks, and Charlotte turned her gaze away from him and toward Lanie who continued picking dandelions not far away.

"Do you realize the last time you pinched me was the time your doll went for a swim in the pond?"

Charlotte faced him again. "I'm sorry. I shouldn't have pinched you. I'm hardly a young and immature school girl who pinches people anymore, even if they do deserve it for nearly drowning my doll!" She paused. "And today for insinuating I had hair like Miss Barry's."

They both laughed then, their voices blending together.

"Seems like yesterday we were just young'uns in Willow Falls," said Tobias.

"It does. I remember being Lanie's age."

"Do you ever think about moving back to Willow Falls?"

Charlotte moistened her lips. "I do from time to time. I'm not sure yet if I'll stay in Prune Creek permanently or if I'll return home. I do miss my family, but if I can visit them often, I think I might like to stay here for the foreseeable future."

Something about her answer pleased him.

CHAPTER TWENTY-ONE

TOBIAS BID CHARLOTTE AND Lanie farewell and was about to enter the shop to return to work when Sheriff Rettig and another man whom Tobias didn't recognize approached him.

"Hello, Sheriff."

"Hello, Tobias. This is Deputy Ortiz, and he'd like to speak with you for a moment."

Tobias couldn't imagine what the deputy might need to speak with him about. "Hello, Deputy. How may I help you?"

"Mr. Hallman, I was one of the deputies who was involved in bringing the Kragel-Fraley gang to justice."

"Kragel-Fraley gang? Is that..."

"Yes. Mr. Fraley was the man you had an altercation with on the train from Nelsonville to Prune Creek. We've had him and his gang on wanted posters throughout Wyoming, Montana, Idaho, and South Dakota. It's my understanding that you helped a bad situation from getting worse aboard the train."

"Yes, sir, but I was only doing what any law-abiding, able-bodied man would do."

The deputy stroked his jaw. "Humility. That's an admirable trait. Unfortunately, as you know, there were no other able-bodied men in the passenger car you were in. The passengers overall were few as is often the case for the route between Nelsonville and Prune Creek. As you are also aware, the two elderly men onboard were injured at the hands of Fraley."

"Have they recovered fully from their injuries?"

Deputy Ortiz nodded. "They are in the process of doing so. The Kragel-Fraley Gang had been planning this robbery for some time, and it worked in their favor because of the lack of capable men aboard. As such, things could have been much worse. Their plans were for Fraley to rob the passengers on the train while the Kragel Brothers intended to completely derail the train and steal the mail, any money in the safe, and any other items of value. It was a well-orchestrated strategy." He paused. "We've been on the lookout for these men for two years and had joined with the lawmen in Willow Falls, Nelsonville, Poplar Springs, Bowman, and Prune Creek in an effort to apprehend them."

"My friend is a deputy in Poplar Springs—John Mark Eliason—and I'm from Willow Falls and am friends with Sheriff Townsend there as well."

"Both good men. Speaking of lawmen, the railroad is fixing to hire a few agents for this stretch. Never thought it was needed before this and one other incident. Trains have been robbed much more frequently in the middle and southern parts of the state than here, but alas, the Driessen-Evers Railway Company figures it's time for this route to have an agent as well."

"Has the gang been apprehended?"

"The Kragel brothers were initially taken alive at the crossing where they planned to derail the train, and one decided to engage in a shootout." The deputy briefly stared into the distance. "Unfortunately for him, it didn't end well."

Tobias was grateful the gang's plan had been foiled before it could put Charlotte, Lanie, and the rest of the passengers in danger. "And Fraley?"

"Amazingly, Fraley survived when you threw him from the train." Ortiz smirked. "Yes, we heard about the fight that occurred on the platform. Well done. Anyhow, because you hindered his movements—he suffered a broken leg and dislocated ribs among other things—and because of you notifying the law at the depot between Nelsonville and Prune Creek, we apprehended him. He and the surviving Kragel brother will be tried in a court of law. My guess is they'll be found guilty and either sent to prison or most likely hanged. This train heist was not their first, and they have committed numerous other crimes, including murder, as well."

Tobias blew out the breath he'd been holding. "That's good news. Those men also attempted to harm a female friend of mine outside of Nelsonville. I wish I'd known they were a wanted gang." How many times had Tobias rehashed in his mind what could have happened if he hadn't attempted to look for Charlotte?

"That doesn't surprise me one bit. These men are ruthless, and your friend would not have been the first woman they attempted to harm—or succeeded in harming. Did you know there was a reward for the capture of the gang?"

"I didn't realize that, but with their apparent notoriety, it doesn't surprise me."

"Many folks had a hand in those captures, and the reward money was divided among them. Here's your share." Ortiz handed Tobias two five-dollar bills. "Thank you for your assistance."

"I—thanks. But maybe I should share this with my friend, Charlotte. She assisted in thwarting Fraley's plans." He again thought of Charlotte's bravery and how her courage saved his life.

Ortiz shrugged. "Divide it as you wish. Tell her thank you as well." The deputy turned to Sheriff Rettig. "I best be on my way if I plan to make it halfway home before nightfall." He touched the brim of his hat. "Thank you again, Mr. Hallman, for giving me the chance to perform a more pleasant job duty."

Sheriff Rettig patted him on the back. "Good job, young man. I knew we were gaining a respectable resident when you moved to Prune Creek."

Tobias watched the two men leave. He stood, stunned about the reward money. If he hurried, he could catch Charlotte and offer her half of the reward money or maybe he'd wait until this evening when he went to the aunts' house for supper.

Charlotte transferred the dandelions to a large pail, gave Lanie a bath, and assisted the aunts with the meal before retreating upstairs. She re-braided her hair, wound it again in a coiffure, pressed the wrinkles from her skirt, and returned downstairs just in time for Tobias to arrive.

"Can we talk for a minute on the porch?" he asked.

Charlotte sat on one of the weathered rocking chairs while he took the other.

"I was paid a visit today from Deputy Ortiz who helped apprehend the Kragel-Fraley Gang." Tobias proceeded to update her on who the gang was, their capture, and the condition of the passengers who'd been injured.

"I'm so thankful the passengers will make a full recovery."

"Yes."

"And that the gang was caught." Charlotte shivered, remembering the frightening incident when she'd first encountered the gang. "I wonder if their wanted posters were among the ones hanging outside the sheriff's office in Willow Falls."

"Could be. Ortiz mentioned a reward, then proceeded to give me my share. I thought I should split it with you seeing as how you saved my life that day when you distracted Fraley." Tobias handed her a five-dollar bill.

Her jaw dropped in surprise. While she figured there was a reward, Charlotte hadn't imagined she had been instrumental enough in the outlaws' capture to secure a portion of it. "Thank you, but please keep my share."

"But I wouldn't have succeeded in removing Fraley from the train without your help."

"Keep my portion to assist you in securing a home for Lanie."

It was Tobias's jaw that now went slack. "Are you sure?"

"Absolutely. I know you're anxious to find a home, what with the boardinghouse not allowing children."

He offered her a grin that made her stomach flutter. "I appreciate that, Charlotte." He stared toward the mountains in the distance. "I've always wanted to find some land and build a house. I aim to talk to Mr. Wubbenhorst at the bank tomorrow to see if anything is available. But with me having a mortgage on the shop, I'm not sure he will oblige in giving me a second loan."

Charlotte hadn't known of Tobias's plans, but it made sense since he couldn't stay at the boardinghouse and Lanie couldn't live with the aunts forever. "If nothing else, you could find a larger place to rent in the interim."

"Yes, and the reward money will help with that. Thank you, Charlotte." He paused. "Neither my parents nor Chester and Paulina ever owned their homes but instead always either rented or were allowed to board there as part of working on the ranches. I've always wanted to own my own place. You know, somewhere to raise a family and pass to the children when I'm gone. Not that I—I mean it's only Lanie and me, and we don't need to own our house, but it's always been a dream of mine." Red crept up Tobias's handsome face, and he cleared his throat.

Charlotte could understand having dreams. She had a few of her own. "There's nothing wrong with having aspirations and plans for the future."

"Do you ever dream about the future?"

Charlotte's eyes widened. She hadn't expected him to ask her that question.

"Forget I asked you. It's not my business."

"I don't mind you being privy to some of my dreams and ambitions." Cyrus's face flashed through her mind. She'd heard far more often than she would have liked about how lovely Cyrus and Violet's wedding was and how thrilled folks were that they'd found each other and fallen in love.

Fallen in love while Cyrus was courting Charlotte.

Now Charlotte agreed with the townsfolk that Cyrus and Violet did make a grand couple and were perfect for each other, but at times the pain of betrayal still lurked in Charlotte's heart. She released a deep breath. "Some dreams *don't* come true. The future doesn't always occur the way we hope.

"Like you marrying Cyrus?"

Tobias's voice was calm. Gentle. And from his wrinkled brow and the warmth in his tender gaze, she knew he wasn't asking to be nosy, but rather because he cared. "Before Cyrus decided he wanted to marry Violet."

"Charlotte..."

"My family, especially John Mark, knew Cyrus wasn't the one for me. They waited patiently while I learned that. They were right when they said I wouldn't heed their warnings. I was blinded. Blinded by what I thought was love. And prideful in thinking I knew best." She sighed. "I envisioned Cyrus and I married and raising our children in a home on his parents' sizable ranch. I would join the Willow Falls Ladies Society and send donations to missionaries and assist with fundraisers in the church to benefit those struggling in our town."

"You can still join the Willow Falls Ladies Society when you return."

"True. And if I permanently return to Willow Falls, I do aim to do that. If not, I'll join the society here. My parents have always instilled in me the importance of supporting those who seek to bring the Gospel to the lost and to help those less fortunate. And I have and will continue to do that. I just...I just had it all planned out how my life would go. The husband, the children, caring for a home...but then I remembered that God is the One who plans our steps and who plans our futures. He always knows what's best, even if we don't see it at the time." She paused, wondering why she had shared so much. "I'm sorry, Tobias. Girlish notions, I'm sure."

Tobias's gaze held hers. Did he think her daft for sharing her heart? If only she could take back her words. She felt her face flush, a warm heat that started at her toes and rose to her face.

"There's nothing wrong with those dreams except being married to Cyrus. Reckon that sounds more like a nightmare."

Charlotte giggled, grateful for the relief from her embarrassment. "That *is* reminiscent of a bad dream. I have no idea why I thought he was a fine catch given what I knew about him, and I'm thankful for the Lord's Providence in that I didn't marry him after all."

"I'm glad God knows what's better for us more than we do. And, Charlotte?"

"Yes?"

"I'm sorry about Cyrus and Violet. For what it's worth, I think they do make a perfect pair. You know how John Mark, Russell, and I never cared much for Cyrus and his bullyish ways in school, and I'm confident only someone like Cyrus could cotton to Violet."

"You don't think I'm daft for believing I was in love with someone like Cyrus?"

"No. We all have those moments when we're not thinking correctly. The important part is that you realized your error before it was too late."

The sincerity in his voice warmed her heart. "You're a good listener, Tobias. Thank you."

"Anytime."

"Tell me about your dreams. Besides owning the blacksmith shop and building a house on some land and having a family."

Tobias crossed an ankle over his knee. "I would like to be the kind of pa my own father was. To love the Lord with all my heart, and to love and care for a family. To work hard to support them." He shrugged. "I hope to raise Lanie in a way that would make Chester and Paulina proud. To give her a happy life to make up for the loss she faced."

"Lanie is blessed to have you. I know you'll do a commendable job raising her and helping her overcome her grief."

"I hope so."

"I have confidence in you."

Something flickered in Tobias's eyes. "Thank you, Charlotte. Thank you for having confidence in me."

"You're welcome." And she meant every word.

CHAPTER TWENTY-TWO

TOBIAS PLANNED TO PORTION out the reward money. After calculating his tithe to the church and deducting it, he put two dollars and thirty cents in his savings account at the bank to go toward the rent of a new home. Then he strolled to the mercantile to pay his bill in full and purchase some items, including some fabric for a new dress, enough for both Lanie and Charlotte.

As one who had only a brother, he was inept at knowing what type of fabric to purchase. Perhaps Judith could be of assistance. He perused the tastefully arranged options, noting the sign indicating it was five cents per yard.

"I'll be happy to help," said Judith, who bustled over to the bolts of fabric and smoothed a wrinkled hand across the top of a folded blue piece of material. "Might I ask who this is for?"

Tobias cleared his throat. "Uh, it's for Lanie and Charlotte."

Something about Judith's quirked eyebrow gave Tobias concern as to whether he should return when Judith attended a sewing meeting and her husband, Hugh, was in charge.

"Lanie and Charlotte?" Judith tapped a finger to her chin. "Hmm. Well, this peach calico is lovely. It's muted and sub-

dued, but bright all at the same time. It would complement Charlotte's complexion."

The peach color *would* complement Charlotte's complexion. He thought of her pretty face with her sparkly
eyes fringed with long lashes and the way her lips curved
when she smiled. Lips he'd like to kiss if given the chance.
Heat scalded the back of his neck and rose up his face.
"I—well—I hadn't noticed Charlotte's complexion seeing
as how I don't know much about complexions and such."

Judith's mischievous grin indicated he failed to be
persuasive. "Be that as it may," she said, "I do believe this
calico would be the best choice."

"All right."

"Might I inquire as to why you're purchasing fabric for
Charlotte? Your niece I understand, but Charlotte..."

"Lanie adores Charlotte, and this way, their dresses
can match."

Judith carried the bolt of fabric to the counter and
faced him. "That's quite kind of you."

Tobias stuck his fingers between his collar and his
neck. While Judith's words might seem innocent enough,
he had a suspicion Judith figured there was more to the
story than what Tobias shared. And there was, although
he truly couldn't wait to see Lanie's face when he delivered the material for matching dresses.

He opted to change the topic. "Yes, well, I'll also be
needing some canned goods, sugar, flour, and baking
powder." Wouldn't the aunts be thrilled when he delivered a basketful of provisions to them? They'd dutifully
not only fed Lanie but also provided food for him many a
time for supper.

His total left him with three cents, and he reached into the glass container and withdrew licorice candy as a special treat for Lanie, Charlotte, and himself.

Lanie tugged on Charlotte's dress. "Aunt Charlotte, Aunt Charlotte!"

"What is it, Lanie?"

"Uncle Tobias is coming down the road in the wagon." She tilted her head to one side. "Why do you think he's driving the wagon?"

Charlotte finished scrubbing a pair of stockings on the washboard and stood. "I'm not sure. Shall we go greet him?"

Lanie's vivacious nod of her head said more than words ever could, and she reached for Charlotte's hand. Together, they hastened toward the front of the house just as Tobias arrived.

He bounded from the wagon, a wrapped item in his hand. "Hello, Charlotte and Lanie."

"Uncle Tobias, why are you driving the wagon today?"

"Because I have a surprise for you." He handed them the flat wrapped package.

Together, Charlotte and Lanie tore gently at the brown paper, revealing vibrant peach calico fabric. "Tobias, it's lovely," Charlotte said, smoothing her hand across the top of the fabric.

"I figured you two could make matching dresses."

Lanie squealed. "A new dress? Matching? Aunt Charlotte, can we go make them right now?"

"We can't make the dresses today, but perhaps tomorrow after our chores, we could start on your dress." She looked up into Tobias's warm gaze. "Thank you. That was so thoughtful. How did you ever know this would be my favorite color?"

Tobias beamed. "I did have some help from Judith, so hopefully it's the correct yardage." He ambled toward the back of the wagon and pulled out a crate packed with food items. "I also purchased some necessities for the aunts."

Charlotte noticed how his shirt stretched across his muscular back when he carried the crate.

"They will appreciate that so much."

"Yoo hoo!" called Aunt Myrtle from the porch. "Are you coming to eat? I don't want supper and the huckleberry bread I made to get cold."

Lanie skipped toward the house with the fabric in her hands. "I love Aunt Myrtle's huckleberry bread almost as much as her huckleberry pie."

"There are other options, right?" Tobias asked.

Tobias pondered which bank to visit first. Wisdom dictated he stop at the one where he already held an established account for the mortgage on the shop. He strode down the boardwalk, greeting passersby and entered the Bank of Prune Creek. Three employees tended the bank, including the manager, Mr. Wubbenhorst, who invited him to his desk in the far corner.

"What can I do for you, Mr. Hallman?"

"I was wondering if there might be any properties for sale with a cabin and some acreage."

Mr. Wubbenhorst, a man in his fifties with a mustache that curled on each end, steepled his fingers. "Are you thinking of purchasing a place to live?"

"Yes, sir."

"Are you certain you can afford some land with the mortgage on your blacksmith shop?"

Tobias raked his fingers through his hair. "That's my hope, Mr. Wubbenhorst. I'd like to find a place that already has a home, even if it's small."

Mr. Wubbenhorst rubbed his jaw. "Land is currently at ten dollars an acre."

Tobias attempted not to wince. Although he had a steady number of jobs scheduled into the immediate future, purchasing land would remain a struggle.

"We only have one property available at present that includes a home. The Rives place is for sale, but such an extensive parcel would be far beyond your means."

Mr. Wubbenhorst's presumption was an accurate one. Tobias could no more afford the Rives place than run for president of the United States. But he'd not give up. If he aspired to be a landowner, he'd best concoct another plan. "And is there acreage available without a house?" Surely he could trade Mr. Stickney at the lumber mill for some materials to build a home.

"There is a homestead consisting of three hundred acres, but again..."

Could Mr. Wubbenhorst see Tobias's dejection? "You're sure there's nothing else?"

"The only other option is a house and lot at the eastern end of Fourth Street for four hundred and fifty dollars."

Tobias sat up straighter in his chair, attempting to recall what was at the eastern end of Fourth Street as he rarely frequented that part of town. "I could take out a loan for that."

"Unfortunately, I've already had someone make an offer. I'm not sure you'd want it anyhow, seeing as it's in poor condition and the lot is miniscule. Plus, it's across from a house of ill repute."

There was no way Tobias would raise Lanie in a home across from a brothel.

Mr. Wubbenhorst extended his hand. "Don't despair, Mr. Hallman. I'm sure something will become available. As with all things, such concerns are best left in the Lord's hands."

"Yes, sir, you are correct. Thank you for your time."

Tobias fought the discouragement that settled deep within him and prayed again for something to become available.

CHAPTER TWENTY-THREE

TWO DAYS LATER, TOBIAS couldn't wait to see Charlotte's face when she saw her surprise.

He parked the wagon he'd rented from the livery. She would be so happy to see her brother and nephew.

"Haven't been here in a while," said John Mark.

"Is this where my other aunts live?" Ambrose asked, his face obscured by his oversized cowboy hat.

John Mark chuckled. "Yes. These are your great-aunts."

"How many aunts do I gots anyways?" Ambrose took a flying leap off the wagon. "And is that my cousin, Lanie, over there?"

Tobias appreciated that the Eliason family had taken Lanie into their home and into their family after Chester and Paulina died. Although, from what Charlotte said, Lanie had long called her 'Aunt Charlotte'. "You're right, that is Lanie."

John Mark kneeled to Ambrose's height. "Now remember, Son, you need to be a gentleman."

"I know, Pa. I will. I pwomise."

"We're going to wait here for a few minutes because Aunt Charlotte doesn't know we're here, and it's a surprise."

"A surprise? Don't worry yourself none, Pa, I won't tell a soul."

Tobias observed the interaction between John Mark and Ambrose. "Not sure if you know this or not, John Mark, but you're sounding an awful lot like your own pa."

"I've heard that a time or two." John Mark shrugged. "What better man to emulate?"

"That's true. I've always respected and admired your pa, even when he was meting out punishments."

John Mark slugged him in the shoulder. "In hindsight, we deserved those punishments."

"I wouldn't have said so then, but now I tend to agree."

They both laughed, and John Mark lifted his bag from the back of the wagon. "I'm surprised the aunts were able to keep Charlotte in the house."

"And away from the window. I can't wait to see her face."

A few moments later, Aunt Fern brought Charlotte, her eyes covered with a bandana, to the back of the house where Lanie, Aunt Myrtle, Quimby, and Stanley waited. "All right, now, you can open your eyes and remove the bandana," Aunt Fern directed.

Charlotte did as she was told, and Tobias would remember the expression on her face for as long as he lived. Her eyes twinkled, and a joyful smile crossed her face. She ran toward John Mark and Ambrose and captured them in a hug. "I have missed you both so much!"

A muffled voice sounded in all of the excitement. "Aunt Charlotte?"

"Yes, Ambrose?" Charlotte took a step back.

"Thank you, ma'am. You was smotherin' me there for a minute."

"I'm just so, so happy to see both of you. What a splendid surprise!" She turned toward Tobias. "Thank you for this delightfully unexpected event."

Her face shone and Tobias's breath hitched. He thought she might run toward him and offer him a hug as well. Charlotte's beauty had never been wasted on him, but the joy that radiated from her made her all the prettier. "I'm glad you're pleased."

"Oh, I am! But where's Hannah?"

"Ma is staying with her until the baby comes, which should be in about a month. Not sure Pa will be able to survive without Ma, but I sure am grateful she's there to help. It's been a blessing, especially for Hannah, not ever having her own ma, and she and Ma have grown close."

Charlotte nodded. "Ma is the perfect one to care for her."

"She is. Ambrose and I will return in a few days, so it eases my mind to have someone there with her while we're here."

Aunt Myrtle introduced John Mark and Ambrose to Quimby and Stanley. "Would you care for some lemonade after that long journey?" she asked.

"You're a great aunt and all for askin', but me, I'd rather go play with my cousin, Lanie." Ambrose tilted his hat back on his head. "Got me one question, though. Why is it that all my cousins are girls?"

Aunt Myrtle laughed. "Perhaps you'll have a little brother."

"That's what I been praying for. Long and hard in my time with the Good Lord, I been praying up a storm that He gives me a little brother. The way I figure it, it'll be about a month or so and then we can start playing sheriff."

"But goodness," said Aunt Fern. "Are you sure you want to wait that long?"

"No, but Pa says I gotta learn patience. Ma and I been talking about names for the baby too."

"What will you name him?" Lanie asked.

"Deputy. I think it's a right fine name, and then when we play, he'll be Deputy Deputy."

Lanie giggled. "You're silly, Ambrose. Deputy isn't a name."

Aunt Fern and Aunt Myrtle brought glasses of lemonade and set them on the table.

Charlotte took a sip. "Thank you again, Tobias. This is a wonderful surprise."

Was it wrong to want to kiss her on that beautiful smile? To declare his love for her? To ask her to court him right then and there in front of her family?"

Tobias chastised himself. Besides other reasons, the fact that she might not feel the same for him forced him back to reality. "You're welcome."

"Say, you wanna play sheriff and you can be the bad guy?" Ambrose asked Lanie.

"Not really. Can we play something else?"

"No..." Ambrose glanced up and caught John Mark's eye. "Uh, sure, yes, we can play something else."

"Wanna play hide and seek?"

"Sure. I can be the sheriff, and you can be the bad guy, and I can try to find you."

"Ambrose..."

Ambrose peeked up at his pa. "All right, sure. We can play hide and seek, and you don't gotta be the bad guy."

"Come on!" Lanie beckoned him, and together they raced toward the far edge of the property.

"Mind if I kidnap your brother and take him fishing?" Tobias asked Charlotte. "I promise I'll have him back before supper."

Tobias and John Mark sat on the banks of Prune Creek. "I was sorry to hear about Chester and Paulina," said John Mark.

"Thank you. It's been difficult."

"I imagine so. How is Lanie handling it?"

Tobias stared out across the sparkling waters. "She's having some nightmares, and she won't allow anyone to fix her hair since Paulina was the last one to braid it for her. Reckon she'll be all right, but it's going to take time."

"I imagine it will."

"How are things in Poplar Springs?" Tobias asked.

"Going well. Since Roessler and his cronies were arrested, things have eased a bit, but it's still one of the more lawless towns in Wyoming. The sheriff has hired a few more deputies, and Silas and Nowell help from time to time."

"And Hannah, Ambrose, and the baby? I still can't believe my best friend is married with a child and another one soon to be born."

John Mark shook his head. "I still can't believe it. I worry sometimes about not coming home and leaving Hannah a widow. As Pa would say, give those worries to the Lord, and I do try to do that. I'm relieved to know that if something were to happen, Hannah, Ambrose, and the baby would have somewhere to go where they'd be cared for."

Tobias thought about John Mark's words. Charlotte's and Lanie's faces flashed through his mind. While he'd always figured he'd get married and have a family, he hadn't thought about all of the specifics, such as where his wife and children would go if something were to happen to him. "I'm sorry I didn't make it to your wedding."

"We had a small wedding in Poplar Springs, and then Ma decided we needed a potluck to introduce the townsfolk to Hannah. Speaking of families, is there something I should know about you and Charlotte?"

"Why do you ask?"

"I see the way you look at her. I know you two have never been particularly fond of each other, but it seems something has changed."

"I think I've loved Charlotte for a long time."

John Mark faced him, eyes wide. "*Loved?* I was talking about a fondness for her."

"We've grown closer these past couple of months, and now with what's going on with Lanie...I care for her a lot. I never thought I'd have feelings for her given how annoying she was during our growing-up years, but, yes, I do love her."

Saying the words aloud made it somehow more cemented in Tobias's mind.

"Have you told her? Asked her to court you?"

Tobias took a deep breath. "No. I'm not sure she feels the same for me. I don't want her to think I only want to court her and subsequently marry her so Lanie will have a ma."

"That's not the case?"

"No. All these feelings for her started before Lanie came to live with me." He thought of her compassion and care for his niece. If Charlotte did accept his proposal, she would make a loving and doting mother. "If I did ask her to court me, would I have your blessing? You know I'll treat your sister with the respect she deserves." Tobias figured seeking Reverend Solomon's blessing would be far easier than attaining John Mark's.

"Cyrus really hurt her. I'm glad they never married."

"I would never hurt her." But the expression in John Mark's face, with his eyebrows raised and his mouth in a firm line, reminded Tobias that, while he himself was muscular and strong, he was no match for John Mark. "I promise I would never hurt her. If she'll have me, I aim to love her and take care of her all the days of our lives. We might argue from time to time, but I would never hurt her or allow anyone else to hurt her."

"From time to time? You two argue all the time, or you once did."

Tobias thought back to many witty barbs they'd traded. "That's true. But something has changed between us. I can't explain it. I think it first happened when we visited Willow Falls after Chester's and Paulina's deaths."

John Mark said nothing for some time, only reeled in the fish that wiggled on his fishing line. Should Tobias have waited for another time to ask? He'd known John Mark nearly all his life, but this was the first time he'd ever been filled with trepidation while speaking with him.

Finally he spoke. "Charlotte is still attempting to recover from a broken heart from that ne'er-do-well, Cyrus."

"I would never hurt her. Besides, I know her brothers would kill me, or at least maim me if I did."

The corners of John Mark's eyes crinkled. "We would do that without a doubt."

"You have my word that I will love and honor her."

"You still have to obtain my parents' blessings, but I reckon you have mine. I know you'll take good care of her." John Mark smirked. "I'm just wondering why you waited so long."

Charlotte and John Mark settled into rocking chairs on the porch after supper and after putting Lanie and Ambrose to bed. The aunts bustled about before settling in the parlor with their stitching, and Tobias, Quimby, and Stanley had left for their respective homes.

The sun had begun to set, a vivid orangey-purplish hue that lit the sky as though God had dipped His paintbrush into the paint jar and created it just for their viewing pleasure.

"I'm so glad you and Ambrose are here. I wish Hannah could have come. Are you excited about the baby?"

"Very much so. Nervous too. Ambrose is six-years-old and is easy to care for in many respects. But a baby?" John Mark exhaled a deep breath. "Not sure I know much about babies other than what I've learned from being around Caleb and Annie's girls."

"You'll be a magnificent father, John Mark, and Hannah will be a wonderful mother. You both have already proven that with Ambrose. He seems to be doing so well."

John Mark leaned back and clasped his hands behind his head. "That little boy has been through so much in his life, but God's hand has guided him the entire time. It's only by His grace we were able to adopt him and give him a good home. He's had some difficulty understanding he isn't allowed to run free like he did when his grandpa was alive. God was watching over him for sure, especially in a town like Poplar Springs. He would be out late at night all by himself, and sometimes he had no food."

"God certainly knows what He's doing when He provides parents for children, whether through the traditional way or through adoption."

"That He does. We know that first hand with Caleb. I can't imagine our lives without him."

Charlotte didn't remember much about when Caleb came to be their brother. To her, he'd just always been a part of their family.

They sat for a few moments, both of them rocking in their respective chairs. The scent of rain rode on the gentle breeze, and Charlotte inhaled. It was good to have John Mark for a visit.

"It seems you and Tobias are getting along better as of late."

"We are—we have been for some time. He's not quite as exasperating as he once was— perhaps it's due to the fact he's older now. But it was quite a shock to realize we both resided in Prune Creek. The aunts invited him for supper soon after I arrived, and I had it in my mind what and who I imagined the smithy to be. I was astounded when I opened the door to see Tobias Hallman standing there." Charlotte laughed as she recalled the day that now seemed so far in the past.

"I'm sure his presence has caused you much consternation." John Mark pivoted his gaze toward her, a smirk lining his face. "So, do you have feelings for him?"

Charlotte nearly choked on nothing at his question. "Feelings for him?"

"Yes, you know…"

"I—we have become good friends in recent days."

John Mark stopped rocking his chair. "Yes, you've insinuated as much. What are your thoughts about Tobias?"

Good ol' John Mark. Still as ornery as ever. "As I mentioned, we have become good friends in recent days."

"And?"

"And he has become somewhat of a pillar of the town."

"You've never been successful at hiding your true feelings, Charlotte. Something tells me you've grown fond of Tobias."

There was truly nothing that got past John Mark. No wonder he was such an effective deputy. "I was *also* about to say that I have no intention of falling in love again after what Cyrus did. It's not worth the broken heart."

"Two things regarding that matter," John Mark said, holding up a hand. "Number one, that happened for the best. It would have been a grave mistake for you to marry Cyrus. And two, Tobias is nothing like Cyrus."

"Do I detect that my big brother has become a matchmaker?"

John Mark chuckled, and for a moment, he resembled a younger Pa, only with darker hair. "No, Sis, your big brother has not become a matchmaker. Although, Tobias is my best friend, and if you do decide to grow fond of him, I won't argue. However, if he ever hurts you..."

She'd long appreciated the protectiveness of both John Mark and Caleb. "Well, thank you for your thoughts on the matter. I shall take them into consideration."

"Does that mean you might be fond of Tobias?"

Charlotte slugged her brother playfully in the shoulder. "Such a persistent sort! No, it does not." But even she knew she wasn't an effective liar, so she turned to peer in the opposite direction. Time for her to change the topic. "I'm really thankful you and Ambrose were able to visit. I've been a little homesick lately."

"It's hard being away from home. I find myself missing our family a lot. If there was an opening at the sheriff's office in Willow Falls, I might consider us moving there. But we recently were able to get a mortgage on the house we were renting, so for the time being, we'll be staying in Poplar Springs."

"I love it here with the aunts, but I do miss home."

"The good news is that with talk of a railroad spur finally coming to Poplar Springs, Ma and Pa can visit much more easily."

They sat there deep into the night chatting, laughing, and reliving days past, and while Charlotte hadn't revealed her true feelings about Tobias to John Mark, she imagined he suspected how she truly *had* grown fond of Tobias.

CHAPTER TWENTY-FOUR

HEAVINESS CLENCHED TOBIAS'S HEART as the ominous words, *Petition for Emergency Temporary Guardianship* blurred before his eyes. Not one minute ago, Sheriff Rettig handed him a thick stack of papers, expression pinched as he said, "Tobias Hallman, you've been served."

Praying he merely misread the words and misheard the sheriff, Tobias again perused the first few paragraphs of legal jargon, although the punch to his gut warned him his fears were correct.

Warring emotions—fear, anger, and confusion—clouded his thoughts at the real possibility of losing his niece. Anger emerged as the forefront emotion as he rifled through the rest of the papers, one of which was labeled, *Petition for Adoption.*

As though he'd hand over Lanie without a fight.

"I'm sorry, Tobias. One of the things I dislike about being a sheriff is serving papers, especially those that don't bear good news."

"*Petition for Emergency Temporary Guardianship?*" His caustic tone caused a casual observer on the boardwalk to glance his way. Tobias slammed the papers against his leg. "There is no way I'm going to relinquish Lanie to Morgan and Antonia."

Sheriff Rettig's brow furrowed. "I'm assuming there will be a court hearing."

Tobias read the words on the service of process. "The court finds good cause to set an expedited hearing as it is in the child's best interest that the matter be resolved quickly." Yes, he wanted it resolved quickly as well. "But in the meantime?" He examined the documents, his heart racing and fury threatening to erupt. "In the meantime, I have to deliver Lanie tomorrow morning to the Thiessens where she'll live until the court hearing?" He flipped through the pages and noted the hearing was set for next Tuesday. "No. I won't do it."

Sheriff Rettig's mouth sank into a sad smile. "As a father, I understand. As a man who cares about what's best for a child, I understand. Knowing you and the man that you are, I understand. But as a lawman, I'm commissioned to abide by the law and carry out justice. You will have to deliver Lanie to them, but Lord willing, it's only temporary. At least the hearing is less than a week away."

Tobias appreciated Sheriff Rettig's sympathy and his attempts to ease the situation, but it didn't alleviate the stressful thoughts ramming through his mind. "Thank you, Sheriff."

"I do intend to be present when you meet with the Thiessens tomorrow morning. Apparently they are residing at the Hitzs' home while staying in Prune Creek."

"I didn't even know they were here." When had the Thiessens arrived? How had they learned about Chester's and Paulina's deaths? Tobias blew out a deep breath. "They're not the kindest of people."

"I'm sorry to hear that. I best be on my way. The missus and I will be praying." Rettig touched the brim of his hat and walked slowly towards the sheriff's office.

Tobias sat on the bench inside the blacksmith shop and braced his face in his hands. Tomorrow morning he would take Lanie to the Thiessens. She wouldn't understand his reasoning for doing so and would likely feel abandoned. How could he explain to her that it was not *his* choice to have her go with Morgan and Antonia? That he would do anything to keep her from experiencing any further pain?

The tension in his neck increased. He also had to hire an attorney—hopefully Quimby—to fight this matter. Where would he get the funds to do so? He thought of the things he could sell—his horses, his tools. But he owned so few possessions.

The Thiessens likely had hired a powerful attorney who would do his best to fight for them given the fact he would be paid an exorbitant amount of money by his wealthy clients.

Lord, please help me.

It had been enough when his parents died. Then Chester and Paulina. Then nearly losing Charlotte to a ruthless gang of outlaws and almost losing his own life on the train. Now he had to give his niece to people who would never love her. The next step for them would be to adopt her, and he would lose her forever.

Where are You, Lord, in all of this?

Ever since he'd surrendered his life to Christ as a young'un, Tobias had relied on God. He'd grown in his faith, doing his best with the Lord's help to overcome the intense grief over the loss of his parents, brother, and sister-in-law.

But now, as he sat alone with silence surrounding him, Tobias's faith threatened to crumble.

Charlotte was hanging laundry on the clothesline when she spied Tobias riding up the road. Her stomach did a somersault at the sight of him. She'd been hoping he'd come for supper tonight.

Lanie emerged from the house from assisting Aunt Fern. She half-skipped, half-ran towards Tobias.

When he dismounted, Charlotte noticed something was awry. Slumped shoulders replaced his strong posture. He crouched down to hug Lanie, and as Charlotte drew closer, she noticed lines of worry framing his eyes. Lanie was prattling on about her exciting day learning to churn butter with Aunt Fern and how she'd learned to write a few letters of her name from Charlotte's earlier instruction.

Tobias stood, and his eyes connected with Charlotte's. "Lanie, I want to hear all about your day, but first, I need to talk with Aunt Charlotte."

"All right."

"Charlotte, could we go for a walk?"

"You and Aunt Charlotte are going for a walk?" Lanie asked. "Can I come too?"

Charlotte kneeled to Lanie's height. "We'll be back soon. In the meantime, would you mind going in and letting the aunts know we'll return soon for supper?"

"I can't go?"

"Not this time. But we will go for a walk tomorrow and see the remainder of the wildflowers. Perhaps we'll see another fawn."

"I like how they have spots on them. Uncle Tobias, me and Aunt Charlotte saw two baby fawns, and they had spots on them. They were twins."

Tobias grinned, but the smile failed to reach his eyes. "We'll be back soon, Lanie."

Lanie stuck out her bottom lip. "All right. I'll go in and tell the aunts."

Tobias didn't speak until they were past the barn and headed in the opposite direction of town. They traipsed through a meadow until they reached the pond. "Charlotte..."

"Tobias, what's wrong?"

He massaged his temples, the appearance of an intense burden resting on his shoulders. "Paulina's sister, Antonia, and her husband, Morgan, have filed legal paperwork for emergency temporary guardianship of Lanie."

"What? No. They can't have her."

"I was served paperwork today about three hours ago." He removed his hat and placed it on an upturned log. "Their goal is to adopt her."

Charlotte placed a hand on his arm. "We can't let that happen."

"Believe me, Charlotte, I don't want it to happen. But I feel helpless."

"I don't understand. How did they know Lanie was here? I'm assuming they'll be arriving in Prune Creek to attend the hearing?"

Tobias focused on something far into the distance.

Had he heard her? "Tobias?"

"They're here in Prune Creek. I have to deliver Lanie to them tomorrow morning at the Hitzs' house."

"No." Charlotte bit back the tears. "There must be something we can do. We could hire an attorney."

"With what funds?"

"We'll raise the money. We can sell things and ask for help from others."

"I've had plenty of time to think about it since Sheriff Rettig served the papers. I'd like to hire Quimby, but I'm sure it'll be a cost I can't afford."

Charlotte offered a prayer heavenward. "The aunts and I and my family in Willow Falls and Poplar Springs—we will all help you. We'll also have an event to raise money. Perhaps a bake sale, we just won't sell Aunt Myrtle's cooking." Charlotte hoped her quip about Aunt Myrtle would alleviate the stress of the situation for a brief moment, but Tobias barely cracked a smile.

"I have some tools I can sell, and I can sell my horses and wagon."

"Tools you need to run the blacksmith shop?"

"Yes, but I can buy them again once I get Lanie back."

Charlotte shook her head. "Tobias, no, you need those tools, and your horses and wagon too. We will figure out another way. There must be something we can do."

"I don't even know how I'm going to tell Lanie." Tobias kicked at a dirt clod.

"That's something to pray about, along with this entire situation. But, Tobias, God wasn't caught unaware. He knows this is happening and the repercussions for especially Lanie, but also you and all who love her. We need to begin collecting prayers."

One corner of Tobias's mouth upturned slightly. "You sound like your pa."

Charlotte didn't want to tell him she was struggling with the entire situation as well. "Thank you. That's a compliment. I think you should discuss the issue with Quimby, Stanley, and the aunts and see if they have any ideas, especially Quimby."

"Will you come with us tomorrow when I have to deliver her to Morgan and Antonia?"

"I will most definitely accompany you, and furthermore, I will be here to help in any way possible."

"I think we ought to hire Quimby," suggested Aunt Myrtle two hours later after Lanie had been settled into bed. "He'll know what to do."

Aunt Fern shook her head. "Lawyers are expensive."

"It will be difficult for Tobias to win against those Thiessen folks. They'll have the best lawyer money can buy. I say we hire Quimby. We can all contribute the best we can." Aunt Myrtle placed a hand on Tobias's arm. "We'll find a way."

"I agree with Aunt Myrtle. We should hire Quimby. He's well-versed in the law, and there's no way we can win without him." Charlotte searched Tobias's eyes for what he may think of the idea. Sorrow swam in their depths, and her heart broke for him. And for Lanie.

There had to be a way.

Tobias nodded. "Thank you, everyone."

"It's settled then," said Aunt Myrtle, "we'll invite Quimby for supper tomorrow evening and ask how we might retain him."

Aunt Fern folded her hands on the table. "All right, I agree. We'll do whatever it takes. There are things we can sell if need be."

"I don't want any of you to have to sell anything," began Tobias, before he was hushed by both of the aunts.

But as Charlotte peered around the humble home, she knew not much remained to be sold. But there was one thing she could sell. She fingered her amethyst necklace. Tomorrow she'd pay a visit to the mercantile and see how much money she could procure from one of her most precious possessions.

CHAPTER TWENTY-FIVE

"BUT WHY DO I have to go to their house?" Lanie asked as they traveled toward the Hitz home where Morgan and Antonia were temporarily staying.

"They want to spend some time with you." Tobias pulled his hat lower over his forehead. No sense in Charlotte and Lanie seeing his struggle of maintaining his composure over the entire ordeal with Morgan and Antonia.

Lanie peered up at him from her place wedged between him and Charlotte. "Will it be like a 'venture?"

"Yes, it will be an adventure." *A gloomy adventure.* Tobias thought of Lanie staying with the Thiessens, and emotion burned in his chest. They no more cared for Lanie than they did him.

They rode the rest of the distance in silence, Tobias unsure of how to properly explain to Lanie what all staying with the Thiessens entailed. He attempted to ignore the possibility that he might not get her back.

The extravagant stone house soon came into view, its expansive porch, blue shutters, and immaculate landscape setting it apart from ninety-nine percent of the other homes in Prune Creek, or likely Wyoming for that matter. Tobias was familiar with the wealthy Hitz family, although he'd never met them.

Tobias brought the horses to a halt and sat for a minute, wishing he'd awaken from the nightmare he and Lanie found themselves in. "I will need to talk to the Thiessens," he said, noting that the sheriff was already there and perched on his horse just beyond the barn.

"Lanie, why don't you and I go collect a few wildflowers? There are some in the meadow over there," said Charlotte, pointing to an area beyond the Hitz property.

"Yes, before they're all gone!" Lanie clapped her hands. "Maybe we can even take some to Aunt Fern tonight. She loves flowers!"

He caught Charlotte's eye. They both knew Lanie wouldn't be returning with them.

Tobias climbed from the wagon and assisted Charlotte and Lanie before straightening his shoulders and proceeding toward the house.

"Hello, Tobias," greeted Sheriff Rettig.

"Sheriff."

His steps nearly faltered when he noticed Charlotte and Lanie in the distant field swinging arms, and Lanie likely talking nonstop. How could he let her go?

Morgan and Antonia emerged from the house and stood on the porch. Antonia's sour expression on her face displayed her ill disposition. She looked down her nose at him, her thinly-veiled disgust surging to the forefront. Morgan retrieved a cigar from the pocket of his daytime suit, a suit costing more than Tobias made in a year in wages. "You're two minutes late."

When Tobias said nothing, Morgan continued. "We would prefer to travel home to Chicago, but because jurisdiction is here in Wyoming, we'll remain here until the adoption proceedings are complete. The Hitz family rented us their home while they're on holiday in Europe. A rather unimpressive and undignified abode, but it's better than the alternative of staying in a hotel. Now, where is the child?"

"She's gathering wildflowers and will be here shortly. Would you reconsider and allow Lanie to stay with me?"

Morgan drew closer and blew a puff of smoke directly into Tobias's eyes. "You? Hardly. No court would see fit to give some poor and nearly destitute plebeian with no social graces and no wife custody of a child in need of a suitable home. What Antonia and I can offer her is far superior than anything you could provide."

"Lanie is every bit as much my niece as she is yours. Paulina loved Chester, and Chester loved Paulina. Our family may not have a lot of money, but we do have a lot of love, and that's far more important." Tobias's pulse sped even faster. "Besides, I've been a part of Lanie's life since she was born. She barely knows you and Antonia."

Morgan harrumphed. "*Your* niece? Such a downward spiral in society Paulina took when she decided to marry into your family. Removing Lanie from the Hallman family and this lawless society is paramount if we are to give her the life she deserves."

"You mean to send her away to a boarding school so you and Antonia can't be bothered with her? Just like you do with your own children? Just like Paulina and Antonia's parents did to them?"

Antonia gasped and covered her mouth.

"How *dare* you!" Morgan's lip curled as he sneered. "It is unequivocally and unquestionably none of your business what we do with our children. Nor how Antonia and Paulina's parents educated them as young women. You are nothing but an uncouth and uneducated fool."

Tobias clenched his fists at his sides. He fought the pride that rose within him. He may not have studied at a university or received degrees like Morgan had, but he could build and fix anything and had an impeccable work ethic.

Morgan's eyes bugged, the darkness in their depths more apparent with their magnified size. "You're nothing but a simpleton, Mr. Hallman."

"I might be a simpleton, but I am educated enough to know that Lanie deserves to be raised in a loving home, not sent off to school because you and Antonia only care about appearances."

"How dare you!" Morgan said again, his face just inches from Tobias's. "Sheriff, I demand this man be removed from my presence. It is clear as the nose on his face that he is ill-suited to care for the child."

"But at least Lanie will be loved."

A vein Morgan's forehead pulsed. "You will *not* insinuate the child won't be loved. You will *not*."

"I just did."

Morgan's fetid breath—smelling of stale cigar smoke—and his intense stare did little to intimidate Tobias. They stood nearly nose to nose, Tobias's heart pounded in his chest. His body tensed, and heat flushed through him. He ought to pray the Lord would hold his tongue.

Were Charlotte and Lanie still in the meadow? What would Lanie do when forced to stay with the Thiessens?

He would fight for her. Fight to raise her the way Chester and Paulina would have wanted her raised. Fight to keep her from the likes of Morgan and Antonia. He tightened his fists.

But he would not fight Morgan with his fists. He would fight him in court and spend ample time in prayer. Tobias's shoulders tensed. He'd never wanted to execute his wrath on someone before as much as he did Morgan. To lambaste him about his thoughts on the matter. To prove that being a blacksmith and swinging a hammer for hours on end had built not only muscles and strength but also tenacity.

Sheriff Rettig stepped toward them. "Let's stop this right now, gentleman."

"No one deserves an upbringing with you and Antonia," Tobias growled.

"Uncle Tobias!"

Lanie's excited call drew Tobias's attention from Morgan to his niece, who raced toward him with two fistfuls of dandelions. She dashed up the steps, her face glowing. "We picked enough to make jam and some extras for Aunt Fern." Lanie swiveled her attention from Tobias to the sheriff, then to Morgan, and finally Antonia. She sectioned some of the flowers and handed a cluster to Antonia. "Here are some for you, too."

Antonia recoiled. "No thank you. Those are nothing but weeds."

"They're not weeds, ma'am. They are flowers. Pretty flowers that God made. My ma says dandelions remind her of sunshine because they are yellow and look like they're smiling."

"Nonsense, child." Antonia pursed her lips.

Lanie's lip quivered, and she blinked. "But they're pretty."

There were times in his life that Tobias knew that the only way he could survive the insurmountable difficulty of holding his tongue was because of God's grace.

This was one of those times.

He glowered at Antonia, then spoke softly to his niece. "Lanie, Aunt Charlotte and I will take some to Aunt Fern. You are right. She will love them."

"And then we can make dandelion jam again. 'Member how tasty it was, Uncle Tobias?"

"Yes, it was." Tobias kneeled and faced Lanie. "Remember when I said that your Aunt Antonia and Uncle Morgan would like you to visit with them?"

"But I don't want to visit with them."

"I know, but it will be an adventure, remember?"

Lanie's thin shoulders shook, and a tear trickled down her face. "I don't want to have a 'venture with them. I want to go home to Aunt Myrtle and Aunt Fern's. I want to help Aunt Charlotte collect eggs and see if there are any tomatoes in the garden. I want to stay with you, Uncle Tobias." She clung to him, pleading. Begging.

"There has to be a better way," Tobias said, his voice sounding more confident than he felt.

"There is no other way," snapped Antonia. "We have the court document that gives us temporary guardianship of her until the hearing. Step aside. You're only making things worse."

Paulina had a gentle nature, riled when someone threatened or harmed someone she cared about, but Tobias's sister-in-law had none of the vindictiveness Antonia possessed.

"I can't let you take her." Tobias prayed for the words to speak—words that would not dishonor his Lord. For Tobias knew without God's intervention, he would say something he would regret—and something that would not be in alignment with his profession of Christ.

Morgan gestured to Sheriff Rettig. "It's time to interpose."

"What's the harm in allowing Lanie to stay with Tobias until the hearing?" The sheriff asked. "Seems to me it makes more sense than to uproot her."

Charlotte held Lanie close. "This makes no sense at all. Please allow her to stay with Tobias until the hearing. Besides, all of this talk is upsetting to her." Like a mother hen, Charlotte stood protective, her glare boring into Morgan.

"And who are you to make an assessment as to our feelings for the child?" Morgan checked his pocket watch. "This fiasco has been allowed to continue for long enough."

"I'll not let her go," Charlotte whispered.

And Tobias was reminded all over again why he loved her.

"Tobias and Charlotte..." began Sheriff Rettig. He rubbed the back of his neck. "They have a court order."

"Lanie," said Tobias, opening his arms to her. She flew into them, and he scooped her up and held her close. "Aunt Antonia is your ma's sister. She would like you to visit for a while. But I'll come see you."

"I don't want to stay here. Don't make me stay here," Lanie wailed.

Tobias held her tighter, begging the Lord to intervene. "I love you, and I'll be back to visit you," he repeated, his tone low and, he hoped, reassuring.

"And I love you too, Lanie," said Charlotte, as she stepped near them. Tobias reached an arm around her and he and Charlotte clutched Lanie.

Sheriff Rettig tapped Tobias on the shoulder, remorse in his gaze. "It's time."

Never had Tobias felt so helpless. So distressed. So guilt-ridden as on that day when he watched Morgan and Antonia drag Lanie into the house while she cried.

And never would he forget the look of anguish and torment on Lanie's face.

The tears that she'd attempted to hinder flowed freely once the Thiessens ushered Lanie into the Hitz home.

"Charlotte," Tobias croaked, his voice dull and flat.

"I am so sorry," she answered, as the tears emerged forcefully and her body shook.

"What can I do?"

Charlotte took a step toward him and placed a hand on his arm. "We will get her back."

Tobias's clenched fists and the tears in his eyes that he tried so hard to hide proved his despondency.

"We will get her back," Charlotte said again. "God will help us."

But in this moment of turmoil, her own faith felt shaky.

CHAPTER TWENTY-SIX

CHARLOTTE TOOK A DEEP breath and entered the mercantile. She rubbed her finger along the edges of the amethyst necklace as she often did, then pressed it more closely to her heart.

It's only a possession, Charlotte.

A Bible verse from the book of Matthew floated through her mind: *Lay not up for yourselves treasures upon earth, where moth and rust doth corrupt, and where thieves break through and steal.*

Lanie's wellbeing was of far more worth than a necklace.

Lord, please help me accomplish this task.

Judith looked up from her ledger. "Well, hello, Charlotte. What brings you in today?"

"Hello, Judith." Charlotte had hoped it would be Judith rather than her husband. Not that Hugh wasn't a kindly gent, but he might be more challenging to persuade than Judith. Charlotte placed her necklace on the counter. The purple heart shimmered in the sunlight that streamed through the window, and she was reminded anew what a beautiful gift it was. "I was wondering if I might sell this to earn some money for an important cause."

"We don't normally buy things other than food items."
Judith's soothing voice did nothing to alleviate Charlotte's overanxious nerves.

"I understand, but I was wondering if you might make an exception."

Judith's brow furrowed and she lifted the necklace. "It's lovely."

"Yes. It was from my family." For a moment, she was taken back to her sixteenth birthday. Ma, Pa, John Mark, Caleb, and Annie crowded around the table. Charlotte closed her eyes and waited as patiently as she possibly could for Ma to place the gift in her outstretched hands.

Charlotte loved surprises.

Even before she opened her eyes, Charlotte dared hope it was the exquisite necklace she'd seen at Morton's Mercantile two weeks ago. Surely it was, for the rectangular-shaped box resting in her palm could fit a necklace just like the amethyst one she'd scrutinized two weeks prior. She'd begged Mrs. Morton to allow her to hold it for the teeniest of moments.

Of course Mrs. Morton acquiesced, and Charlotte had even tried it on for good measure. Purple was Charlotte's favorite color, and amethyst was her birthstone. The pearls bordering the heart provided an elegant contrast.

Ma and Pa had purchased the necklace for her, a gift that meant all the more because her parents could scarcely afford any type of gift other than a simple one, let alone something so elegant and pricey.

But Ma had taken in extra sewing, and Pa had taken on an extra job to pay for it. No, they hadn't informed Charlotte of the extra work, but she *had* overheard her brothers discussing it. Brothers who had also contributed to the necklace's purchase.

"You must really need the funds to want to sell it."

Judith's voice interrupted Charlotte's musings, and she returned to the present. Lanie's face flashed in Charlotte's mind. Her mournful eyes. Her begging Tobias not to leave her with her aunt and uncle. "Yes, very much so."

Judith said nothing, and Charlotte surmised the kind woman wanted her to elaborate on why she needed the funds. But it wasn't Charlotte's place to do so. Instead she once again did her best to persuade the owner. "I do think you'll be able to sell it. It's real amethyst and pearls and boasts such an ornate chain." Charlotte's voice shook. Ma and Pa would understand her predicament and the need to sell the cherished possession, but why then was it so hard to part with the necklace?

Sentimental reasons.

And because Ma and Pa sacrificed so much to purchase it for you.

And because you love the necklace and have worn it every day without fail since your sixteenth birthday.

Thoughts flooded her mind, and with effort, Charlotte shoved them aside. "Would you be able to give me a fair price?" How much would Quimby charge to provide legal services? Would the selling of her second-most treasured possession—after her Bible, of course—even make enough of a reduction in the cost for them to be able to afford to hire him?

She blinked, willing the tears not to fall. They must do all they could to help Lanie. Charlotte waited expectantly as

Judith further inspected the necklace. "Just a fair price is all I'm asking."

"All right, we will make an exception because it sounds as though you are in desperate need."

"Yes, ma'am, I am, and I thank you for making an exception."

Judith moved the necklace to the side and opened the cashbox. She handed Charlotte the money. "Was there anything else?" Judith asked.

"No, I best be on my way." Charlotte grasped the money in her hand, took one more wistful glance at the necklace, and stepped out of the mercantile and onto the boardwalk.

"Hello, Charlotte."

She turned to see Tobias. While his voice might sound buoyant, she knew it was a façade, hiding the pain of losing those he loved and potentially losing Lanie as well.

"Hello, Tobias."

"Are we still meeting with Quimby tonight?"

Charlotte squeezed the dollars tightly in her hand. "Yes. Aunt Myrtle invited him to supper. We'll discuss our plan with him then."

Tobias released a deep breath. "I sure hope he can help us."

"Yes, I do as well. I'm positive he will do what he can to assist us."

He took a step toward her and searched her gaze. "Is something wrong?" he asked.

Before their new friendship, Charlotte would have tossed aside—or most likely cringed—at the thought that Tobias understood her so well that he could detect when something

240

was amiss. But now she knew it to be true. Their friendship had changed so much of their relationship.

She paused before answering for surely Tobias would also detect a bold untruth. She couldn't very well say nothing was amiss. "Just thinking about Lanie."

That was for certain true. The girl was on Charlotte's mind often.

"Yes, me too. I keep thinking of how little I have to offer her in comparison to Morgan and Antonia."

"Tobias, you have so much *more* to offer her than Morgan and Antonia. You have been such a profound part of her life. You love her, and she loves you. You can offer her a loving home and raise her the way her parents would have wanted her to be raised. There is *no* comparison."

His face brightened at her comment. "Thank you, Charlotte. For everything."

"You're welcome. Now, I best be on my way. The aunts have a list three miles long of chores for me to undertake before supper tonight. I do believe our dear Aunt Myrtle is quite smitten with Quimby because everything has to be just so before he can arrive this evening." Charlotte attempted to laugh, but even to her own ears, it sounded strained.

"Ah, yes, the aunts. And Aunt Myrtle in particular." Tobias's face relaxed into a smile, the creases of worry in his brow temporarily disappearing. "I'll see you tonight then, Charlotte." He tipped his hat and sauntered in the opposite direction.

Charlotte offered another prayer heavenward as she made her way up the hill. *Lord, please, please let Quimby be amenable to helping us. And please let us be able to afford him.*

Tobias was becoming accustomed to eating at the aunts' house. Not that he minded. While the meals at the boardinghouse were sufficient, the company was far superior at Aunt Myrtle and Aunt Fern's. Although tonight he would be discussing a burden weighing heavily on him.

He had two dollars and some odd cents in savings, and despite Charlotte's objections to the contrary, he could sell some tools, his horses and the wagon. Perhaps he could take on a second job on a ranch after his day of blacksmithing was over.

Lanie was worth every sacrifice.

As he rode his horse past Quimby's house, he noticed the place appeared to be in immaculate condition. Maybe there were some interior repairs he could do for the attorney in exchange for his representation in court. Tobias had always worked hard and, as Pa always mentioned, was quite capable.

He would do whatever it took to win custody of Lanie.

Minutes later, Tobias tethered his horse and plodded up the stairs to the aunts' house. He could hear voices inside, most notably Aunt Myrtle's nervous giggle. He was far from an expert on matters of romance, but Tobias figured the woman was—as Charlotte would say—enamored. Tobias chuckled. It was likely the elderly lawyer was just as smitten with Aunt Myrtle as she was with him.

Charlotte met Tobias at the door before he could raise a hand to knock. She looked pretty tonight in her pink skirt and white blouse. Not that she wasn't always pretty, for she was. He'd determined that long ago.

"Hello, Charlotte." He opened the door and walked into the house. Something about her was different, although he couldn't articulate what. Had she changed her hair?

"Hello, Tobias. Haven't seen you in a while," she quipped, and Tobias was reminded what a great sense of humor she had. "Although I did see someone of your likeness on the boardwalk just today." She stepped to the side and he entered.

"Tobias," gushed Aunt Fern. She clutched his arm and led him to the table, although he already knew where his seat was. Right across from Charlotte where the aunts had settled him the first day he'd arrived and discovered she was their niece.

Before he sat, Tobias shook Quimby's hand. "Good to see you again, son," the older man said.

Aunt Fern took her place between Charlotte and Aunt Myrtle. "Supper will be but a few more minutes, so savor the remaining seconds of your life before you eat Myrtle's cooking."

Aunt Myrtle elbowed her sister. "There will be none of that, Fernie."

"Fernie?" Quimby asked. "Is that your nickname, Fern?"

"No, it is not. Myrt only calls me that when she wishes to be an irritant." Aunt Fern cast a glowering look at Aunt Myrtle.

Aunt Myrtle sat up straighter in her chair and peered across the table at Quimby. "Thank you for coming to supper tonight, Quimby. We actually have something of utmost importance to discuss with you. A serious matter."

"Is everything all right? And where is Lanie?"

"Tobias, would you care to explain?"

Tobias offered a prayer heavenward and turned to face Quimby. "As you know, my brother, Chester, and his wife, Paulina, recently passed due to the influenza epidemic in Willow Falls, and Lanie has come to live here with the expectation of her living with me as soon as I can secure a home for us."

"I'd heard the loss of life from the influenza in some parts of the state was extreme. Please accept my condolences for your loss."

"Thank you, sir." Tobias's voice broke, and he took a deep breath in an effort to maintain his composure. "I have decided that I would like to seek custody of her and raise her as my own."

"Lanie is fortunate to have you, and it should be no problem at all to prepare the paperwork to make everything legal."

Tobias shifted in his chair. "We've encountered a problem. Paulina, Lanie's ma, has a sister named Antonia Thiessen. She and her husband, Morgan, filed paperwork for emergency guardianship. I had to deliver Lanie to them at their temporary residence at the Hitz home here in Prune Creek until the court hearing on Tuesday. They reside in Chicago."

Quimby stroked his chin. "I see."

"Morgan and Antonia raising Lanie would not have been what my brother and sister-in-law would have wanted. Paulina and Antonia were estranged and have been for some time."

"Was there a will detailing Chester and Paulina's wishes?"

Tobias shook his head. "No, sir. My brother and his wife were poor folks. He worked as a hired hand on a ranch in Willow Falls where they were given room and board and some pay in exchange for his work. I doubt they would have thought about where Lanie would go if something happened to them."

He tapped his fingers on the table. How could he explain to Quimby that *he* was the one who ought to raise Lanie even though he had so much less than the Thiessens to offer? Charlotte's words from earlier today filled his mind. *"Tobias, you have so much more to offer her than Morgan and Antonia. You have been such a profound part of her life. You love her, and she loves you. You can offer her a loving home and raise her the way her parents would have wanted her to be raised. There is no comparison."*

Her words, along with the slight nod of her head for him to continue, emboldened him. "Paulina and her sister, Antonia, have never been close. When Paulina decided to marry my brother, Chester, her parents and Antonia estranged themselves from her. To my knowledge, Paulina hadn't seen Antonia for years until they saw each other by accident in Cheyenne. I'm not sure if the two sisters attempted to mend their relationship or not." He paused and took a drink of the water Charlotte offered him. "Paulina was close to my parents, especially my ma. She was like a sister to me. My parents passed and then it was just the four of us."

"Do you think Tobias has a chance of winning custody of Lanie?" Charlotte asked.

"There will be some concerns the judge will have. For instance, Tobias isn't married. Where will Lanie stay while he's working? Right now Tobias lives at the boardinghouse. That's sufficient for him, but insufficient to raise a child there, what with only one room, and a small one at that. Yes, he will soon move to the apartment above Stanley's barbershop, but in the meantime, Lanie has been residing with non-family members."

"Stanley mentioned the family in the apartment would be moving within the month." Tobias wished he could find a house for him and Lanie. That would bode much better in the court's eyes.

The aunts stood to retrieve the meal. "You do believe he has a chance, don't you?" Aunt Fern asked.

"Yes, I do," answered Quimby. "This is a matter to hand over to the Lord, but yes, I do think he has a chance."

"I know the hearing is in only a matter of days, but would you represent me?" The words tumbled from Tobias's mouth, and he held his breath.

Quimby took a few seconds to answer. "Yes. Yes, I will represent you."

Charlotte placed a few dollar bills and some coins on the table in front of Quimby. "Will this be sufficient for you to begin?"

Tobias knew his jaw slacked when he saw her place the money on the table. "Charlotte, you don't have to..."

"I want to, Tobias. It's important to me that Lanie is adopted by you. She deserves the kind of home you can give her."

Emotion welled in his throat. He'd found a good friend in Charlotte. "Thank you. I appreciate this."

"We'd like to help as well," insisted Aunt Myrtle, carrying a steaming pan of some sort of concoction to the table.

"Indeed," agreed Aunt Fern. She set the pitcher of milk in front of Tobias.

"Thank you, all of you. And I have some money to add as well." He reached into his pocket and produced the two dollars and change he'd withdrawn when he closed his savings account today.

Quimby cleared his throat. "This is all fine and well, but I plan to take this case pro bono."

"Pro bono?" Aunt Fern asked.

"Yes, it means that I plan to do it for free."

Had Tobias heard him correctly? "Free, sir?"

"Indeed. I will file any necessary and appropriate paperwork in response to the documents you were served, and I will represent you at the hearing. Now, I believe Myrtle has made a delicious meal. Shall we say grace and partake?"

But food was the last thing on Tobias's mind.

For the first time since being served the papers from the Thiessens' lawyer, he had a glimmer of hope when it came to adopting Lanie.

Charlotte hardly slept that night. She kept thinking of how gracious Quimby was for offering to help them for free.

And how she would need to retrieve her necklace, provided it hadn't sold.

After a restless night of tossing and turning, Charlotte sprang from bed and quickly dressed. She joined the aunts to say grace for breakfast before devouring the toast with huckleberry jam Aunt Fern had prepared.

"Where are you off to in such a hurry?" Aunt Myrtle inquired.

Charlotte laced up her brown boots. "Please don't worry. I need only to tend to an errand in town. I'll be back soon for chores."

"Be careful," said Aunt Fern.

"I will. Be back soon!" Charlotte bolted out the door. If she arrived as soon as the mercantile opened, there was a chance Judith hadn't yet sold her necklace.

Oh, to have it again!

She lifted her skirt and began running down the hill toward town, her reticule with the dollars and coins clutched firmly in her grasp. Wagons and horses passed by her and the dust plumed in the air. Perspiration dripped from her forehead from the combination of the already-hot early morning sun and the fact she was running faster than she had in a long while. As a matter of fact, she hadn't run this fast since Tobias used to chase her around the playground at school. He'd been so annoying then, terrorizing her with worms and his pet snake. She'd never liked snakes, still didn't. And she'd never understood why anyone would want to have one as a pet. Charlotte shivered despite the heat as she thought of his striped brown and greenish snake he'd named Slithers.

Slithers had found his way onto her chair at school one time, and she'd shrieked so loudly when first noticing his presence that she was quite sure those as far away as Nelsonville or Poplar Springs heard her.

Thankfully Tobias had changed since those days. Charlotte now found herself appreciating his friendship and perhaps longing for more someday.

The dry dirt, combined with loose gravel caused Charlotte to slide and nearly plunge to the hard ground. She righted herself and continued on her way.

Nothing would stop her from arriving in town as efficiently as possible.

Charlotte glanced both ways for oncoming traffic then crossed the alleyway and slowed to a stop. She took several deep breaths, willing her lungs to cooperate after her expedient travel. She passed the church, blacksmith and barbershop, the boardinghouse and the restaurant, the livery stable and Quimby's office, and finally arrived at the mercantile.

Thankfully the only other customer was Tobias, who stood perusing the men's boots.

"Hello, Charlotte, is there something I can help you find?" Judith asked.

Charlotte peered behind her at Tobias. She'd rather he not know about the necklace, so she lowered her voice. "Yes, I was wondering if my necklace has been sold."

"Actually I have someone interested in purchasing it for his wife. He'll be back within the hour."

Something akin to a heavy weight pressed on Charlotte's chest. "Might I renege on my offer and purchase back the necklace?"

"I'm so sorry, Charlotte, but I promised Mr. Lund he could buy it when he returned." Judith's brow crinkled. "I'm so sorry," she repeated.

"But I have all of the money you paid me." Charlotte hurriedly opened her reticule and placed the dollars and coins on the counter. "Please. The necklace means a lot to me."

To her credit, Judith did not chastise her for selling the necklace. Instead, the kindly woman offered a sympathetic smile. "I wouldn't feel right going back on my word."

Tears pricked Charlotte's eyes. It would be difficult, but she would have to accept Judith's answer. She struggled to avoid letting her emotions get the best of her and was about to leave when Tobias sidled alongside her.

"Is this the necklace you always wear?" he asked.

"Yes."

"I thought something was different about you. It was that you weren't wearing the necklace."

If Tobias sought to make her feel better about the situation, he was not succeeding.

"Judith, I have an extra two dollars and some odd cents I'd be willing to add to the amount Charlotte is paying for the return of the necklace."

"Tobias..."

Tobias held up a finger. "And I know your wagon wheel has needed to be fixed for some time. I will fix it for you for free in exchange for the necklace."

"We do need our wagon wheel fixed and what with my husband being unable to fix it himself...I—the difficult part is that I've already promised to sell it to another. He's a good customer, and I don't wish to be dishonest," said Judith.

"I'll fix something for the man too, free of charge."

Tobias's generosity, coupled with the determination in his gaze endeared him to her. How had she not known the man he truly was? "Tobias, that's a lot of work."

"Yes, and the necklace will be worth it. I would be happy to explain the situation to this man and help to rectify things if need be." Tobias paused. "Here's the two dollars and some odd cents." He plunked the money on the counter with Charlotte's.

His voice was kind, but persuasive. For a moment, Charlotte recalled when he'd evaded punishment a time or two during his school years due to his charming demeanor.

"No, the money from Charlotte and the wagon wheel will be sufficient. Will you promise to speak to Mr. Lund about it? He'll be here within the hour."

"I will. Please send him to the blacksmith shop, and thank you, Judith."

Emotion choked Charlotte, and for a moment, she was unable to speak. Finally, she found her voice. "Thank you, Tobias. Thank you, Judith."

"Here, I'll help you with the necklace." Tobias clasped the hook, his touch causing a shiver to travel down her spine.

They walked together out of the mercantile and toward the blacksmith shop. "Thank you again, Tobias."

"You're welcome. Glad I could help. Why were you selling your necklace anyway? If you don't mind me asking."

"I had something important I needed to pay for." She was thankful when Tobias didn't probe further.

Tobias clasped his hands behind his head and sought sleep that night. It hadn't been easy not seeing Lanie. There was no love in the hearts of the Thiessens, and it concerned him that Lanie would be emotionally neglected, especially at a time when she needed caring folks who loved her more than ever. Tomorrow he would attempt to visit Lanie and reassure her the best he could. Would Morgan and Antonia allow him to visit her? He'd already tried twice to no avail when no one answered the door at the Hitz house.

He wasn't prone to worry, but he did agonize over whether they had taken Lanie to Chicago. Surely even they wouldn't do that, especially since the hearing was in only a few days.

At least Quimby would be representing him in court, and he offered to do it for free. Tobias would think of something to repay the man for his generosity as he knew preparing for a court case was time consuming.

It was then that a random thought occurred to Tobias. He figured he knew why it was that Charlotte sought to sell her prized necklace her family had purchased for her years ago.

When he prayed that night, he added in a prayer of gratitude for the woman he had come to love.

CHAPTER TWENTY-SEVEN

TOBIAS STALKED UP THE stairs of the Hitz home where Morgan and Antonia temporarily resided while the Hitz family was out of state. The extravagant stone house boasted something no other home in Prune Creek had—a wooden and brass doorbell. He pressed the button, causing an ominous chime to sound on the other side of the door. Tobias took a step back and awaited an answer.

Would they be home?

If so, would they allow him to see Lanie?

A tall maid in her forties dressed in a black dress with a white apron opened the door. Her gaze traveled the length of him, and she wrinkled her nose and tilted her chin upward. "The owners are not hiring at this time," she said, her tone brusque as she started to close the door.

Tobias pushed on the door gently to keep it ajar. "I'm not here for a job, ma'am."

The maid's expression indicated she didn't believe him. "Well, then, we are not interested in whatever you are selling." She again attempted to close the door.

This time, Tobias put his foot between it and the doorframe to keep it from closing all the way. "Ma'am, I am not trying to sell something." It took restraint on his part not to allow his annoyance to show.

"Then what *are* you here for?"

"Are Morgan or Antonia home?"

The woman scowled. "What sort of business would the likes of you have with Mr. and Mrs. Thiessen?"

Antonia appeared beside her. "It's fine, Kremena. I'll take care of it, thank you."

"As you wish, Mrs. Thiessen." Kremena stood a second longer before tossing one more disapproving glance at Tobias.

"What is it you want, Mr. Hallman?" Antonia asked.

"I'd like to see Lanie."

Indecision lined Antonia's solemn features. "I believe it's neither wise nor prudent. The child is experiencing trouble adjusting as it is. Besides, we plan to leave for Chicago the day after the court hearing awards us custody. Pray tell, what good will it do for you to see her?"

Because she's my niece? Because I have every right to see her?

Tobias attempted to squash his frustration; a feat achieved only by prayer. He took a deep breath. "It would do no harm for me to see her. After all, I am her uncle."

"A dismal state of affairs to be sure. If only Paulina hadn't chosen to take leave of her senses."

He knew where this conversation would lead, and it would do nothing to further the opportunity to see his niece, so Tobias attempted a different tactic, although he refused to grovel. "Antonia, I'll only stay a short time. Please."

Antonia directed her attention first to the left, then to the right, before settling on Tobias again. "All right, but keep the visit brief. Morgan will be home soon, and I highly doubt he will appreciate seeing you here." She continued, her tone curt, "You can wait in the parlor. Right this way."

Antonia led Tobias into an elaborate room with expensive furnishings, including a glass-fronted wooden hutch, vases, an imposing bookshelf, and a polished square grand piano. He took a seat on an ornate light blue sofa that he feared wouldn't accommodate his weight.

"Kremena," Antonia called.

The dour-faced servant returned and bowed slightly. "Yes, Mrs. Thiessen?"

"Would you please fetch the child and have her convene promptly in the parlor?"

"Yes, ma'am."

Kremena turned on her heel and hurried around the corner.

"Remember, Mr. Hallman. Do keep it brief."

Nervousness, fear, concern, and exhaustion spread through him. He'd been unable to sleep well since delivering Lanie to the Thiessens. If it hadn't been for the considerable job he'd undertaken and promised a customer to complete swiftly, he would have attempted to visit a second time yesterday. He saw Lanie before she saw him, and guilt assaulted him when his nearly unrecognizable niece staggered toward the parlor.

Had there been anything he could have done to avoid Lanie living with the Thiessens?

Finally, she lifted her chin and saw him. "Uncle Tobias?"

In less than a second, she flew into his arms. He stood, lifted her, and swung her around. "Lanie," he croaked.

Antonia stood in the doorway, a shallow dip of a frown on her face. She said nothing but observed a moment longer before disappearing elsewhere.

Lanie's tears dampened Tobias's shirt, and he held her close, willing that the entire situation was only a bad dream.

"Uncle Tobias," Lanie sobbed. "When can I leave this place?"

He attempted to release her so they could sit on the sofa, but she held fast, her arms tightening around his neck. He held her, prayed to the Lord for wisdom in answering Lanie's question, and for God's mercy in returning her to him.

The grandfather clock in the far corner indicated the time, and several more minutes passed before Lanie pulled back and searched his face.

The sight of her caused his heart to constrict.

Lanie's blonde hair was fashioned into one tight French braid wrapped around her head. Her droopy brown eyes shimmered with tears, and her pale face gnawed at him. Were they taking appropriate care of her?

"Why don't we sit on the sofa?" he quietly suggested.

Lanie acquiesced, and they took a seat.

"I don't like it here," said Lanie. "I miss you and Aunt Charlotte and Aunt Myrtle and Aunt Fern." Her lower lip trembled.

"I know. We miss you too."

Lanie dipped her head. "I don't want to stay here. Kremena is mean, and Aunt Antonia..." Her skinny shoulders shook. "Aunt Antonia told Kremena to fix my hair like this." She patted the braid. "I told her no because—because Ma fixed my hair 'afore, and I wanted it to stay that way. The way Ma fixed it. And it pulled my hair really bad and hurted when Kremena fixed it."

Tobias balled his fists. It was just like Antonia to not see the importance of allowing Lanie to keep her messy braids in honor of the last time Paulina had fixed her hair. "I'm sorry, Lanie."

"And I don't like the food here. It doesn't taste good like Aunt Myrtle's."

"But you are getting enough food to eat, right?"

Lanie nodded. "Yes, but Aunt Charlotte would say it's untasteful."

"Distasteful?"

"Yes. That's what Aunt Charlotte would say. But she's not here." Lanie began to sob again.

Antonia stood in the doorway. "As I mentioned previously, Mr. Hallman, I don't believe this is a prudent idea."

Tobias held up a hand. "We're fine."

Antonia appeared to want to say more but instead had the decency to remove herself from the room.

"Have you done anything fun at all while you've been here?" he asked Lanie.

His niece shook her head. "No. Nothing fun at all. See those doll babies over there?" She pointed to a crib with a variety of porcelain and rag dolls.

"Yes."

"I can't even play with those. There are no dollies here, and I miss my doll."

Tobias wished he would have thought to bring Lanie's doll from the aunts' house. "Maybe I could bring you your doll."

"Aunt Antonia will say 'no'. That is her favoritist word."

What type of upbringing did the Theissen children have? Tobias figured it was better they were always away at a boarding school. "I'm sorry, Lanie."

"Let's just go to the aunts' house. I promise I'll be good."

Her words froze his heart midbeat. "Lanie, you aren't here because you weren't a good girl."

"Then why am I here?"

Her eyes searched his. How could he tell her? *Lord, help me with the words.*

"Aunt Antonia and Uncle Morgan want to visit with you. Remember when we talked about that before I brought you here?"

Lanie shook her head. "I don't like Uncle Morgan. He has a mean voice."

Tobias knew that Lanie would never be physically harmed in Morgan and Antonia's care, but he wagered that Morgan's harsh tone and Antonia's emotional distance wasn't a suitable environment for Lanie.

"Did I ever tell you the story about when your pa was a little boy?"

Lanie drew her head back. "Pa was a little boy?"

"He was once upon a time."

"And did you know Ma when she was a little girl like me?"

Tobias nearly chuckled at her inquiry. "No, I didn't know your ma until she was a woman. But once upon a time your pa and I were little boys. We lived on a ranch in Willow Falls."

"The town where some of my cousins and my grandma and grandpa live."

"Yes. And it was a ranch that our pa worked on, and we lived in a house there."

"Was it a big house like this one?"

Tobias recalled the house, more like a shack, that Ma and Pa resided in during his growing-up years. It was part of the room and board Pa received for working the ranch, and Ma made it as homey as possible with their meager funds, but it only felt like a home because his family was there. "No, it was small."

"Like Aunt Annie and Uncle Caleb's house?"

"Smaller than that."

Lanie squinted. "The size of my room at the aunts' house?"

"About that size."

"That's small, Uncle Tobias. How did you and Pa fit?"

The house had been cramped, but since his parents had few possessions, it hadn't mattered. "It was crowded, but one day after your pa and I finished chores, we played hide and seek because that was our favorite game."

"That's my favoritist game too. I like to play it with my cousins."

"One time it was your pa's turn to hide. I closed my eyes and counted to ten, then went to find him."

Lanie's eyes rounded, and for the first time since he'd arrived to see her, there was a hint of happiness on her face. "And did you?"

"Well, I looked all over. I looked in the barn, in the loft, in the house, and behind the grove of trees, but I couldn't find him."

"He was losted?"

"He wasn't lost, just a really good hider."

Lanie nodded. "We played hide and seek with my boy cousin, Ambrose, once, and he was a good hider too. 'Cept it was because he was in the kitchen eating the cookies Grandma Lydie made."

Tobias laughed. John Mark's son proved that the saying about the apple not falling far from the tree was accurate in their family. "I'm glad you found him."

"Did you ever find Pa?"

"I was worried at first." As though it were yesterday, Tobias recalled thinking his older brother was missing forever. Had he walked to town? Visited the neighbors? Had Tobias just not seen him when he searched in all the likely places? "I said 'ollie ollie oxen free'!"

"Me and my cousins say that too."

"Your pa didn't answer, so I said it again, even louder. Still no answer. I was just about to tell our ma when I thought of one more place to look."

Lanie leaned forward, her mouth formed in an "o".

"Our wagon was parked not far from the barn. So I climbed up and peered into the back. Lo and behold, there was your pa, sleeping in the back of the wagon, just snoring away."

Lanie giggled. "Were you 'prised about that?"

"I sure was. It took me some time to wake him from his slumber. I think he was dreaming about fishing or something because he sure was sleeping hard."

"That sounds like Pa."

Tobias glanced up to see Antonia in the doorway, her arms folded across her chest and an indiscernible expression on her face. How long had she stood there listening to his and Lanie's conversation?

"It's time for you to leave now, Mr. Hallman."

Lanie's renewed sobs as he left without being able to promise she'd someday be able to leave the Theissen's shredded his heart.

Chapter Twenty-Eight

TOBIAS SAT IN THE chair next to Quimby behind the table in the Prune Creek County Courthouse. He jiggled his knee, anxiety permeating through him. What if Morgan and Antonia were awarded custody of Lanie? What if he failed her? Failed Chester and Paulina?

Morgan narrowed his eyes at Tobias before taking his own seat between his attorney, Mr. Stewart, and Antonia at the opposite table.

The bailiff announced, "All rise", and everyone in the courtroom stood as the judge entered.

After Judge Voetberg took his seat behind the bench at the front of the courtroom and everyone was seated, he announced, "We are here for the matter of the adoption of Layna Paulina Hallman."

The proceedings started with Mr. Stewart calling Morgan to the stand. Morgan reiterated his high-society standing, his wealth, and the fact that he was the father of two children. Antonia was called second. "No further witnesses at this time," Mr. Stewart said before Quimby called his first witness to the stand.

Tobias wiped his sweaty palms on his trousers, stood, and walked to the stand where he promised to tell the entire truth.

Quimby then proceeded to ask him a myriad of questions. "We have several letters from townsfolk indicating you are an upstanding citizen. Please tell us about your move to Prune Creek, why you moved to this town, and where you resided before moving here."

Tobias answered Quimby's questions, outlining his dream of becoming a blacksmith, why he chose Prune Creek, and his plans for the future. He discussed the friends he'd already made, including Charlotte, Aunt Myrtle, and Aunt Fern, and their desire to assist in raising Lanie if need be.

Mr. Stewart was a short-statured, fine-boned man with an elaborate gray-brown beard that came to two forked points and was attached to sideburns and a finely groomed mustache. He approached the witness box, his eyes rounded and beady, making his hard, unblinking stare all the harsher. "Mr. Hallman, please tell the court where you live."

"I currently live at the boardinghouse on Second Street."

"A boardinghouse?"

"Yes, sir."

Mr. Stewart stroked one fork of his long, coarse beard. "Do you think that a boardinghouse is a suitable place to raise a young girl?"

"I am in the process of renting a space above Stanley Gormon's barbershop."

"Curious. And will the space have adequate living quarters?"

"It does. It's currently rented by a family of five."

Mr. Stewart raised his brows into his graying hairline. "You mentioned in prior questioning that you are a blacksmith. It appears you owe a substantial amount on the mortgage for the blacksmith business you purchased."

"I do, but I make regular payments, always on time. I aim to pay extra each month so the mortgage will be paid in full sooner."

"Hmm. Are you married, Mr. Hallman?"

"No, I am not."

"Do you plan to someday marry?"

Tobias's eye caught Charlotte's. Would she someday be amenable to marrying him? "Yes, sir, I do. When the Lord sees fit."

"With a profession of such magnitude, where do you anticipate the child staying while you are working since you do not have a wife to care for her?"

"I have enlisted the assistance of three friends—Charlotte Eliason and Myrtle and Fern Beauchamp." He hoped his use of educated vernacular made him sound more intelligent and capable of caring for Lanie. Tobias had Annie to thank for always assigning large vocabulary words in school.

"Mr. Hallman, how would you describe your standing in society?"

An efficient perusal at Morgan and Antonia proved they failed at hiding their smug expressions. Antonia tilted her chin upward and looked down her nose, while Morgan held his fixed stare on his expensive pocket watch. For them, the only thing that mattered was wealth. Tobias recalled Paulina's story of her family estranging themselves from her when she chose to marry Chester. "I am a Christian who attends church regularly. I have developed friendships in Prune Creek and have many friends in my former towns of residence in Willow Falls and Cheyenne where I did my apprenticeship. One of those friends is Sheriff Townsend in Willow Falls and Deputy Sheriff John Mark Eliason in

Poplar Springs. Reverend Solomon Eliason in Willow Falls can also vouch for my trustworthiness and my character."

"Such a shame we are in Prune Creek rather than Willow Falls, and none of those individuals are here to vouch for you." Mr. Stewart shook his head. "Mr. Hallman, are you familiar with the laws that dictate the proper way to care for a child in the State of Wyoming?"

Tobias could figure out how best to raise a child based on his knowledge of the Bible and his own upbringing. "I know there are laws, yes."

"In Chapter Thirteen, Section 2291, of the Revised Statutes of Wyoming, it details that if one has custody, it is unlawful to endanger a child or allow a child to live somewhere where their health and life could be jeopardized. Do you believe that allowing the young child to reside in a boardinghouse is safe?"

"As I mentioned, sir, I am in the process of securing living quarters above the barbershop."

"Yes, but in the meantime, she will reside at the boardinghouse, is that correct?"

Tobias pondered for a moment how much Morgan and Antonia were paying Mr. Stewart to represent them in this case. Obviously the man had experience in manipulation. "No, she will temporarily reside at the home of Myrtle and Fern Beauchamp while we finalize the move to the barbershop."

Antonia gasped and placed a hand over her mouth. Mr. Stewart strode toward her. She whispered something to him, and he again faced Tobias. "Would you say it is fair to the child to be raised by two older women of whom she has no relation while you determine a place for her to reside?"

"Sir, they take excellent care of her and love her as if she were their own niece. And it is only temporary. In two weeks' time, I will have secured the living quarters above the barbershop."

"In the same section of the Revised Statutes of Wyoming, it discusses withholding the proper sustenance, clothing, and shelter for the child. Your Honor, we request that the Court take these findings into consideration when making a judgment. I have no further questions for the witness."

Tobias's emotions of irritation, anger, frustration, and helplessness meshed into one. Quimby, calm as always, addressed the court and requested a redirect of Tobias. When it was granted, he asked, "Mr. Hallman, would you say you also have townsfolk who reside in Prune Creek who could vouch for your character and integrity?"

"Yes, sir."

"No further questions of this witness."

After Tobias returned to his seat behind the table, Quimby called Sheriff Rettig to the stand. He was sworn in, and Quimby conducted his questioning. "Sheriff Rettig, how long have you known Mr. Hallman?"

"Since he moved to Prune Creek earlier this year."

"As a lawman, you no doubt know the intricacies of the town and those who abide by the law, those who don't, those of upstanding character, and those with a lack of character."

Sheriff Rettig nodded. "Yes. I feel I know everyone in town reasonably well seeing as how I've been a lawman here for the past eight years."

"Can you please tell me what you know of Mr. Hallman?"

"He is an upstanding citizen who assisted in helping thwart an outlaw's plans to rob the train. He also provides outstanding work as the blacksmith. He attends church, and I have never once seen anything objectionable in his character, nor has he spent time in the saloons to my knowledge."

"Has he ever resided in the Prune Creek jail?"

"No, sir."

Quimby tapped his chin, waiting several seconds before continuing. "Sheriff, were you present on the day that Layna Paulina Hallman was delivered to the Hitz home to be under the temporary guardianship of Morgan and Antonia Thiessen?"

"Yes, I was."

"What was your opinion of the ongoings of that event?"

Mr. Stewart nearly stomped to the front of the courtroom. "Objection. Calls for speculation."

"Sustained," said Judge Voetberg. "Mr. Quimby, please rephrase your question."

"Yes, Your Honor. Sheriff, what did you observe about the ongoings of the event?"

Sheriff Rettig took a deep breath. "When I was asked to be present on the day the girl was delivered to the Hitz home, I was not impressed by the Thiessens' actions or words."

Quimby perched near the witness stand. "How so?"

"They seemed harsh. Unloving." Sheriff Rettig faced the judge. "Your Honor, I'm a pa myself. Kids need love and a tender approach, especially when they're in pain as Miss Lanie is after losing her parents. I didn't see that love and tender approach in Mr. and Mrs. Thiessen."

Morgan uttered something indiscernible. Antonia dabbed at her eyes with a lace handkerchief likely for dramatic effect.

"No further questions of this witness," said Quimby, his erect posture adding to his already considerable height. "Your Honor, the court wishes to again call Mrs. Thiessen to the stand."

"With all respect, Your Honor, she has already been questioned," Mr. Stewart protested.

"Mr. Stewart," said the judge, "as a practicing attorney in Chicago, no less, with the license to practice in several states, including Wyoming, you are fully aware that a witness may be recalled. Please take the stand, Mrs. Thiessen. May I remind you that you are still under oath."

Quimby strolled toward the front of the court, his casual swagger proving his composed and placid disposition. "Good afternoon again, Mrs. Thiessen. Can you tell me a bit about your relationship with Lanie's mother, your sister?"

Mr. Stewart stood. "Your Honor, is this line of questioning really necessary?"

"I'll allow it. Please proceed with answering the question, Mrs. Thiessen."

Antonia glanced about the room with a wistful gaze. "My dear sister, Paulina, and I were very close. It was a dreadfully painful circumstance when she passed." Antonia dabbed at her eyes again with her handkerchief. "I hadn't even the chance to tell her goodbye."

"How long had it been since you'd last seen Paulina?"

Antonia blinked. "Far too long." She faced Judge Voetberg. "You see, she married and moved to Cheyenne, so we were no longer able to spend as much time together as we previously had."

"How long would you say?" asked Quimby.

"I had not seen her in four years."

Quimby nodded. "Four years. And did you make an effort to visit her in Cheyenne or did she come to visit you in Chicago?"

"I did see her in Cheyenne about four years ago when Lanie was just a baby. I was so utterly thrilled to be an aunt. Paulina and I were our parents' only children."

"I see. How did you know she had moved to Willow Falls?"

Antonia pooched her lower lip. "We didn't know at first, and it devastated me when I hadn't heard from her in some time. You see, formerly, we frequently wrote letters back and forth."

Tobias suppressed the urge to roll his eyes at Antonia's false sincerity. While Paulina had not shared much about her upbringing and estrangement from her family, Chester mentioned their family had never been close.

"How did you discover she moved to Willow Falls?"

"Morgan hired a detective."

"Please do correct me if I am mistaken, Mrs. Thiessen, but if you and Paulina were close, why would your husband find it necessary to hire a detective to determine Paulina had moved to Willow Falls? Wouldn't you be adept at knowing her whereabouts?"

"I—the postal service does take time to deliver the mail, what with this being the Wild West." Antonia took a deep breath. "And then...and then, she passed so suddenly." Her voice quivered and she blinked rapidly, focusing on Judge Voetberg while doing so.

Quimby appeared unaffected by Antonia's show of emotion. "Please tell the court why you and Mr. Thiessen wish to adopt Lanie as your own."

"For one, she is all that I have left of my sister."

"And?"

"And?"

"Are there other reasons?" Quimby turned and faced the audience in the courtroom while awaiting Antonia's answer.

"Yes." A flicker of irritation flashed in her eyes. "Morgan and I want to give Lanie the best life possible. We can give her everything she could want. She will also be able to spend time with our children, her cousins."

When they aren't away at boarding school, Tobias mused.

Quimby placed his hands behind his back and paced back and forth. His intended prolonging of further questions created even more tension to permeate throughout the courtroom. Tobias prayed again that the Lord would see fit to give him the opportunity to raise Lanie.

He turned around to gaze at the townsfolk in the courtroom gallery. Many had come in support, promising to speak on his behalf if necessary. His attention settled on Charlotte. He'd known her long enough to know the expression on her face was one of encouragement and support. She smiled, and he remembered all over again why it was he had come to love her.

And how he would declare his love for her once this debacle with Morgan and Antonia concluded.

Finally, Quimby stopped pacing and stood again facing Antonia. "Mrs. Thiessen, can you tell me about the inheritance from your parents?"

Her voice rose an octave. "The inheritance from my parents?"

"Objection, Your Honor," interrupted Mr. Stewart. "How is Mrs. Thiessen's inheritance relevant to this case?"

269

Judge Voetberg addressed Quimby. "Do you have a reason for this line of questioning?"

"I do, Your Honor. It's paramount to the case."

"I'll allow it."

Quimby again asked the question. Antonia set her mouth in a firm line. "When Mother and Father died, they left both Paulina and me an inheritance."

It was obvious that Antonia wished to evade any further inquiries pertaining her parents' will. Tobias wondered, too, why Quimby remained resolute in urging her to continue. "And what was that inheritance?"

Mr. Stewart again attempted to interrupt, but the judge ordered Antonia to continue.

"I received our family home in Chicago. Paulina received our home in New York."

Tobias's jaw dropped. He'd never known about the inheritance. Had Paulina even known? If so, why hadn't she and Chester moved to the home or at least sold it to alleviate some of the monetary hardships they faced?

Quimby tapped his chin. "Yes, and if Paulina was to pass away, who would receive the home in New York?"

"Lanie." Antonia lifted her chin. "Paulina and I had fond memories of that home, and Morgan and I hoped to take Lanie there to spend the summers."

"Can you tell the court the property's address?"

Antonia briefly narrowed her eyes at Quimby. "Of course I can. The address for the home in Chicago is 879 North Davis Street. The address for the home in New York is Forty-five East Eighth Avenue."

"Since you and your sister were close, I presume you would be able to ascertain if a signature is hers."

"Yes, I could."

Quimby returned to the table and retrieved a sheet of paper. "Is the address on this document as you testified?"

"Yes, it is."

And is the signature that of Paulina Hallman's?"

"Yes, that is Paulina's signature." Antonia leaned forward, obviously attempting to read more than just the signature. "What is that document?"

"It is a deed."

"A deed?" Mr. Stewart's tone rose several notches. "Surely, if Mr. Quimby has paperwork to be admitted into evidence, he would follow proper procedure."

Murmurs filled the courtroom.

Judge Voetberg hit his gavel on the bench, causing those in the gallery to quiet. "Mr. Quimby?" asked Judge Voetberg.

"Your honor, I did not believe the paperwork would be an issue until Mrs. Thiessen stated that Paulina inherited the house. As such, I am marking the deed to the property in New York as Exhibit A. We offer Exhibit A into evidence."

Judge Voetberg nodded. "Paperwork is admissible and shall be admitted into evidence. Please proceed."

"Thank you, Your Honor. Mrs. Thiessen, what if I was to tell you that the house is no longer Lanie's?"

Antonia sucked in a deep breath. "Whatever do you mean?"

Quimby held up the sheet of paper. "I have it on good authority that Paulina donated the home to an orphanage in New York."

Several gasps filled the room, most notably Antonia's.

Judge Voetberg pounded his gavel. "There will be order in the court."

The audience hushed, and Antonia finally spoke. "I don't understand."

"Apparently your sister had a heart for the less fortunate and determined that the New York Home for Orphans and Foundlings would be a suitable beneficiary of the property."

Mr. Stewart stood. "Your Honor, with all due respect, I do doubt Mr. Quimby's claims."

"Mr. Quimby," the judge asked, "Do you have proof that Mrs. Paulina Hallman donated the home to the orphanage?"

"I do."

"Your Honor," interjected Mr. Stewart, "As Mr. Quimby *surely* knows, all evidence and documentation must be provided beforehand."

"Mr. Quimby?"

Quimby placed the sheet of paper on the bench before Judge Voetberg. "You will find all that you need to know here. In answer to your question, Your Honor, I had no reason to produce the deed of the New York home prior to this time because I had no reason to believe it would be an issue. However, Mrs. Theissen stating on record that Mrs. Paulina Hallman inherited the house, providing the address of the New York house, and verifying Paulina Hallman's signature, allowed me grounds to produce the deed."

Mr. Stewart cleared his throat. "Your Honor..."

"The court finds that the deed to the house in New York and the accompanying paperwork is admissible." Judge Voetberg adjusted the spectacles on his bulbous nose.

Tobias held his breath.

Charlotte leaned forward and squeezed his arm.

And Quimby's former stoic expression boasted a bud of a smile.

"Your Honor," squeaked Antonia. "Perhaps it is best that Lanie be remanded to an orphanage rather than allowed to stay with Mr. Hallman."

Mr. Stewart's panicked gaze settled on Antonia. "Your Honor, may I speak with my client in private for a moment?"

Judge Voetberg allowed a brief recess before reconvening. "I'm about to make my decision. Is there anything else you would like to add, gentlemen?"

"Is it the court's understanding that you no longer wish to adopt the child?" Quimby asked.

Antonia, who had again taken the witness stand, nodded. "We no longer wish to adopt her."

Mr. Stewart asked if he might add some clarification to Antonia's statement. When given the opportunity, he said, "Your Honor, Morgan and Antonia Theissen wish to withdraw their petition to adopt Layna Paulina Hallman."

"Request is granted," said Judge Voetberg.

"Your Honor," said Quimby, "In the Compiled Laws of Wyoming in the Adoption Chapter, Section Nine, it states that if both parents are dead and there are no known relatives of the child, or if the relatives are unwilling to adopt the child, then the county commissioners shall intervene. However, in this case, while Layna Paulina Hallman's parents are both deceased and one relative does not wish to adopt the child, we *do* have a relative who is willing to assume control of the child. That relative is Tobias Hallman. Nothing further, Your Honor."

Quimby returned to the chair beside Tobias.

"Mr. Stewart, do you have anything to say before I make my judgment?"

"Yes, Your Honor." Mr. Stewart stood and faced the gallery. "I would again reiterate that Mr. and Mrs. Theissen are expecting that the minor child, Layna Paulina Hallman, be placed in the best possible home. That best possible care is not with Tobias Hallman. Rather, it would be in an orphanage where an upstanding and perhaps high society family could adopt the child. Yes, there is a living relative. However, I would suggest that asking the commissioners to intervene and inquire as to their thoughts on the matter would be a worthwhile endeavor."

"Will that be all, Mr. Stewart?" the judge asked.

"Yes, Your Honor."

Judge Voetberg nodded. "Very well. It is the opinion of the court, based on the fact that Mr. and Mrs. Thiessen no longer wish to pursue the adoption of Layna Paulina Hallman and have withdrawn their petition, and given that there is, in fact, a relative who does wish to raise the child as his own, the Court recognizes there are no longer two parties wishing to proceed with the adoption of the child. As such, it is the Court's decision that paperwork be filed posthaste for Mr. Tobias Hallman to adopt the child. Further, so as not to disrupt the child's life any further, the Court finds that in the interim, guardianship is awarded to Mr. Tobias Hallman. That will be all."

"Celebration party at our house!" exclaimed Aunt Fern over the loud rejoicing from nearly everyone in the courtroom.

"Everyone is welcome to join us for some delicious huckleberry pie. I also have some leftover huckleberry muffins," chirped Aunt Myrtle.

Aunt Fern addressed the crowd with a confident, "And please, fine folks, don't worry that those are the only offerings."

Antonia approached. Tobias. "May I speak with you for a moment?"

"Yes?"

"I just want you to know that I truly did love Paulina."

Without awaiting his response, Antonia joined Morgan as they left the courtroom.

And Tobias had never ridden his horse as fast as he did the day he retrieved Lanie from the Hitzs' house.

Chapter Twenty-Nine

Tobias returned to town after leaving Lanie at the aunts' house for the day while he was at work. He planned to stop at Stanley's barbershop for a much-needed haircut, but when he arrived, Quimby and Stanley were standing against the counter, their voices hushed in serious conversation.

Stanley looked his way first.

"Hello, Tobias. Here for your haircut and shave?"

"Yes, sir." He greeted Quimby before taking a seat in the chair and taking note of his unkempt appearance in the mirror in front of him. He hadn't slept well last night, allowing his mind to exhaust him with continual concerns. Concerns he ought to have put before the Lord, like how he would provide for Lanie, making the blacksmith shop successful, and proposing to Charlotte and hoping she would trust he wasn't like Cyrus. Then there was loud and rowdy noises from the saloon across the street, unusual for a Thursday night, but someone mentioned some new fellows had ridden into town. A dog howling early in the morning woke him from a slumber that started a mere two hours before it ended.

The dark circles beneath his eyes told of his fatigued state. Good thing he scurried away from the aunts' house this morning before Charlotte could see him. "Definitely need a haircut and a shave." He rubbed his jaw, noting how it grew in unevenly. Ma would have his hide and then some if she saw how he'd allowed his hair to grow longer than he ought, causing one to think he might be a ruffian. Add to that his three-day growth of whiskers and Tobias might as well be on a wanted poster.

"Perhaps we should discuss this matter with the young Tobias," suggested Stanley. His brows pulled together. "After a haircut and shave."

"How are things with Lanie?" Quimby asked, taking a seat in an out-of-place wooden chair with faded brown velvet cushions.

"Going well. It's been a month since the hearing, but I'll be forever thanking God for allowing me the opportunity to raise her. I couldn't have done it without your help, Quimby. And I don't know what I would have done if you hadn't offered to allow me to rent the apartment above this barbershop, Stanley."

Stanley draped a white towel across Tobias's shoulders. "Happy to help," he said. "Although I do know that it can get a mite bit loud at times with the saloon across the street."

"Last night was one of those nights." Tobias rubbed his left eye. "Can't say as I had much shuteye, what with that and a howling dog early this morning."

Quimby chuckled. "Prune Creek may not be a lawless and disorderly town like Poplar Springs, but it does have some moments where things are less than tranquil."

Stanley began to cut Tobias's hair, making the improvement profound even with a few snips. When he finished with the shave, Tobias paid him the discounted haircut and shave price of fifteen cents for the shave and thirty cents for the haircut.

"How about we discuss the matter at the restaurant?" suggested Stanley.

"What matter?" At the mention of eating, Tobias's stomach rumbled.

Stanley chuckled. "Sounds as though someone is prit near starvation."

"The bread and coffee this morning was severely lacking," said Tobias. "I was almost wishing for Mrs. White's unappetizing fare at the boardinghouse."

Quimby grinned. "Are we to understand that you're not a chef?"

Tobias patted his stomach. "Not even close. A man could starve attempting to live on my cooking. At least Lanie eats well-rounded meals at the aunts' house."

Stanley placed a wooden "closed" sign in the window, and Tobias stood and brushed off his trousers. Quimby and Stanley were adept at making him curious. "The matter?" he asked again.

Quimby unfolded himself from the displaced chair. "I hope you have an appetite, Tobias, as I'll be treating us all to the second-best breakfast this side of the Mississippi."

Stanley smirked. "Let me guess. Myrtle cooks the best breakfast."

Tobias wasn't sure he'd seen many men blush, but Quimby's weathered cheeks turned a bright red. "Could be. Tonight can't come soon enough when I again partake in some of Myrtle's homemade huckleberry pie. I'm hoping she'll bake some biscuits too."

Stanley blanched, his wrinkled face turning from a habitual smile to a frown. "You, Myrtle, and Lanie are the only ones who appreciate Myrtle's huckleberry pie and biscuits."

"Or any of her cooking for that matter," added Tobias. He resisted the urge to cringe.

"Myrtle, Lanie, and I wouldn't argue. It leaves more for us."

Stanley opened the door. "More stomachaches, that is." He chuckled. "All of this talk of food is making me overly hungry. What's say we get ourselves some breakfast before they start serving the noonday meal."

A few minutes later, Tobias joined the two men at a table in the corner of the restaurant. While Quimby and Stanley were old enough to be Tobias's grandfathers, he'd grown to appreciate their wisdom, company, and especially their friendship. He recalled something Ma had said once, her sweet and demure voice ringing in his ears as if she'd said it just yesterday. "Sometimes the Good Lord places folks in our lives who become far more than mere friends."

Such was the case with Quimby and Stanley. It was almost as though they truly *were* Tobias's grandfathers or uncles.

Tobias took a drink of coffee after placing his order for the daily special—scrambled eggs and pancakes.

Stanley peered at Tobias through his spectacles. "Have you invited yourself to the aunts' house for supper tonight?"

"Is there supper tonight?"

"There's always supper," said Quimby. "We'll be there."

Tobias didn't worry about inviting himself. Ever since Aunt Fern said he was welcome for supper anytime and Aunt Myrtle had vehemently agreed, Tobias hadn't given it a second thought. He often brought food to assist with feeding everyone, as did Quimby and Stanley.

Back when he and Charlotte were foes, Charlotte once mentioned he possessed a habit of causing a kerfuffle due to his arrival at the aunts' house for supper. He chuckled to himself at the memory. His feelings for her over the past months had certainly changed, and he hoped hers for him had too.

Quimby interrupted Tobias's musings. "We're making plans for a special evening."

"Oh?" Maybe Tobias *shouldn't* invite himself. He didn't want to intrude.

"Do you think Fern cottons to me?" Stanley smoothed his non-existent hair with his hand. "I am handsome, charming, and kindhearted. I've been an elder twice so far at church, I try my best to be thoughtful and generous, and I am the best barber in Prune Creek."

"Yes, you do give good haircuts," added Quimby.

"Yes. Yes, I do, and all for a reasonable price with a discount if someone asks for a shave at the same time." Stanley stared at Tobias, his eyes magnified beneath smudged spectacles. "And I own a nice home. Smaller than Fern is accustomed to with the Peabody house, but nice all the same." He paused. "You don't suppose Fern will be disappointed it's not like the Peabody house, do you?"

Tobias had seen Stanley's house many times on his way to the aunt's home. A tidy cabin at the far end of Main Street, it boasted a small front porch. "I don't think she'll be disappointed with your house. I think she cottons to you, and yes, you're what the womenfolk would say is a 'fine catch'."

Stanley's face and bald head took on a reddish hue. He sat up straighter in his chair, his short stature still no match for Quimby's and Tobias's heights. "I *am* a fine catch. And do you think Myrtle cottons to Quimby?"

Quimby, much more reserved than his best friend, leaned back in his own chair. "I have much to offer a woman like Myrtle. I, too, have been an elder at the church and presently serve as such. I also serve as the Chairman of the Prune Creek Founder's Day Committee. I'm caring, hardworking, intelligent, and I, too, have a nice home."

Quimby's house was similar to the Peabody's home in appearance, although half the size.

"You would be a fine catch for Myrtle. But you two don't have to convince me. It's the aunts you have to convince."

"Well, we aren't as young as we once were." Stanley's gray brows bunched together, causing his bald head to wrinkle.

"No one is as young as they once were," said Quimby. "But it's never too late to find true love."

"True, true." Stanley tapped his fingers on the table. "Do you think they'll say yes?"

Tobias nearly choked on his coffee. "Say yes?"

"The young Tobias here doesn't realize we're about to make the biggest decisions in our lives." Quimby said.

"We're thinking of proposing to the aunts tonight."

Tobias stared at the men across from him. Totally opposite in every sense with Quimby tall, thin, and refined; and Stanley short, slightly round, and witty. Quimby had an overabundance of gray hair, while the only hair on Stanley's head was sideburns and a mustache. "Proposing?" he asked.

"One of the worries that's caused a commotion in my mind is what if Myrtle says yes to Quimby, but Fern says no to me." Stanley turned to face Quimby. "Not that I wouldn't want Myrtle to say yes to you and all, and you are deserving of such a fine woman, but what would I do if Fern says no?"

He took a deep breath. "Reckon I don't want to make a fool of myself."

"You could always pester her until she says yes," teased Tobias. "She didn't like you much at first, but things have changed. Now she speaks with you all the time, and I see the way she smiles when she's around you."

Quimby's eyebrows rose. "It would appear Tobias has been paying close attention to things of a romantic nature."

"No, I just—" Tobias fiddled with the button on his shirt. "I just think you don't have to worry, Stanley. Fern likes you."

"You could ask Charlotte for her hand as well," suggested Quimby.

Tobias felt the heat crawl up his neck. When he proposed to Charlotte, if he ever worked up the gumption to do so, he wanted it to be a special moment just between the two of them. "I...no."

"We're thinking of a double wedding. At least that's what the womenfolk call it," said Stanley. "There's nothing that says it can't be a triple wedding."

"Yes," agreed Quimby. "So what do you think? We've seen the way Charlotte smiles when she's around you."

Stanley chuckled. "That is true."

"I won't be asking Charlotte to marry me tonight. However, I do think you two should ask Myrtle and Fern."

"Hopefully they say yes," Stanley tapped his fingers in a rhythmic pattern on the table.

"Seems you're getting somewhat mushy in your old age," joked Quimby.

And as they sat and chatted and ate breakfast, Tobias reckoned that securing the friendships of Quimby and Stanley was a pure blessing.

Charlotte saw Tobias from her place on the porch as he rode toward the house. She held a hand to her heart, noting how the beat of it increased upon seeing him.

Her growing feelings for him had progressed over time, and now she was sure she loved him.

Did he feel the same?

Surely after knowing him her entire life, she could rest assured he was nothing like Cyrus. And surely she could confidently place her heart in his hands without fear.

"There's Uncle Tobias!"

Charlotte joined Lanie as she dashed down the steps to meet Tobias.

Tobias dismounted and walked toward them. The navy-and-beige plaid shirt he wore accentuated his strong broad shoulders and slim waist. He'd cut his hair and shaved. How had she not truly noticed his rugged handsomeness in all the years of knowing him? Or maybe she had but instead determined his ability to be a dunderhead in those days wasn't worth that second glance.

"Uncle Tobias! Uncle Tobias!" Lanie ran toward him, and he lifted and swung her around, eliciting enthusiastic giggles.

He stopped spinning Lanie and placed her on her feet. His eye caught Charlotte's, and he held her gaze, even while Lanie tapped him on the arm and persisted in her goal to attain his attention. Warmth spread through Charlotte, and she thought she should perhaps turn from him, lest he see the red that surely infused her face.

"Hello, Charlotte."

"Hello, Tobias." Charlotte wondered briefly what it would be like for him to circle his arm around her waist, hold her close, and tell her he missed her.

Such fanciful notions!

She for certain ought to discontinue her loyal reading of the sweet and tender romance novels lining the parlor shelves.

"Uncle Tobias, do you like my dress?"

Tobias averted his attention to Lanie. "I do. You look very pretty."

Lanie curtsied, just as Charlotte had shown her earlier when they pretended to be in the queen's court and prepare for afternoon tea.

Tobias bowed and extended his hand toward her. Lanie took it, and he twirled her.

And Charlotte was reminded again that one of the things she loved about Tobias was his caring heart toward those in his life.

When he finished twirling Lanie, she spoke again. "Aunt Charlotte and me made my dress today with the lovely cow-ico you bought for us. She says my stitching is im-pessive and that I'm going to make a fine seam-stess one day."

"I agree with her. You did a fine job on your dress."

"Yes, and next we will sew Aunt Charlotte's dress so we will match."

Tobias chuckled, causing Charlotte to laugh as well. He took another step toward her. "Thank you for teaching Lanie to sew."

"My pleasure. She is an expedient learner and quite adept at her stitching. I believe someday she'll be as good of a seamstress as..."

"Grandma," announced Lanie.

"Yes, Grandma." Charlotte smiled at her young charge. Everyone who'd ever met Lanie adored her, and Ma was no exception.

Charlotte and Tobias stood facing each other for a moment, neither of them speaking while Lanie prattled on about the other things she and Charlotte had done that day. Mundane chores, really, such as washing and hanging the laundry and the thrill of finding seven ripe tomatoes in the garden. Charlotte's breath hitched. Why was it in times like these, that her mind thought of what it would be like if Tobias were to kiss her?

But goodness, Charlotte! You really have become a giddy and lovelorn buffoon.

She was staring. Definitely staring. She distracted herself by fidgeting with her necklace and shifting her gaze toward the cows in the neighbor's field.

"Thank you," Tobias said, causing her again to meet his eye.

"You're welcome." When it occurred to her she had no idea why he was thanking her, Charlotte squeaked, "Thank you for..."

"For taking care of my niece day after day. For teaching her how to sew and garden and how to be an honorable young lady."

"You're welcome," Charlotte repeated. "It is my pleasure, and Lanie is such a sweetie. I do adore her."

Tobias offered her a crooked smile. "That she is." He extended both elbows. "Well, my ladies, shall we go inside for supper?"

Lanie placed her hand through his left elbow. "We can stay for supper?"

"Yes, we can."

He leaned toward Charlotte as she placed her hand in the crook of his right elbow and whispered, "Did I sound like Ferdinand just then? All proper-like?"

Heat traveled in a slow wave up her cheeks. Goodness, but what was the matter with her? This was Tobias—Tobias Hallman—after all. How many times had she been near him in all these years? Too many to count. She took a deep breath, begging herself to sound somewhat coherent. "Well, Ferdinand is not actually proper-like as he works in the silver mines and has attained limited schooling, but he is a gentleman. So, yes, you are just like Ferdinand in that way."

Tobias smirked. "Am I as dapper?"

"Well..."

"Who's Ferd-nan?" Lanie asked.

"He's a character in a book, and yes, Tobias, you do resemble his gentlemanly ways."

"I reckon I never did ask if the love of his life got away. Didn't he run after her and tell her he loved her?"

Charlotte attempted to ignore the tingling that zipped up her arm as she rested her hand on his brawny forearm. "You would have to read the book to determine the answer."

His crooked grin drew her attention. He was standing so close, their heads mere inches from each other. In the love stories, this was the time the hero asked the heroine if he might kiss her. If only she and Tobias were in the pages of a love story.

"Don't imagine I'll be reading any of your romance novels anytime soon," Tobias finally said, his voice a husky timbre that exuded a mixture of warmth and teasing.

"No, I don't imagine so." Her own voice emerged as a soft squeak that varied in pitch between the five simple words.

Lanie tugged on Tobias's arm. "Come on, Uncle Tobias, the sooner we eat supper, the sooner we can have huckleberry cupcakes."

Disappointment shadowed his face. The same disappointment Charlotte herself felt. She would have not complained an ounce if they stared into each other's eyes late into the evening.

You really must stop swooning, Charlotte. It's unbecoming of a refined lady. Her inner voice chastised her, and she nearly tripped on the first stair onto the porch.

Tobias's quick reflexes allowed him to steady her by wrapping his arm around her. "Watch that step there," he whispered, amusement in the depths of his eyes.

"I, um, yes. There is a step there."

His eyes traveled to her lips then to her eyes, or maybe she just imagined it.

"There you three are," twittered Aunt Myrtle. "We thought perhaps you'd gone to town to eat at the restaurant."

"No, Aunt Myrtle, we would *never* do that," giggled Lanie. "We would miss the huckleberry cupcakes we made today."

The way Aunt Myrtle bunched her mouth to one side and squinted her eyes toward Charlotte almost made Charlotte dissolve into laughter. "We're coming, Aunt Myrtle."

"Seems to me there might be some lollygagging out here between two *certain* individuals. If you continue to dawdle, supper will arrive and depart before you've nary stepped a foot onto the porch."

"We're sorry, Aunt Myrtle. We wouldn't want to miss supper," said Tobias, his voice thick with charm as the three of them strolled up the stairs and into the house.

Tobias took his place at the table at the only place left—between Charlotte and Lanie. Not that he minded. He was struggling this evening to keep his mind on anything *but* Charlotte.

Lanie nearly bounced out of her seat in excitement as she chattered about the huckleberry cupcakes she and Aunt Myrtle made from the fresh berries they'd picked yesterday. There were times when he was taken aback by a facial expression she made, one that was so like Ma's or Chester's. Other times, he could clearly see a strong resemblance to Paulina in his niece's features.

If only they'd lived. Realizing he'd never see his brother or his parents again this side of Heaven was jolting, especially when thoughts of them arrived unannounced.

So far things had progressed well with Tobias caring for Lanie with the exception of his ineptness and her occasional nightmares. Never would such a feat have been possible without the Lord's intervention and Tobias's continual reliance on Charlotte and the aunts.

His awareness of Charlotte sitting next to him—the reminders of how he'd longed to kiss her outside when he'd first arrived, the aroma of her lavender perfume, and how being with her brightened his day consumed his thoughts. Her dainty hands with slender fingers and slim wrists and the way her eyes lit when she smiled captured his attention. He could almost see the way she would twist her mouth to one side when deep in thought.

The shifting of the table drew Tobias from his thoughts and toward Stanley, who had accidentally bumped the table, causing a minute amount of milk to slosh over the side of the pitcher. He stood, adjusted the pitcher, and swiped the spilled milk with a cloth. "Sorry about that," he said, returning to his seat.

It didn't surprise Tobias that Stanley was nervous given he and Quimby planned to ask for the aunts' hands in marriage. Stanley squirmed constantly in his chair, his eyes darting about—when they weren't fixed on Aunt Fern.

He and Quimby couldn't be more opposite in appearance and personalities. But Tobias observed that Quimby was also more riddled with anxiety than Tobias had ever known him to be in the brief amount of time knowing him. Like Stanley, he also wore spectacles, although with much thinner glass, but tonight Quimby consistently adjusted his spectacles and cleared his throat several times in just a few minutes.

Tobias could hardly fault them for their nervousness. He was apprehensive just thinking about asking Charlotte to court him, let alone asking for her hand in marriage. Holding her and kissing her were thoughts that remained in his mind throughout each day. He wanted to pull her to him, to tell her he loved her and had loved her for far longer than he'd realized. Tobias wasn't sure how she felt about him or if she even wanted to take a chance on courting someone after that dolt, Cyrus's, actions.

It amazed him that the woman the Lord might have meant for him was right beside him and had been in his life for all these years.

After everyone settled in place, Quimby offered to bless the food. Lanie grabbed Tobias's hand. "And you hold Aunt Charlotte's," she directed.

Tobias's gaze met Charlotte's, and he hesitated. Did she want to hold his hand even if it was as they prayed? When she smiled at him—a smile that did something weird to his insides—he took that as an affirmation and clasped her smaller hand in his own. Without thinking, he gently caressed her hand with his thumb before thinking better of it and ceasing.

Charlotte's hand felt natural in his, and he wondered what it would be like to hold it often and walk with her along the acreage of their property. To dream of a future together.

Mushy. That's what John Mark and Russell would call him if they were there. They'd also refer to him as an addlepated dunderhead with no hope. Ridiculous. A feebleminded lunkhead.

Tobias inwardly cringed. Romantic notions were for women, not blacksmiths who prided themselves on being manly.

Quimby prayed, and Tobias closed his eyes and dedicated the time to the Lord, agreeing in gratitude for the food and for the makeshift family God had given him. He finished the prayer with his own petition to the Lord for help in raising Lanie and for courage to ask Charlotte for her hand in courtship if that was the Lord's will.

He was sorry when the prayer ended and he had to release Charlotte's hand.

Lanie scarfed her meatloaf and potatoes, and Tobias pondered whether to suggest she slow down a bit, but he changed his mind when he witnessed the joy on her face when Aunt Myrtle brought the huckleberry cupcakes to the table. There would be plenty of time to train her in proper manners.

"Uncle Tobias, would you like a huckleberry cupcake?"

The thought of eating Aunt Myrtle's baking caused something akin to indigestion, but he had no willpower to resist Lanie's expectant pleas.

"Yes, Uncle Tobias, won't you try just one?" Charlotte teased.

"He won't be trying just one," said Aunt Myrtle, who had taken it upon herself to pass out two muffins to each person. "These have all the requirements to be entered in the county fair."

Aunt Fern harrumphed. "Most folks in Prune Creek are wise enough to know that if they value their delicate constitutions, they'll avoid anything baked by one Myrtle Beauchamp."

"You're just jealous, Fern. I've always been the better baker. Remember when Ma would encourage us to bake for the church potlucks? My offerings were always the most well- received."

"Well-received by those who arrived late, were half-starved, and had no other choice but your unpalatable offerings."

Aunt Myrtle's eyes enlarged and she pressed her lips into a slim line. "Well, I never! You know that is absurd and far from the truth."

Instead of apologizing, Aunt Fern laughed, her amusement joined in perfect chorus with Stanley's loyal chuckle.

"I would have to respectfully disagree with you, Fern," said Quimby. He took a bite of one of the cupcakes and closed his eyes. "Myrtle and Lanie, I do believe these are sure to win a blue ribbon."

Lanie squealed. "Can we enter them, Aunt Myrtle?"

"I don't see why not." Aunt Myrtle placed an arm around Lanie.

"I can see why not. The poor folks of Prune Creek deserve long and healthy lives. Who are you to cut those lives short?" Aunt Fern took a bite of the cupcake, presumably so Lanie's feelings wouldn't be hurt, but the expression on her face indicated she'd not be taking a second bite.

Quimby started on his third cupcake. "You're a fine cook, Myrtle."

"And your brains are addled from all of Myrtle's cooking." Aunt Fern shook her head. "But goodness."

Stanley chuckled and looked at Fern with adoration. "You have such a pleasing wit, Fernie."

Aunt Fern puffed up and squared her shoulders. "Yes, I do, don't I?"

"No, you don't," countered Aunt Myrtle. "And 'Fernie'? I thought you didn't cotton to that name."

Charlotte leaned toward Tobias, her whisper tickling his face. "She likely cottons to it *only* when Stanley refers to her by that name."

Tobias laughed. "That's likely the truth."

"Are the cupcakes good, Uncle Tobias?" Lanie asked, oblivious to the meaning of the banter between the aunts.

Tobias took another bite and swallowed the dry, bland dessert, resisting the urge to wash it down with a full pitcher of milk. "I'm proud of you for learning how to bake, Lanie."

Lanie wrapped her arms around his neck and planted a kiss on his cheek. "I can make these for you all the time at our 'partment."

"Perhaps when you are a bit older, I reckon that would be a nice gesture." Hopefully by then, Lanie would have perfected the recipe.

Aunt Myrtle thrust her shoulders back and held her chin high. "Tobias and Charlotte, do tell the story again of how my prized cookies took down a notorious outlaw."

"Pshaw, Myrt," admonished Aunt Fern. "Your cookies only took down a notorious outlaw because they were so hard, rough-textured, and overcooked."

"Well, I never. You are such a disagreeable sort, Fernie."

A broad smile tugged at Stanley's lips. "I don't think you're a disagreeable sort, Fernie."

Aunt Fern fluttered her lashes at Stanley. "Thank you, Stan."

When they finished eating and Tobias had choked down the tasteless cupcakes, Quimby announced he and Myrtle would be taking a stroll.

"And we're going to relax on the porch," said Stanley, pulling out Aunt Fern's chair and assisting her as she stood.

Charlotte stacked a few plates. "We'll clear the dishes."

A few minutes later after Tobias, Charlotte, and Lanie had cleaned the table, Tobias witnessed Stanley on one knee on the porch. "Charlotte, look!"

Charlotte followed the direction he pointed. "Oh! I hope she says yes!"

Charlotte placed the extra chair in the parlor and peered out of the west window. "Tobias!"

He was instantly at her side just in time to witness Quimby on one knee proposing to Aunt Myrtle.

"I wonder if they're going to have a double wedding. Wouldn't it be a remarkable notion that the aunts would marry on the same day after waiting all these years for their true loves?" She did her best not to swoon, but the musings about a wedding with Aunt Myrtle and Aunt Fern as brides warmed her heart. Especially Aunt Fern, who vowed never to fall in love again after Mr. Wilkins broke her heart.

Tobias chuckled. "Yes, it would be."

"The aunts are going to get married?" Lanie sidled up alongside Charlotte, her eyes doubling in size.

"Maybe so." Charlotte stooped to Lanie's height. "Wouldn't that be magnificent?"

A crease formed in Lanie's brow. "Will Grandpa Solomon marry them?"

"Wouldn't it be marvelous to have him and Grandma and all of your cousins attend the wedding?"

"Yes!" Lanie clapped her hands together. "All my girl cousins and even my boy cousin, Ambrose."

"And Ambrose might even have a baby brother or sister by that time."

Lanie scrunched her nose. "Like Baby Evangeline?"

"Yes."

Charlotte folded Lanie into a hug and held the little girl close. A bond had developed between them, and for the first time, Charlotte realized just how much Ma loved her because that was the way she felt about Lanie, even though she wasn't her mother.

When she released Lanie, Charlotte stood and nearly bumped into Tobias.

"Oh! Sorry." She took a step back, and he reached for her hand.

What if Tobias proposed to her like Stanley and Quimby had to the aunts? What if her one true love was standing before her? The one God meant for her all this time, but for years she'd been too blind to realize? Her breath hitched.

Tobias cupped her chin with his hand. Would he kiss her? Declare his love like Ferdinand had in Charlotte's favorite novel? Ask for her courtship? Or immediately ask to marry her?

"Are you going to sleep already, Aunt Charlotte?" Lanie's voice interrupted the moment, and Charlotte's eyes fluttered open. She stared deep into Tobias's eyes, a twirl of excitement settling in her stomach.

"Thank you," he said.

Not the words she was expecting.

"I know I already said it, but thank you for caring for Lanie and for being there for her."

"Oh, well, yes, you're welcome." Would Tobias now ask if Charlotte would aid him in raising Lanie after they married?

Tobias leaned closer. "I love it when you twist your mouth to one side like that when you're in deep thought."

"I do that?"

"Yes, you do."

The sound of the door opening regrettably drew them apart. "You'll never guess what just happened!" Aunt Fern stood just inside the doorway, her arm linked through Stanley's.

Stanley's grin covered the entire expanse of his face. "She said yes. My Fernie said yes."

Aunt Fern tossed him an adoring glance. "Of course I said yes, Stanley Gormon. How could I say anything else?"

Charlotte rushed toward them. "We are so happy for you!" She hugged a beaming Aunt Fern.

"Yes, well, I always knew Stanley was a good man."

Stanley placed a kiss on Aunt Fern's flushed cheek. "I always did know you'd take a liking to me."

Aunt Myrtle and Quimby entered the house a few moments later, Aunt Myrtle's contagious laughter ringing throughout the house as they emerged into the kitchen. "You'll never believe what Quimby just asked me."

Quimby winked at Tobias. "She said yes."

"Quimby just proposed to you?" Aunt Fern's eyes rounded beneath her spectacles.

"He did, and I, without even the slightest bit of hesitation, affirmed that marriage to him was something I would wholeheartedly consent to."

Quimby leaned toward Stanley and whispered loud enough for all to hear, "Glad you found the courage to ask her. I wasn't sure you'd carry through on our plan."

"Oh, I carried through with our plan, all right," Stanley whispered back.

"And?"

Aunt Fern placed a hand on her ample hip. "But goodness. I'm standing right here, Quimby. Stan did ask for my hand in marriage, and I accepted his offer without even a hint of reservation."

Charlotte hugged Aunt Myrtle and congratulated her, and Lanie dashed forward for her own hug from the aunts. "Is Grandpa Solomon going to marry you?" she asked.

"Wouldn't that just be the most ironic thing?" Aunt Fern shook her head. "The dear man whom Myrtle nearly caused to meet his early demise with her huckleberry pie all those years ago in Willow Falls would be the very one who would marry us."

"He's a dear man, but I did not nearly cause his demise. You're just jealous because I was the first to discover he was the one true love for our Lydie."

That caused a discussion between the aunts before Quimby cleared his throat and interrupted their bickering. "Stanley and I were discussing this matter, and we'd like to suggest a double wedding."

Aunt Fern and Aunt Myrtle exchanged a hug. "I'm all right with that if you are, Myrtle."

"I'm more than fine with it, Fern."

And as Charlotte observed the joy on the faces of her dear aunts, she knew without a doubt that only the Lord could have orchestrated such a happy ending for two of her favorite people.

CHAPTER THIRTY

CHARLOTTE FINISHED STIRRING THE pancake batter and wiped her hands on her apron before removing it and hanging it on the hook in the kitchen. "I'll be back soon," she said, pressing the wrinkles from her skirt.

Aunt Myrtle peered up from her sewing. "We'll start breakfast in about a half hour to give you time to return."

Aunt Fern folded the laundry from yesterday's wash. "Thank you for preparing the pancake batter, Charlotte. That prevents anyone from developing a gastrointestinal illness from Myrtle adding the ingredients."

"When the Good Lord was handing out senses of humor, He must have skipped plumb over you, Fern," said Aunt Myrtle.

Aunt Fern shrugged, then eyed Charlotte. "My, but doesn't Charlotte look like me when I was younger?"

Charlotte inhaled a sharp breath. She'd been told she favored the Eliason side rather than the Beauchamp side. Surely Aunt Fern's eyesight was failing.

Aunt Myrtle rose and peered at Charlotte as if to inspect every detail of her face. "I don't agree with you often, Fern, but I do agree this time. Charlotte does resemble you." Aunt Myrtle lifted her chin. "And I shall try, though it be difficult, not to be envious."

"Well, my beloved aunts," Charlotte said, attempting not to allow her dismay to show, "I best be on my way."

The crisp morning air, indicative of fall soon arriving, caused Charlotte to tug the wrap around her shoulders as she hurried to town. During this time of year, the mornings lent a chill in the air, while by the afternoon, temperatures soared to a comfortable warmth.

Time passed since the blessing of Judge Voetberg's ruling for Tobias to adopt Lanie. Every day Charlotte thanked the Lord for answering her prayers for the precious orphan girl.

Several minutes later, she waited outside the apartment above Stanley's barbershop to retrieve Lanie. Usually, Tobias would bring her to the aunts' house, but today Charlotte needed to tend to errands in town.

"Aunt Charlotte!" Lanie flung herself into Charlotte's arms.

"I have some errands to tend to and thought you'd like to join me."

"Yes!"

Tobias stood near Charlotte. She inhaled the pleasing smell of soap and noticed how dapper he looked in his tan plaid shirt.

Lanie tapped Tobias on the arm. "I don't have to go back to those people's house, do I?"

Charlotte heard Lanie's pleas about never returning to the Thiessens every day when Tobias left for work. It broke her heart that the young girl had endured additional heartache at the hands of her relatives.

"No, you don't ever have to go back." Tobias answered patiently as he did each time she asked. He lifted Lanie into his arms. "I love you, Lanie, and I will see you this evening for supper at the aunts' house."

Lanie placed a kiss on Tobias's cheek. "I love you too, Uncle Tobias. You're my favoritist uncle, and tonight we are going to have some of that scumpcous dandelion jam me and Aunt Fern made."

"I look forward to it, especially if my favorite niece helped prepare it." He set Lanie on the ground and twirled her once before facing Charlotte. He lifted a finger and stroked her cheek.

Her breath caught, and she wished they weren't on the boardwalk in the middle of Prune Creek. Perhaps then, he would ask to court her. He took a step towards her, and she again wondered what it would be like for him to kiss her. To bid her farewell until he arrived home after work to *their* home. To plan a future with him as his wife. To raise Lanie together.

Such romantic notions best belonged in the pages of novels rather than in real life, and Charlotte aimlessly picked at a seam on her skirt to avoid Tobias seeing the flush she knew surely infused her cheeks.

"See you tonight," he said.

"Yes, I'll see you tonight."

She and Lanie proceeded first to the post office where a letter from Ma awaited her. Charlotte held the envelope to her chest, a twinge of homesickness settling although less so in recent weeks. Perhaps Prune Creek would become her permanent home.

"Who's it from?" Lanie asked, interrupting Charlotte's introspections.

"It's from Grandma."

"Will you read it to me?"

Charlotte tore the seal and removed the letter, her mother's flowing handwriting leaping from the page.

My Dearest Charlotte,

I hope this finds you doing well. How are the aunts? Lanie? And dare I ask how Tobias is doing?

We are doing well. Pa has begun to use his cane less and less. He's back to his healthy self and is again preaching every Sunday. The girls are growing like weeds, and Baby Evangeline has added words to her vocabulary.

We were thrilled to receive your letter with the delightful news of the aunts' upcoming nuptials. Of course Pa would love to marry them, and we would be ecstatic to have the wedding here in Willow Falls next spring. Who would have thought the aunts would have found true love? But as they say, you're never too old to find the one God has planned for you.

Please do write and tell us how you fare. We miss you so.

With much love,

Ma

"The girls are growing like weeds?" Lanie asked, her brow furrowed.

"It means they're growing fast. Grandma would be amazed to see how you've grown these past weeks."

Lanie stood on her tiptoes, although it didn't add much height to her petite frame. "When I grow up to be a woman, I'm going to be just like Grandma, and I'm going to bake tasty treats like Aunt Myrtle."

Charlotte giggled at Lanie's declaration, and they walked to the mercantile to deliver the eggs. Charlotte chatted with Judith while Lanie perused the candies and fabrics.

"Aunt Charlotte, aren't these ribbons pretty?" Lanie held up a purple ribbon.

"Oh, my, yes. Those are beautiful."

Lanie ran her finger along it, her blonde brows knitted together. "Aunt Charlotte?"

"Yes?"

"Can we get a ribbon?"

There was scarcely enough money for necessities, let alone frivolities, but Lanie's expression caused Charlotte to strategize a way to purchase the ribbon nonetheless.

"If we got one of these ribbons," continued Lanie, "could you braid my hair and put it in the end like Ma used to do?"

Charlotte choked back the emotion close to the surface. Lanie wanted her to braid her hair? "I would be honored to braid your hair."

"And can we put these purple ribbons in my braids?"

Charlotte again peered at the price. Surely just this once she could use some of the egg money for such an important purchase. "Yes, I think that would be delightful."

Lanie jumped up and down. "Thank you, Aunt Charlotte!"

Judith whispered to Charlotte, "Did you know we are having a sale today on ribbons? If you buy one, you get the second one for free."

"Oh, Judith, you don't have to do that."

"Consider it a gift."

Charlotte peered into the face of the woman who exhibited kindness so often to those around her. "Thank you, Judith."

Yes, the town of Prune Creek was definitely beginning to feel like home.

Tobias finished a project for a customer and wiped the sweat from his brow. Blacksmithing was hard work, but he wouldn't have it any other way. He peered around the blacksmith shop at the stone fireplace, the projects in various forms of completion, the horse shoes, the axe he'd just sharpened, and his numerous tools including tongs, a vise, anvil, shovels, knives, and pokers. When the option to purchase the business became available, Tobias wasn't sure he could afford the mortgage and wasn't sure he could continue the tradition of running it successfully as the former owner had. Yes, it would be years before the loan was paid in full, and if commerce waned, such a feat would be a challenge.

But he'd vowed to build his life on the hard work of the blacksmithing profession. He was content here. Grateful to the Lord for His Providence and the wisdom to create, forge, and be a contributing member to the town. Grateful the Lord saw fit to allow him to raise Lanie.

Charlotte's image flitted through his mind. He planned to ask for her hand in marriage soon. Would she accept? Would she want to move back to Willow Falls? If so, he'd sell the shop and work for the blacksmith there. While that wasn't his first choice—he'd much rather stay in Prune Creek and be his own boss—Tobias would do just about anything for the woman he had grown to love.

CHAPTER THIRTY-ONE

CHARLOTTE LOOKED FORWARD TO Tobias's arrival each evening for supper. She'd grown accustomed to his presence and had long lost her heart to him.

He dismounted and strode toward her, a grin on his face.

"Special delivery for Miss Charlotte Eliason." He handed her a letter.

"Thank you."

Charlotte could barely contain herself as she swiftly tore open the envelope from Hannah. Could it be the news she longed to hear? Her hands shook as she unfolded the letter.

Dearest Charlotte,

John Mark and I are excited to share the news that you are again an aunt! We are thrilled to add Russell John Mark Eliason to the family. Everyone has taken to calling him "Little Russell". I, of course, am biased, but I do believe he is the most beautiful baby I have ever seen. I can't wait for you to meet him. He has John Mark's hazel eyes, and Ambrose says he has his ears. I'm so grateful that Lydie was here with me and will stay for another week until we are settled.

How are things in Prune Creek? How are the aunts? How are Lanie and Tobias?

Do take care and write soon.

With love,
Hannah

Charlotte held the letter to her heart. Hannah had become so much more to her than a friend. She'd become a sister, just as Annie had. The entire family embraced Hannah and Ambrose as their own, and now Charlotte couldn't imagine life without them.

And to think that Charlotte was an aunt again! If only they lived nearby. She offered a prayer thanking the Lord for Little Russell's safe arrival.

"Is it good news?"

Charlotte returned to the present. Being John Mark's friend, Tobias would want to know about the baby as well.

"Yes. Hannah and John Mark had their baby!"

"They did?" Both corners of his mouth lifted.

"A little boy, and they named him Russell John Mark Eliason."

A flash of sadness again crossed his face. "That's an apt name for him." He paused. "Well, I'll be. I still can't believe John Mark is a pa again." He rubbed the back of his neck. "Just yesterday we were..."

"Making nuisances of yourselves?"

"Something like that." He cleared his throat. "And Hannah? She's doing well?"

Charlotte nodded. "She is. Honestly, Tobias, I can't wait to see them all again."

Charlotte assisted the aunts with clearing the table after supper then stepped onto the porch. She ambled toward the railing and peered into the distance. The leaves were beginning to change, a sure sign autumn would arrive soon. She needed to make a decision about whether to stay in Prune Creek or return to Willow Falls before snowstorms precluded easy travel.

The decision was both complicated and difficult.

The door squeaked, and she turned to see Tobias. "Care for some company?" he asked.

He wore a blue and gray plaid shirt that accentuated his broad shoulders, and his thick ruffled hair, warm eyes, and handsome smirk drew her in.

Charlotte attempted not to stare.

"I—yes, I would like some company."

He started toward her, then pivoted back to the door. "I'll be right back."

Tobias reentered the house, and Charlotte noticed through the front window him speaking with Aunt Myrtle. She nodded and gestured with her hand as if shooing him away. He chuckled in response.

Charlotte redirected her attention toward the barn just as Tobias reemerged.

"Were you spying on me, Charlotte Eliason?" One side of his mouth turned upward, and his eyes lit.

"I most certainly was not, Tobias Hallman."

Tobias chuckled again. "Would you care then, Miss Elia-son, to join me in an after-supper stroll?"

Charlotte found it ever more difficult to resist his charismatic charm. He offered his elbow, and she placed her hand through it, noting the warming shiver caused by his closeness.

They started toward the western edge of the property, past the fence, the garden area, and the barn. "Nice night for a stroll," Tobias said as they edged their way down the road.

"Yes, it is." Why was she suddenly so nervous around him?

"You look so beautiful tonight."

"Thank you," she squeaked. From his close proximity, she was aware of the woodsy fragrance of the soap he used and the deep golden brown of his eyes with a dispersion of yellow flecks. Eyes that gazed deep into her soul.

His perusal of her traveled from her eyes to her mouth. Charlotte involuntarily closed her own eyes for the briefest of seconds. When she opened them again, Tobias leaned toward her. "Charlotte?"

"Yes?"

"May I kiss you?

She nodded and was about to answer when his lips claimed hers. His arms circled her waist and drew her to him, and Charlotte's legs threatened to buckle beneath her in response. She clasped her arms around his neck, a twirl of excitement in her middle. Whatever she envisioned it to be like being kissed by Tobias Hallman, this far surpassed anything she could have imagined.

The kiss ended all too soon, and Tobias gently released her. He studied her for a moment, his eyes searching hers.

Would he kiss her again?

Ask her to court him?

Tobias blew out a deep breath. "I know Cyrus broke your heart. I know he was unfaithful and wasn't the man he claimed to be."

Charlotte did *not* wish to think of Cyrus at this moment. Not after that exhilarating kiss.

She recoiled in distaste. "Why are we talking about Cyrus?"

"I just want you to know I'm nothing like Cyrus."

Charlotte shook her head. "I know you're nothing like Cyrus."

"And I know he broke your heart and that you don't want to ever trust someone again. And I know I can be a dolt sometimes."

Charlotte nodded mutely, still holding her breath. Had the air gotten thinner?

"You don't have to agree with me." He smirked.

"I—well..."

He directed his attention toward the mountains to their left before returning his attention to her. "Do you remember Ferdinand?"

"Ferdinand?"

"Yes, your hero in the book you've read twelve thousand times."

"Oh, yes. That Ferdinand. Yes—I remember him." The composed Charlotte would tell him she *hadn't* read the book twelve thousand times, but rather a mere four, five once she finished it this most recent time. But she wasn't the composed Charlotte. Instead, she found herself somewhat flustered. "I—I remember Ferdinand." Why was it she sounded like a blundering fool?

The self-assured Charlotte would not be stuttering all over herself like a muddleheaded and befuddled buffoon.

But at this moment, Tobias standing so close and her mind still reeling from the kiss, she was hardly composed.

The glint in Tobias's eyes told her he was enjoying her nincompoopish behavior.

Nincompoopish?

"I—pray tell, what does Ferdinand have to do with our conversation?" There, that sentence resembled a somewhat coherent thought.

"Weren't you worried that Ferdinand would allow his one true love to get away?"

She narrowed her eyes at him. "Yes."

"And weren't you wanting the handsome and heroic Ferdy to run after the stagecoach?"

"Ferdy? Yes, he needed to run after the stagecoach and let his true love know he loved her and not allow her to ride back to Topeka. Not when he loved her with all his heart."

"You always were one for swooning, Charlotte."

She enjoyed their bantering back and forth. "You wouldn't understand."

"Perhaps not. I'm not accustomed to such drivel."

Silence between them ensued. Only the sound of a horse neighing nearby, a bird chirping, and the faint strains of Lanie's giggles could be heard. He reached toward her and tenderly stroked her cheek with his finger. Affection glowed in his eyes.

"Charlotte, will you court me?"

"Yes," she breathed.

"Yes?" he asked, uncertainty in the depths of his gaze.

Her breath hitched. "Yes, Tobias, I will court you."

He stole another kiss, and Charlotte melted into his arms, wondering if he had, in fact, really asked her or if it had been her imagination. "I intend for this courtship to someday lead to marriage."

She nodded mutely in agreement.

"I'll ask your parents for their blessing, and Caleb, too."

"And John Mark?"

"Already asked him." He paused, his eyes searching hers. "If you want, I will sell the shop and we can move back to Willow Falls."

"Willow Falls?"

"I know you miss your family."

"I do. But we can stay here and visit Willow Falls often. I wouldn't ask you to sell your shop. Not after finally being able to fulfill that dream."

Tobias again pulled her closer to him, and she basked in his nearness, hoping he'd hold her in his arms a while longer.

He kissed the top of her head. "Are you sure? Because I could probably work for the blacksmith in Willow Falls."

"I'm sure. I would like to visit my family often if you're amenable, and Lanie can grow up knowing her cousins."

"I'm amenable to that. You're sure you want to stay here?"

Charlotte reached up and traced the scar on the left side of his chin. "Prune Creek with regular visits to Willow Falls would be, as they say, the best of both."

His expression was something Charlotte would remember for all her years.

The train ride to Nelsonville had been uneventful. The Driessen-Evers Railway Company hired an agent, and with the exception of Charlotte clutching his arm on the trestles, the time was peaceful. Lanie, of course, once again saw it as an adventure.

Tobias looked forward to retrieving the remainder of Chester's tools, but more than that, he was anxious to seek Reverend Solomon's blessing.

They arrived in Willow Falls in time for supper, but Tobias found it difficult to eat despite his hunger. While he'd known Reverend Solomon for most of his life, the thought of asking for his blessing to marry Charlotte brought about a whole new set of nerves.

When he entered the barn, the reverend was mucking the stalls. Tobias reached for a rake and assisted him, and the two worked in silent tandem for a few minutes. Tobias noticed Reverend Solomon looked far better than he had the last time he'd seen him. It was reassuring to see that his strength had returned and he no longer had a limp.

"Thank you for the help, Tobias." Reverend Solomon leaned his rake against the barn wall. "How is Lanie?" He took a seat on the wooden bench and invited Tobias to take a seat next to him.

That was something Tobias appreciated greatly about Reverend Solomon. He made one feel comfortable discussing other matters before specifically asking about the topic at hand.

"She's doing much better, but it'll take time."

"Losing her parents, then nearly losing you and having to live with Morgan and Antonia..." Reverend Solomon shook his head. "There have been many answered prayers for her, but she's been through a lot. I take it Morgan and Antonia left Prune Creek?"

"And Wyoming. It's a relief. Lanie still carries some wounds."

"And she will." Reverend Solomon appeared thoughtful. "Just remember in times of doubt, you are the one the Lord chose to raise her. He orchestrated it all, even during those times of grief and times of not knowing what the court's decision would be."

"Thank you, sir."

They sat in silence for a few minutes while Tobias attempted to find the courage to ask his question. He took a deep breath. "Reverend?"

"Yes?"

"May I have your blessing to marry Charlotte?"

Reverend Solomon's eyes crinkled at the corners. "What took you so long, son?"

"I—well, we were foes."

"Funny how God has a way of working things like that out."

Tobias squirmed on the bench. "I promise to love her, take care of her, and to try not to annoy her too much. I will provide for her and bring her to Willow Falls as often as possible to visit."

Reverend Solomon placed a hand on Tobias's shoulder. He closed his eyes for a minute, likely to pray, then spoke the words Tobias had hoped he'd speak. "Lydie and I were wondering when you might ask. You have our blessing, Tobias. You've been like family all these years, so we might as well make it official."

The barn door squeaked, and Caleb entered. "Hey, Pa?"

"Come on in, Caleb. Tobias and I were just talking."

Caleb extended a hand. "Hey, Tobias. Good to see you. What brings you to Willow Falls?"

Tobias figured he might as well seek Caleb's blessing as well. "I—uh—just asking for your pa's blessing to marry Charlotte."

Caleb's eyes bugged. "Reckoned you were fond of her with the way you always pestered her." He clapped Tobias on the back. "It's about time you asked her."

"I have John Mark's blessing. Do I have yours?"

"You do promise to love her and take care of her?"

"I do."

"And bring her to Willow Falls often for visits?"

Tobias hadn't received this much interrogation from Reverend Solomon. "I aim to, yes."

"All right, then. Yes, you have my blessing. Welcome to the family."

Tobias wiped his damp palms on his trouser pants. Did most men experience such apprehension when asking for a blessing to marry one's daughter and sister? He emerged from the barn to see Charlotte standing near the porch visiting with Lydie and Annie.

Would he be worthy of her? Would he make a suitable husband? Would he care for her properly as a husband ought? Be the husband God commanded he be?

She turned then, her gaze connecting with his. She started toward him, wisps of her beautiful blonde hair blowing in the breeze. He admired her lovely face, her slender form, and her vibrant personality. "Did you and Pa have a nice talk?" she asked.

"We did."

"Is everything all right?"

"It is."

They stood facing each other when the thought occurred to Tobias that he might as well ask her right now. Get the nerve-wracking part of it over with.

He kneeled on one knee and heard her sharp inhalation of breath. "Charlotte Lydie Eliason, will you marry me?"

"Yes, Tobias Edgar Hallman, I will marry you."

Tobias leaped to his feet, and in an efficient movement, he swooped her into his arms and swung her around.

After several seconds, Tobias teetered, dizziness setting in. He stopped spinning, but continued to hold her in his arms, his attention never leaving her. "You did say yes, right?"

Charlotte leaned her head back and giggled. "Yes, I did."

"And I promise on my honor that I will do my best not to be too vexatious. I won't tie your braids together, throw your doll in the pond, or allow snakes into our home. I won't hurt you like Cyrus did. I will love you forever."

EPILOGUE
ONE YEAR LATER

CHARLOTTE SAT ON THE upturned log, the baby swaddled in blankets in her arms. "Do you think the girls will be all right?" she asked.

"They'll be fine. We'll only be a few yards away, you'll be able to see them the entire time, and after I take my beautiful bride for a skate, I'll take Lanie on the ice."

Charlotte attempted to dismiss her concerns when she saw the hopefulness and expectation in her husband's expression. He was right. They wouldn't be far from the edge, and she'd looked forward to this moment since last year when they'd skated on the pond not far from the aunts' home—now their home. When Aunt Myrtle married Quimby, and Aunt Fern married Stanley, they moved into the homes of their respective husbands. Never in her wildest dreams did Charlotte think she and Tobias would live in the former Peabody house.

Baby Rebecca cooed as Charlotte set her in the baby cradle on the ground a safe distance from the edge of the pond. Lanie perched on an upturned log, joy written on her face.

"Remember, Lanie, we are just a few steps away and won't be long."

Lanie nodded, her blonde hair covered in a warm woolen hat Ma had made for her birthday. "Don't worry about Baby Rebecca, Mama. I'll tell her some stories."

"I think we have a future writer in our midst," Tobias said.

"And Bunny here will protect us." Lanie patted their golden retriever who wore the new pink scarf Aunt Fern had knitted for her. Bunny's soulful brown eyes and gentle personality helped her easily become a well-loved member of the Hallman family.

Charlotte kissed Baby Rebecca on her chubby cheeks, eliciting a baby giggle, and tucked the quilt more closely around her. She then planted a kiss on Lanie's forehead. "Thank you for assisting with your sister while Papa and I skate."

Lanie's eyes lit. "Will you do spins and twirls?"

"I think we can manage a few of those," Tobias winked at Charlotte. "We're experts when it comes to the ice."

"And then you'll teach me how to do spins and twirls," Lanie said, her adoring gaze on the man who had, in the past year, become a second father to her.

Tobias nodded. "Yes, and then you and I will skate."

Charlotte settled on the edge of a smooth rock to put on her ice skates. Tobias plunked down beside her, his irresistible grin and reassurances calming her new-mother-worries. She knew they had only a short time before Rebecca, who had a voracious appetite, would soon be hungry again. Charlotte's heart warmed. She'd always wanted to be a wife and mother, and the Lord had blessed her richly with their little family.

Four feet away, Lanie was talking to her younger sister, her voice sweet and calm. "And when you get older, you can ice skate too, Baby Rebecca. And wait until you see what I made you for Christmas. You will love it."

Baby Rebecca cooed, and Lanie leaned over and kissed her cherubic cheek. "That's right, little sister. I can't wait for you to be older. Then you can meet all the people who love you. Mama says there are lots and lots of people who love us."

Charlotte's eyes misted. Lanie had come so far in the past year. While the heartbreak of losing her first parents would always remain, Charlotte and Tobias endeavored, with the help of the Lord, to give her a loving and full life as their adopted daughter.

Tobias brushed her lips with his. "What could be better than being here with my girls?"

How had Charlotte become so blessed?

"Do you know who loves you?" Lanie was asking, her voice enthusiastic. "I will tell you a story about everyone who loves you. I think I love you the mostest and also Mama and Papa and Grandma and Grandpa. Aunt Myrtle and Uncle Quimby and Aunt Fern and Uncle Stanley, they love you too. And Aunt Annie and Uncle Caleb, and Lena, Lola, Esther, and Baby Evangeline, although she's not really a baby anymore. And Uncle John Mark and Aunt Hannah and Ambrose and Little Russell." Without so much as a breath, Lanie continued. "And pretty soon, you'll be able to walk around. I have to tell you a secret about our cousin, Ambrose. He's a boy. And he always thinks he needs to be a sheriff when we play. I think boys are nuisances, and Ambrose is plenty ornery, but you'll like him just the same. Our friends Poppi and Freddy also live in Willow Falls where Grandma and

Grandpa and our girl cousins live. They always share their candy whenever we are there."

Tobias reached a gloved hand toward Charlotte's. "Are you ready to ice skate?" he asked.

Charlotte brushed aside a tear that slid down her face with her free hand and stood on spindly blades, her other hand warm in his. They made their way to the ice, their skating abilities nearly as natural as breathing. For years, Charlotte had skated on the pond on her parents' property in Willow Falls. Tobias and many of their other classmates had joined in the fun with Ma providing cups of hot chocolate after the skating.

And now, when they finished, a pitcher awaited them in the sleigh they'd borrowed from Quimby. Charlotte anticipated all of the traditions she and Tobias would share with their own family.

It wasn't long before Tobias twirled her around on the ice. They then skated, him going backwards, her going forward, both of her hands in his. "I love you, Tobias Hallman."

"I love you, Charlotte Hallman."

He captured her in his arms then and pulled her to him, their balance on the ice impeccable. His lips found hers as he held her warmly in his embrace.

And as they took a brief intermission before a second kiss, Charlotte glanced at their daughters on the banks of the pond, then back at her husband.

Tears of joy blurred her vision. Though she'd once thought Tobias an onerous pest, and despite the former heartbreak caused by Cyrus, the past year proved love would come only in God's timing. And His timing was certainly best.

READ A SNEAK PEEK FROM

Love's Promise

WYOMING SUNRISE
BOOK 4

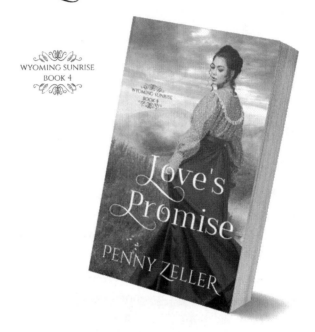

CAN ONE MAN'S LOVE WIN A FRAGILE WOMAN'S HEART?

Coming March 2024

LOVE'S PROMISE

SNEAK PEAK

"GOOD MORNING, GRANDMAMA. HOW is Mr. Alvarado today?" Silas asked as he set a variety of purchases on the counter at the mercantile.

Grandmama peered at something in the distance before answering. "As well as can be expected, I suppose. I'll be glad when Amaya arrives in Poplar Springs. She and her grandfather are close, and I wouldn't want him to pass before she can say goodbye."

"I'm sorry to hear he's not doing well, ma'am. Has Doc given any indication that Mr. Alvarado will recover?"

"He's just not sure. But we keep praying. The Lord is faithful." Grandmama closed her eyes, perhaps to pray once again for her ailing husband.

Silas prayed as well. He had come to know the couple reasonably well in his short time in Poplar Springs and had grown fond of them. He recalled recently when Mrs. Alvarado asked him to refer to her as "Grandmama". Silas had tamped down the emotion that threatened on that day. He'd had to remind himself that referring to her as "Grandmama" as she requested did not take away from precious Oma and what she'd meant to him. Between her expectant gaze and the empty void she'd filled in his life, he'd agreed to Mrs. Alvarado's appeal.

Grandmama's eyes flung open then. "I almost forgot to ask. Would you...could you..."

"Yes?"

"I know this is a lot to ask and you are busy with spring chores on your ranch and helping the sheriff when necessary, but..." Twin lines formed on Grandmama's forehead. "Might you be willing to ride halfway toward Bowman and make sure Amaya's stagecoach arrives safely? Deputy Eliason said there's been an increase in stagecoach robberies."

"Say no more, Grandmama. I will be happy to oblige. When are you expecting the stage to arrive?"

"It leaves Bowman tomorrow morning at 9:00 a.m." She reached over the counter and pinched Silas's cheek. "You're a sweet boy, Silas McFadden."

The endearment reminded him so much of Oma. He swallowed the lump in his throat and focused on the present.

"Thank you," he said. Grandmama needn't know he'd not always been the "sweet boy" she surmised him to be.

Grandmama raised her chin. "Now, I insist you allow me to pay you for your time, or at the very least apply a credit to your account."

"And I insist, Grandmama..."

"Ah, no." She shook her head.

Silas chuckled at the woman's stubbornness. She was all of five feet tall, but a lot of spunk was wrapped in that small package. He briefly wondered if her husband had ever won a disagreement. "The payment I would most like is some of your delicious gateau Basque."

The woman put her hands on her hips. "I was about to argue, but then I remembered how much you love the homemade blackberry-filled tarts."

"Indeed I do."

"All right, then, Silas, it is a deal. Your parents raised a stubborn young man, but alas, whom am I to argue with someone who's doing me a much-needed favor?"

If only Grandmama knew that his parents had nothing to do with his upbringing.

"Thank you for agreeing to see that the stagecoach arrives in Poplar Springs safely. We do not want anything to happen to Amaya and she's been through so much with having lost Russell. Have you met her?"

Silas shook his head. He'd regrettably been out of town on the day of Russell's funeral. "No, ma'am, I haven't."

Silas loaded his pack and gave instructions to his hired hand. Assured his growing ranch was in good hands, he mounted his horse. A ride through the beauty of God's Creation that stretched all the way from Bowman to Willow Falls on the other side and Prune Creek over the mountain was something he never tired of.

After about an hour of riding, Silas eyed the horizon.

Shouldn't he have met up with the stagecoach by now?

The hot Wyoming sun beat down on him, and sweat trickled down his back. He stopped his horse, removed his hat, and wiped the moisture from his forehead. Silas had long ago learned to listen to the sounds around him and to have complete awareness of the ongoings nearby.

Two crows bickered from a nearby tree, their obnoxious calls disturbing the otherwise quiet surroundings. Silas dismounted and placed an ear to the ground.

Nothing.

He scanned the area ahead of him, behind him, and on either side. Too many stagecoaches had fallen into the hands of nefarious outlaws. And while travel by rail replaced much of the need for the stagecoach line, places such as Poplar Springs still waited for spurs to be completed, rendering stagecoach travel a necessity.

Prairie grasses waved in the breeze, and to his right, timbered hills melded into majestic mountains, their tips still covered with snow. Snow that would likely remain throughout the year while the valley below experienced a toss between pleasant and hot summer temperatures.

Silas raked his fingers through his hair. Perhaps the stage had been delayed from its departure in Bowman. If so, concern wouldn't yet be warranted. Or maybe Grandmama mistook the time of its arrival to Poplar Springs. Or maybe Silas harbored a cynical outlook when it came to opportunities for crime. After all, he knew what it was like to live on both sides of the law. He raised his canteen to his lips and guzzled a fair amount of water. Never could the Wyoming heat compare to the Texas heat with its high humidity. Nonetheless, the spring day was uncharacteristically warm.

He mounted his horse, returned his hat atop his head, and continued on his way.

Before he'd become a praying man, Silas depended fully on himself. And the men who pledged their loyalty to him. After surrendering to Christ, that all changed. Now his every breath was dependent on the One who'd given him his first breath.

Antelope on a nearby hill briefly drew his attention from the road. In the sky, several birds circled an area just ahead near where the Poplar River wound through a grove of willows. He squinted, thoughts pummeling his mind. Could be a dead animal. Could be nothing.

Or it could be something he needed to investigate.

Riding with the Poplar Springs sheriff's posse and being deputized when assisting in the search for criminals gave Silas an even keener sense of awareness. Resting his fingers briefly on his revolver, Silas did one more sweep of the area before beckoning his horse and riding at an efficient clip toward the willow grove. Adrenaline coursed through his veins, reminding him that the life he'd chosen as a rancher was much more preferable.

At the crest of the hill, Silas again stopped his horse and inspected the area as far as his eye could see. On the second perusal to the right, he glimpsed something that caused him another, more lingering perusal.

A stagecoach overturned in the middle of the Poplar River, its red wheel still spinning. Silas's heart lurched, an uneasy feeling settling in the pit of his stomach.

"Giddyap!" Silas pushed his horse as fast as safely possible. Minutes later, he dismounted and tethered his horse to a tree. Half-sliding, half-running, he headed down the embankment toward the river, the tall weeds attempting to impede his travel. He nearly tripped when he stumbled on a hole in the ground, likely the home of a prairie dog. The sound of the rushing river, a child's whimpering, and an obnoxious cawing from a well-fed crow flying overhead filled the air.

He wasn't prepared for the site before him, nor the greeting he would receive.

Water rushed through the windows of the stagecoach. A man lay prostrate near the river's edge. To the right, a woman huddled near a wounded man, a young child in her arms.

"What happened?" he muttered, attempting to piece together the scenario that caused the accident.

"Hold it right there, mister."

From behind a tree, a woman appeared, holding a Winchester on him. Her long dark brown hair hung in clumps around her face in disarray, and twigs and leaves clung to her brown skirt.

He raised his hands. "I mean no harm, ma'am." Silas took a step back, his arms still raised. He'd had a lot of guns held on him over the years, but this was the first time it was a woman pointing a shotgun at him.

If you want to be among the first to hear about the next Wyoming Sunrise installment, sign up for Penny's newsletter at www.pennyzeller.com. You will receive book and writing updates, encouragement, notification of current giveaways, occasional freebies, and special offers. Plus, you'll receive *An Unexpected Arrival*, a Wyoming Sunrise novelette, for free.

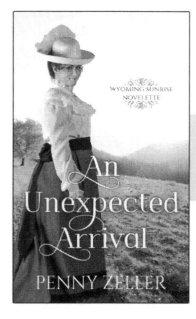

AUTHOR'S NOTE

Dear Reader,

Thank you for taking the time to read Charlotte and Tobias's story. I have anticipated telling their tale from the time
I wrote *Forgotten Memories*. They are just such memorable
characters, and I knew, while it would take them a while,
they would eventually realize their love for each other. Of
course, it did help to have two aunts on the scene orches-
trating a few things.

In the court scene when the Wyoming statutes were referenced, the Compiled Laws of Wyoming and the Revised
Statutes of Wyoming were real publications. I did take a
slight fictional liberty on the latter as those laws were "in
force" December 1, 1899, and *When Love Comes* takes place
in 1895.

For purposes of the story, I also took some fictional lib-
erties with the train scene. For instance, I intentionally did
not have the railroad hire an agent in the beginning to assist
with protecting the passengers. This allowed me to more
easily have Fraley attempt to rob the train. Additionally,
all of the towns, while inspired by real Wyoming towns,

are fictional. Also, for purposes of the story and plot, I skipped some normal legal proceedings and went directly to a hearing after Tobias was served.

Research is such an integral part of writing historical novels. My husband set me up with a second screen that permanently hosts my favorite historical research sites as well as an etymology site to check to see if words were used in the era of my book. I really, really wanted to use the word "preened" for a scene with Aunt Myrtle. Sadly, that word was not in usage until 1903.

While I was in research mode, I discovered a story about a pie eating contest in the late 1800s where some unkind people decided to fill the pies with leather and nails. Yes, leather and nails. Can you believe it? Anyway, the poor, unsuspecting contestants had no idea what was beneath the layer of pie crust until they bit into it (and swiftly for the contest). Needless to say, the perps were in a huge amount of trouble for their antics.

Doc Carver and Adam Bogardus were real sharpshooters. H.R. Prune was a fictional character developed specifically to be the founder of the fictional town of Prune Creek.

Sometimes we authors face some challenges while writing our books. In the middle of *When Love Comes*, I was hit with a bad case of the flu. I don't remember the last time I was as sick as I was this time. Losing two weeks of writing time, I wasn't sure I'd be able to finish the book in time to meet deadlines. But God is faithful. He healed me, gave me the best family ever who cared for me, gave me the ability to continue on with the book, and blessed me with editors, book tour participants, and book launch team members and Peeps who graciously gave me that extra time needed to finish strong.

No story would be complete without some typos along the way. A huge thank you to my beta team and my editors for finding some seriously hilarious mistakes. For instance: my misspellings of Charlotte (calling her Charloote) and Russell (Rullseel). Or the sentence, "Why was it she wounded like a blundering fool?" rather than, "Why was it she sounded like a blundering fool?" And finally, my favorite was when I must have gotten sidetracked because an unfinished sentence graced the page. It read: "her heart raced in her chest as though."

As always, thank you for escaping with me to Wyoming in the late 1800s. I hope you enjoyed reading about the characters as much as I enjoyed creating them. Until we meet again for *Love's Promise*, happy reading!

Blessings,
Penny

ACKNOWLEDGMENTS

To my family for their continued support and encouragement. It's not easy living with an author, especially one who spends a large majority of her hours in another century.

To my husband, Lon, for helping me perfect the train scene with the outlaw. Your knowledge of historical weaponry is always super helpful.

To my daughters for manning the fort while I spent long hours in the office. I appreciate you so much!

To my oldest daughter for spending countless hours brainstorming those couple of "challenging" scenes with me. What would I do without your help?

To my Penny's Peeps Street Team. Thank you for spreading the word about my books. I appreciate your continued encouragement and support.

To my Uncle Tim for all of your help in understanding the history of trains. It was fun catching up with you and picking your brain about all things trains.

To Alexandria Loftus for your continual assistance on the court hearing scene. Your advice and guidance were invaluable. Thank you so much for your willingness to answer my nonstop questions.

To Deb W. for your help in assisting me with the legalities of Lanie's adoption. I appreciate you taking the time to help me even while you were in the midst of arguing a huge case.

To Judith Welbaum for naming Morgan as one of the antagonists in the book. Thank you also for allowing me to use your namesake for the kind mercantile owner.

To Marie Concannon, Head, Government Information & Data Archives, University of Missouri Library. You have been so amazing to work with and are so full of knowledge! Thank you for all of your research help on a variety of topics and other historic details. I will forever have you on "speed dial" for future books.

To Jane Nelson, President, Albany County Historical Society, for assisting me with historic courthouses and for the amazing photo you provided of Albany County's court room in 1887, which provided the inspiration for the courtroom in Prune Creek.

To the Cheyenne Depot Museum staff and volunteers for their assistance in answering my many questions about train history.

To Suzi Taylor, Reference Archivist, Wyoming State Archives, for all of your help in researching early Wyoming adoptions and laws. The Wyoming statutes you provided were especially intriguing and helped so much.

To my readers. May God bless and guide you as you grow in your walk with Him.

And, most importantly, thank you to my Lord and Savior, Jesus Christ. It is my deepest desire to glorify You with my writing and help bring others to a knowledge of Your saving grace.

Let the words of my mouth and the meditation of my heart be acceptable in your sight, O Lord, my rock and my redeemer. - Psalm 19:14

ABOUT THE AUTHOR

Penny Zeller is known for her heartfelt stories of faith and her passion to impact lives for Christ through fiction. While she has had a love for writing since childhood, she began her adult writing career penning articles for national and regional publications on a wide variety of topics. Today, Penny is the author of nearly two dozen books. She is also a homeschool mom and a fitness instructor.

When Penny is not dreaming up new characters, she enjoys spending time with her husband and two daughters, camping, hiking, canoeing, reading, running, cycling, gardening, and playing volleyball.

She is represented by Tamela Hancock Murray of the Steve Laube Agency and loves to hear from her readers at her website www.pennyzeller.com and her blog, *random thoughts from a day in the life of a wife, mom, and author*, at www.pennyzeller.wordpress.com.

WYOMING SUNRISE SERIES

— HORIZON SERIES —

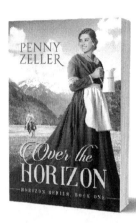

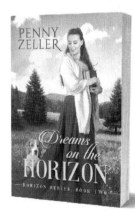

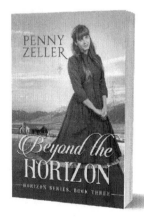

LOVE LETTERS FROM ELLIS CREEK

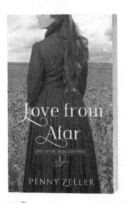

Love in
DISGUISE

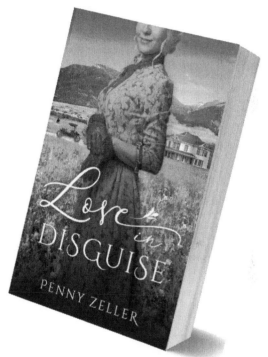

WHO KNEW CONCEALING ONE'S TRUE
IDENTITY COULD BE SO DISASTROUS?

Freedom's Flight

LIVES IN JEOPARDY.

A RACE AGAINST TIME.

WILL MISTRUST PROVE FATAL FOR ALL INVOLVED?

CHRISTIAN
CONTEMPORARY ROMANCE

Love in the Headlines

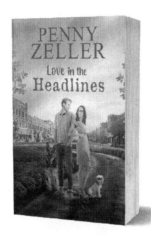

Chokecherry Heights

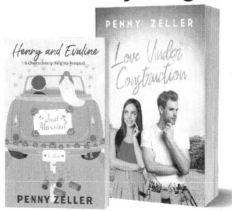